Praise for the previous
JACK FIELD mysteries by
LEE CHARLES KELLEY

"Smart and witty . . . with plenty of plot twists, characters you really care about, and to top it off, a nice fillip of dog lore and dog training; the best I've read in the growing list of mysteries a la canine."
Shirley Rousseau Murphy, author of the Joe Grey mysteries

"A very clever canine caper."
Romantic Times BOOKclub

"If you love dogs and you love mysteries, which I do, this is perfect. The detective/dog trainer, Jack Field, is a great character, utterly charming and disarming, and he is full of doggie facts that I found fascinating . . . Beautifully written, fast-paced, and engrossing. What could be better?"
Delia Ephron, author of *Hanging Up*;
executive producer/screenwriter of *You've Got Mail*

"A terrific story with equally terrific characters."
Rendezvous Magazine

"A great mystery . . . it should also be sold in every pet store in America."
Kevin Behan, author of *Natural Dog Training*

Books by Lee Charles Kelley

DOGGED PURSUIT
'TWAS THE BITE BEFORE CHRISTMAS
TO COLLAR A KILLER
MURDER UNLEASHED
A NOSE FOR MURDER

LEE CHARLES

KELLEY

Dogged Pursuit

AVON BOOKS
An Imprint of HarperCollins*Publishers*

This is a work of fiction. Names, characters, places, and incidents are products of the author's imagination or are used fictitiously and are not to be construed as real. Any resemblance to actual events, locales, organizations, or persons, living or dead, is entirely coincidental.

AVON BOOKS
An Imprint of HarperCollins*Publishers*
10 East 53rd Street
New York, New York 10022-5299

ISBN-13: 978-0-06-073229-5
ISBN-10: 0-06-073229-6
www.avonmystery.com

First Avon Books paperback printing: July 2006

Printed in the U.S.A.

10 9 8 7 6 5 4 3 2 1

Dedicated to the memory of
Charley and Puck . . .

"Outside of a dog, a book is man's best friend.
Inside of a dog, it's too dark to read."

Groucho Marx

Disclaimer

The following is a work of fiction.
Only the dogs are real.

Dogged Pursuit

Prologue

Before I begin, I should tell you a few things that happened before the State Police found the body. I haven't even told Jamie some of them, so if you happen to see her, don't let her know until I've had a chance to explain. The wedding's only two weeks away and it might complicate things.

You see, a few days after our engagement party (which we held in July of last year), I was standing by the front counter of the kennel, putting price tags on the rawhide bins, when Jennifer Vreeland, who was eighteen at the time, came over, walking kind of sideways, the way some teenagers do, her ash blond hair with its pink and green stripes partially hiding her face. When she got close enough, she grabbed my beard with both hands and kissed me.

I pulled away. "What the hell did you do *that* for?"

"To see if I'd like it," she said, and tried it again.

I put the pricing gun on the counter and held her back at arm's length. Frankie, my black-and-white English setter, watched us, his tail going crazy.

"No," said Jen, pushing closer. Frankie jumped up on us. "You're supposed to kiss me back then *I* say, 'It's even *better* when you help.' " She used a low, throaty Lauren Bacall voice.

"Yeah, I've seen that movie," I said, then told the dog, "Okay, off," and he jumped down. "Look, Jen, this isn't Hollywood. You can't go around kissing people. Especially me. I'm engaged, and Leon has a huge crush on you."

"Yeah, so?"

"So, did you stop to think how he might react?"

"No." Her face took on a guilty look as she thought about my sixteen-year-old foster son and his feelings for her.

Gently, I said, "Or were you just doing it because your mother tried the same trick on me last week?"

Her stepmother, Kristin Downey, my ex-girlfriend from college, had tried to make out with me inside the kennel the day of Jamie's engagement party. In a way Kristin's kiss made sense—she has bipolar disorder and I think she'd gone off her meds—but Jen pulled this dumb stunt seemingly out of nowhere.

"She's my *step*mother," she said, turning away. "And I hate her." There was no emotion in her voice when she said it, as if she were discussing the color of Kristin's eyes.

"Why?" I asked.

"Who cares? I just do." She looked down at her boots, angry with herself. "You're not going to tell her about this, are you? Or Jamie?"

"No." I hadn't even told Jamie about Kristin's kiss yet. "We'll pretend it never happened. As long as it doesn't ever—"

"Don't worry, it won't. So, am I fired or anything?"

"No, I just have two rules for you now instead of one: No cracking your gum and no trying to make out with the boss."

"It's a deal," she almost smiled.

"And be nice to Leon. He may act cool, like he doesn't feel things deeply, but he does. He saw his whole family get killed in their apartment in Harlem, you know."

Shocked, she said, "Oh, god, I'm sorry." Her eyes began to well up with tears. "He never told me that."

I'd been revving up to not like the girl anymore; I'd had enough of Kristin's wackiness and didn't need the same sort of antics from one of my employees. But Jen's quick, automatic tears on hearing about Leon's family tragedy made me like her again—a lot. "Yeah, well, he doesn't talk about it much."

"What a terrible thing to have happen to him." She stopped, looked away. "My mother was murdered too, you know."

I was stunned. "I'm sorry. I didn't know that."

"Well, she *was*. She was drowned in a lake, though they never found the man who did it." She sniffled, brushed back the tears with one side of her fist, then touched my arm. "Anyway, I'll be nice to Leon, Mr. Field, I promise."

"That's good. And haven't I told you to call me Jack?"

"Yeah," she said, then laughed, shyly. "But after doing something crazy like this, I think I should call you Mr. Field for at least a week, maybe the rest of my life."

I laughed. "That's all right. You're forgiven."

She thanked me and took Frankie out to the play yard.

I left a little while later for a training session. When I got back, her 1965 rust red International Harvester Scout was no longer parked under the willow tree. Damn, I thought. I was hoping to find out more about her mother's death.

That night Kristin came by to tell me that Jen had gone missing. Her father, Sonny Vreeland, is the heir to a vitamin fortune and she was worried that the girl had been kidnapped. I looked into it. Jen had just gone to New York to be with her boyfriend, Troy, a young actor whose main talent was that he had a movie star for a father. Kristin flew down, dragged Jen back to Maine, and got her enrolled at Colby College.

A few weeks passed and I talked to Jen on the phone a couple of times, trying to figure out a way to get her some more hours at the kennel, but she hadn't counted on making the basketball team. She promised to come visit Frankie when she could, though, and apologized for causing all the trouble. The subject of her mother's death didn't come up.

She would come by at various times during the next year to play with Frankie. She was still embarrassed at being around me, so she timed her visits for when I wasn't home.

Then one afternoon in early October, two weeks before the wedding, I got two phone calls. The first was from Jamie.

"Honey," I said with a sigh, "I can't think about which fondue I want on our wedding cake right now."

She laughed. "It's called a fondant and you know it."

"Whatever. And why isn't it just called icing?"

She'd been bugging me about the style and color of our wedding cake, and I'd been having trouble feigning interest.

" 'Fondue . . . ' " she said, still chuckling, then told me the State Police had just found a young woman's body under a dock in a lake near Vassalboro. Jamie is the state's chief medical examiner and I'm supposedly her advisor in criminology (though she doesn't pay me), so she asked me to come up and observe while they recovered the body and processed the scene.

"A floater?" I groaned, and passed on the invitation.

A few minutes later, though, Kristin called, worried sick about a police report she'd just heard about the same body in the same lake. She was afraid it might be Jennifer.

"Why would you think that?" I asked.

"She's gone again, Jack," Kristin said. "She missed three weeks of class."

"Three weeks? And you're just now telling me this?"

"Don't yell at me. I didn't want to bother you."

"Bother me? What bothers me is that she's been missing for three weeks and I'm just now finding out about it."

"Please don't yell at me, Jack. I *have* to go up there, to see if it's her. I thought you'd want to come too, but I guess I'll just have to get someone else."

I huffed. "Don't be ridiculous, Kristin," I said, "of course I'll go up there. In fact, I'm leaving right now."

I hung up the phone, told my kennel manager, Farrell Woods, to keep an eye on things, ran to the woody, and drove up to Vassalboro as fast as I could.

I told you, I really like that girl.

1

The body was bloated, glistening with lake water, and had a grotesque, waxy appearance, blotched gray and white. I'd never seen anything like it and hoped I never would again. It lay naked on the landward edge of the dock and stank to high heaven—an awful combination of the sick smell of dead flesh and the sodden perfume of fish, algae, and lake water.

I had parked about fifty yards away and was glad I'd had the foresight to buy a pack of menthols before making the drive up 104. I opened the cellophane wrapper with trembling hands—praying this monstrosity wasn't Jen—took out one of the cigarettes, broke it apart, then wedged the pieces, with the factory-cut ends first, into my nostrils.

There were six State Police divers in black wetsuits, having a mug-up (Maine-speak for a coffee break) by the boat ramp, off-wind from the corpse. Why six divers, I wondered.

And, God, I hope that isn't Jen.

Jamie was kneeling next to the body and had her back to me. I couldn't tell if she'd heard me drive up or not, though I assumed she hadn't or she would have turned to greet me.

Five crime scene analysts were hard at work, including a photographer I knew by her first name, Gretchen. She was a pretty, statuesque black woman about Jamie's height (Jamie's 5'11"), who once had a crush on me. Four uniformed troopers and two detectives were also on hand. They were standing around not doing much except trying to ignore the smell.

A trooper came over to stop me but a detective said, "That's okay, Congressman Schiff. He's official."

I wondered at the trooper's odd title, then recognized the other man. "Hey, Sinclair. How's it going?"

Jamie turned and looked up at me, shielding her eyes.

"Well, other than the smell," said Sinclair, "I guess I'm okay. How about you?"

Jamie interrupted our reunion with a loud, happy laugh. "What the hell have you got in your nose, Jack?"

I shrugged, feeling silly. "It's an old cop trick."

She stood up, casually dusted off one knee, and laughed some more. She was wearing chinos and a maroon turtleneck sweater under a barn jacket the color of brown mustard. Her dark chestnut hair, which she usually wore long, had been cut recently to shoulder length. She said it would look better with her wedding dress. I didn't see the need and was still having trouble getting used to the change.

"Can you *breathe* like that?" she asked, smiling.

"A little, though I can still smell the body."

She sighed, and tilted her head toward the corpse. "Yeah, it's pretty bad. It could be a lot worse, though."

I wondered how. And hoped it wasn't Jen. I said, "Any idea yet on how long she's been in the water?"

She shook her head. "Not pinpoint. My guess is probably since late spring."

I breathed a sigh of relief. Good, it *wasn't* Jen.

"Could be even longer," she said. "Some of the fatty tissue has converted to adipocere, and it takes at least five months for that to happen. It also keeps the smell down."

I nodded as if I knew what she was talking about. Or as if I agreed about the smell. "Any ID?"

"Nope. She's a Jane Doe for now."

"Tough break," I said, then looked at the uniformed cop—who was staring at me. "So, you're a congressman *and* a cop?"

He gave me a sour look and started to say something but Sinclair interrupted him with a snort. "Nah, his parents played a mean trick on him. Congressman's his first name."

He stuck out his hand. "Glad to meet you, Detective Field. I've heard a lot about you. And call me Dave."

"Okay. And call me Jack. I'm not really a detective anymore, no matter what my fiancée thinks. So, you never thought of going down to the courthouse to have it changed?"

He gave a resigned shrug. "Wouldn't make much difference now. People'd still razz me about what it used to be."

"Yeah," I said, backing upwind of the body, toward the far end of the dock, "but you could at least upgrade yourself. You could be Senator Schiff. Or Governor."

"Good idea, Jack," said Sinclair, elbowing Schiff. "I think I'll start calling myself Pope Sinclair."

"See what I mean?" muttered Schiff.

Jamie said, "Jack, *now* what are you doing?"

"The breeze . . ." I said, walking a few more steps away. "I want to get upwind of the body." I looked out at the water, which was lit by the late afternoon sun. I noticed a bright spot in the middle of a densely wooded area across the lake, thinking at first it was an autumn leaf fluttering in the breeze, but then it moved deliberately, like someone adjusting a car mirror, and I knew it was sunlight reflecting off glass.

Jamie sighed. "You really are a wimp about this."

"What?" I turned. "You mean the smell? It isn't *that*. Well, it isn't *just* that. The thing is, I don't want it getting into my clothes, not to mention my hair and beard. It's going to drive the dogs nuts if they pick it up on me when I get back to the kennel. Haven't you ever worked on a floater before?"

She gave me a pointed look, then gave the slightest tilt of her head toward the rest of the law enforcement personnel. I guess she didn't want them thinking she was a novice.

"Sorry," I said. "Any idea yet on the cause of death?"

"I'm not sure. There are some marks on her chest. They could be knife wounds, they could be postmortem bites from the fish in the lake." The breeze kicked up and she crinkled her nose. "Got any more cigarettes? And is your stress level about the wedding so bad that you've taken up smoking?"

I said I had a whole pack and that no, it *wasn't,* and no, I *hadn't.* She came over and I removed the pack from my shirt, took out a cigarette, broke it in two and held out the pieces.

"Thanks," she said, "the menthol cream isn't working very well." She pointed to her upper lip, which I now noticed was glistening slightly, then put out her hand, which was encased in a Pliofilm glove, to take the broken pieces.

I stopped her and said, "Here, let me do it for you." I held her face with my left hand and gently placed the ends of the broken cigarette into her nostrils.

She leaned into me. "I guess I *am* kind of new at this."

"You're doing fine." I looked away from the body, disturbed by a memory. "Is there a pattern to the wounds?"

"A pattern?"

I didn't want to entertain the thoughts that had begun to surface, but had to ask about the marks on her chest.

She shuddered—it was an awful thing to think about. "Yes, but it might not have been a deliberate mutilation, Jack. The injuries could've been caused by—"

"—fish bites, I know. You said that." I let out a deep breath.

She must have seen something in my eyes because she let out a deep breath too, followed by an "Uh-oh." She shuddered again then touched my arm. "You've seen this before?"

"No," I shook my head, "it reminds me of an old case."

"Something you worked on?"

"Sort of. We broke it down at a seminar in Quantico about six years ago. I think it was an active case then."

She sighed. "Looks like it still *is*?"

"Maybe. Have them run it through ViCAP to find a match. And try the database in Canada too—ViCCAS. His first victims were killed up in Ontario, I think. How was the body found?"

"A high school kid was swimming and found it. The poor woman had been tied to the timbers under the dock." She got a far-off look in her eyes, picturing how the body had been discovered, then shivered slightly.

"Kind of late in the year for swimming." I looked around but didn't see the kid. "Has he been interviewed?"

"Yeah. Sinclair talked to him and sent him home."

I looked at Sinclair and motioned to him. He came over and made a snide, yet curious, comment about our nosewear.

Jamie shifted her weight onto her other foot.

I tapped out another cigarette and gave it to Sinclair. "Did this kid tell you why he happened to be swimming here?"

He shrugged, broke the cigarette in two, and inserted the pieces into his nostrils. "Thanks," he said, taking a long, deep breath, "that's much better." He looked back over to the beach where he'd interviewed the swimmer, using one hand to protect his eyes from the slanted sun. "Yeah, he told me he swims here all the time. Why? You think he's lying?"

"No," I said, "I think he probably *does* swim here all the

time, but I think our killer knew that, and made a phone call to the kid, telling him there was something valuable under the dock, like a diamond necklace or a gold watch."

"Huh. He didn't say anything to me about it."

"Well, you may need to reinterview him."

"Okay, but how do you know he got a call like that?"

"I don't, but it would fit the pattern of a killer who always wants his victims found on a specific day and time."

The wind picked up and Jamie pushed a stray lock of hair behind one ear. Her head and shoulders were now crowned with late afternoon sunlight. She crossed her arms and said, "Jack thinks it might be a serial killing."

I shrugged. "If it *is,* you'll probably find the victim's clothes buried somewhere about thirty yards from the beach."

He looked out at the half dozen or so (mostly official) cars parked in just that area, close to the creeping afternoon shadows laid down by a nearby stand of pines, and said, "Crap. We'll have to repark everybody and start a grid search. Plus, a lot more cars will be here soon."

"Yeah." I nonchalantly turned to look at the lake. The glint of light was still there. "And listen, I want you to do something, but try not to be too obvious about it, just do it real casual-like: Take a look across the water."

Jamie saw something in my eyes. "What is it, Jack?"

"I'm not sure," I said.

Sinclair nodded, then he and Jamie began to scan the shoreline, very calm and relaxed. We were like extras in a bad movie, pretending to have a real conversation.

"What are we looking for, exactly?" Sinclair asked.

"Sunlight reflecting off some kind of lens."

Sinclair looked and said, "I can't see anything."

Jamie said, "Is that part of the killer's MO?"

"No, it's just an impression I have."

"What kind of impression?"

"I'm not sure. I just have this eerie feeling that the killer is out there right now, watching us."

Jamie shivered again, though the wind was suddenly still.

2

"I'll send a radio car over," Sinclair said, meaning across the lake. "Maybe they can catch him in the act."

"Good luck," I said. "This guy—if it's *him*—is smart. He's been outwitting the experts at the FBI's Behavioral Science Unit for years."

"No kidding," he said, then grumped. "You know, the only thing is, I didn't see the reflection and—"

"I know. It's just a wild hunch on my part."

"Yeah. But if you're right . . ." He smiled and nodded suddenly. "You know what? I'll have them send a couple of cars. Maybe we can box him in."

He went to his unmarked cruiser. Jamie smiled and hugged me lightly. "I'm really glad you came, Jack."

"Yeah, well, the funny thing is," I said about to step, unwittingly, into a minefield, "I wouldn't have come at all, but Kristin asked me to meet her here."

Her smile died a little.

"Apparently," I went on, oblivious, like the idiot I can sometimes be, "Jennifer is missing again."

She frowned. "Oh, no. I hope she's all right."

"Anyway," I went on, giving a nod to the lump that used to

be a human being, "Kristin was worried that this body of yours might be her."

"Well, you can tell your girlfriend not to worry." She put a little English on the word *girlfriend.* "Like I said, this body's been here since late spring, which eliminates—"

"I remember. And she's my *ex*-girlfriend."

She glared at me and shook her head. Then to the photographer—who was finishing her shots of the body—she said, "Gretchen, have you got a Wratten 18 filter?"

Gretchen was surprised by the question. She let go of her 35mm SLR, letting it hang by the strap around her neck, then reached with long, pretty fingers for a pocket in her photo-journalist-style vest, and said, "Uh, sure?"

"Good. Can you shoot the whole body with it?"

"You want me to retake *every*thing?" She wasn't too happy about having to photograph the floater in the first place, let alone having to retake all her shots with a new filter.

"Would you mind?" Jamie asked, though it wasn't really a question. Then she told her to take a series of alternating shots, first with the filter, then the same shot with plain daylight. "Do it for entire body, head to toe."

Gretchen nodded, though she was pissed off at being given the extra work, then pulled a filter holder from her vest.

"What are you thinking?" I asked Jamie as Gretchen cleaned the clear filter then screwed it onto her lens.

Jamie said, "Ultraviolet photos can pick up bruising under the skin up to several months after the original trauma. That, along with the adipocere, I don't know, we might get lucky and find something; rope marks, bruise patterns?"

"Adipocere. That's the second time you said that."

She gave me a smile that wasn't really a smile; her teeth were too on edge. "I'd explain it to you, Jack, but you're only *here* because of your ex-girlfriend, remember?"

"Honey—! Oh, never mind. What is adipocere, please?"

She shook her head at me. "It's what sometimes happens to bodies submerged in cold water. The fat cells go through a process called saponification, where they solidify and become a hard, soaplike substance." She gave a nod to the divers. "That's why it took six men to get her onto the dock."

"I see," I said, though I only halfway did.

"The *good* thing is adipocere retains evidence of things like stab wounds, bullet holes, and—"

"—bite marks?"

"And bite marks. I don't know if we'll be able to use them in court. The adipocere expands over time, making the wound pattern a bit larger than it was originally."

"So"—I changed the subject—"where are you planning to sleep tonight? My place or yours?"

She arched her eyebrows. "Does it really matter?"

"Sure it does," I said. "I need to know where to have the sunflowers and the box of chocolates delivered." (They're her two favorites.) "And by the way," I lowered my voice, "this is one of the reasons I don't like being your civilian advisor in criminology, or whatever it is I'm supposed to be doing. Can you please fire me or someth—"

"Fire you? My god, if you would just do your job because it's your *job,* not because your ex-girlfriend needs you to—"

"Sshhh," I said, and nodded my head toward Gretchen.

Jamie brought it down a notch. "Anyway, the point is you're a crucial part of this or any other investigation. If they actually find the killer hiding out across the lake, watching us . . ." She pointed in that direction.

I pulled her arm down. "Honey, don't point like that. If he's there, you'll give it away."

"Fine," she whispered, "but if they find him and we can somehow tie him to the murder, you would have effectively solved this case."

"Yeah, I guess, but I don't think this civilian advisor thing is a real job. I think it's just a position you made up so that we—" I'd been about to say, So that we could spend more time together. And that was true, and it was based on logic. But when you're already on the wrong side of an argument with a woman, there's no point in using logic; it just pisses them off even more. At least it does Jamie.

Hands on hips she said, "What were you about to say?"

"Nothing. It's just that I'm not that thrilled about standing next to the decomposed, or saponified, body of a naked woman, discussing flowers and chocolates with you."

Gretchen shot me a pointed glance. She wanted me to know she was on my side. I gave her a quick, frustrated look, trying to let her know she wasn't helping any.

Jamie, who'd missed all this, flexed her eyebrows some more and said, "Flowers and chocolates. If you hadn't acted like an ass we wouldn't be discussing them at all. And do you really think that's all it's going to take to make up for—"

"Well," I smiled, "you're allergic to perfume or I'd buy you a bottle of Chanel No. 5. Hell, I'd buy you a whole *case*." In fact, you're going to *need* it after working on a floater, I almost added, but wisely kept my mouth shut.

She nodded. "Is that all?"

"Well, Tiffany's doesn't deliver," I joked, "so I guess a pair of diamond earrings is out of—"

"They *do* deliver, actually. I also like turquoise and silver, in case they run out of diamonds, which knowing you . . ."

I felt my face flush. "Meanwhile," I said, "where do I have the flowers and choco—?"

"I'm staying at your place. Or I should say, our place, since that's what it's supposed to be once we're married and all the remodeling is done." She knelt back down. Over her shoulder she said, "And we need to have a serious conversation about your relationship with this Kristin Downey person."

"Yeah, yeah."

"Don't 'yeah, yeah' me, Jack. I'm serious. Oh, and don't get any ideas about later on." Then she mouthed so I could read her lips, "I didn't shave my legs." With that she turned her back on me.

I laughed. "Like that's going to stop me?"

She swiveled and glared.

I put my hands up. "From getting *ideas,* I mean."

Gretchen tried not to laugh but it was no good. She snorgled (a combination snort and giggle).

Jamie heard her. She focused her hottest glare on the photographer for a moment then went back to the body. Over her shoulder again she said, "You can have all the ideas you want, cowboy. They won't do you any good."

I walked past Gretchen. "Next time," I said, "don't help."

"Hey, don't look at me, *cowboy,*" she said, her big brown eyes all innocent. "I only work here."

"Yeah, well," I said, "at least they pay you."

"Yeah, but not nearly enough for this kind of stuff—which reminds me . . ." She dug into a pocket and produced a business card. "If you guys need a wedding photographer . . ."

I took the card and looked at it, then looked down at the bloated corpse on the dock. "You've got to be kidding me."

She shrugged. "Hey, I'm very versatile."

3

I heard a car coming but didn't want to look, in case Jamie caught me hoping it was Kristin, which I was. But I also didn't want to stay with my nose pointed in the direction of the body, so I slowly turned around.

It wasn't Kristin. It was a red Sting Ray, and she drives a silver Mercedes 450SL. Besides, the vehicle didn't really pull up; it sort of roared through the tall grass and swerved to a stop, trailing a big cloud of dirt road behind it. I knew Kristin wasn't behind the wheel; not unless she was in one of her manic phases, and she hadn't sounded like that on the phone earlier. No, that type of driving comes with a specific personality type, so I shouldn't have been surprised when the car door opened and out popped my old "pal"—Regis.

Randall Corliss, or Regis, as I like to call him (due to the way he dresses), used to be a detective with the Lewiston PD. He was also on the take (allegedly) with a drug dealer by the name of Eddie Cole. The brass in Lewiston found out about it (thanks to me and Jamie's ex-uncle-in-law, Rockland County Sheriff Horace Flynn), and Corliss lost his job. He was also brought up on charges, which apparently hadn't stuck, or he wouldn't have been treating us now to his million-dollar smirk and his shmancy wardrobe.

He closed his car door, twirled his key ring around one finger, like James Arness after shooting a bad guy, then put it in the pocket of his jet black slacks. He wore a shiny black shirt, a bright green silk tie, and a charcoal sports jacket. He's an inch shorter than I am (I'm 6'1"), solid, well-built, with deep brown eyes, dark, wavy hair and a full, dark mustache. The backs of his arms and his fingers had a dark fuzz, just enough to show you how masculine he was. You could practically smell his after-shave over the stink of the body. He checked his watch, adjusted himself, and came around the other side of the car and opened the door for someone.

Kristin Downey got out.

Oh-God-no, I thought. What the hell was she doing with him? I looked at Jamie, who had taken in their arrival and now turned to look at me. I tried to send a message with my eyes—"My life is a nightmare."

She shrugged and lifted her eyebrows. "Hey," they seemed to say, "*I* didn't get you into this mess, did I?"

She was partially right. Kristin Downey seemed to be my own little cross to bear; but on the other hand, I would have never even *met* Regis if Jamie hadn't roped me into helping *her* solve the Marti MacKenzie case. I made a mental note to save that one for our discussion later that night.

Regis saw me and gave his usual salute—hand outstretched, imitating a pistol, with a sudden snap of the wrist. Kristin immediately looked down at her shoes, a pair of Timberland boots actually, with some clever designer type of frou-frou fabric sprouting around her ankles the way the sere, autumn grass beneath her feet made its last stab at the summer sun. She also wore jeans, a T-shirt, and a heavy, gray V-neck sweater.

Congressman Schiff and Pope Sinclair stopped them

before they got close enough to contaminate the scene. I was right behind them. Kristin glanced up, shot me a look, then tilted her head toward the dock, meaning, "Is it Jen?"

I shook my head.

She heaved a sigh, ran to me, and started to put her arms around my waist. "I was so frightened," she said.

I held her away and said something soothing. I looked back at Jamie. She was busy examining the body.

Kristin looked up at my nose and started to giggle. "Is that a cigarette sticking out of your nostrils?"

We repeated the whole cigarette-in-the-nose thing, then she turned to Corliss and said, "It's not her. We can go."

"In a minute, honey," he said, without looking at us. He was busy shooting the bull with Schiff and Sinclair.

Kristin's pale complected cheeks reddened. "Randall," she explained simply, "we're going. Now."

He put a finger up for the two cops, then turned his head slowly to stare her down. He said to the cops, "Give me a minute," then came over and said, "Don't get your panties in a twist." Then looked at me and gave me an eye roll that would have said, "Women . . ." in a sarcastic tone if he'd spoken it.

He looked at my face more closely, then at Kristin's. His nose twitched. I handed him a cigarette and he took it. To Kristin he said, "I need to talk to these guys a minute."

"No. It's not Jen. We're leaving. Now."

"That's not how it goes. I'm working the case. We do it my way. If you want, you can go wait in the car."

He turned and went back to the cops.

I found myself wondering, briefly, how he'd look with his nose broken, and would it go with his mustache, but before I could go after him and crack his face in, Kristin turned her back on him, clutched my arm and said, "Take me home, Jack. Please? I can't be here any longer." I hesitated, looking back toward Jamie. "Just a goddamn ride," she spat, "is that too much to ask?" Then, more softly she said, "I don't want to cause you any trouble, I really don't. I just need to get away from that horrible-looking thing." She meant the body.

"I can't," I sighed. "I have some dogs to pick up."

"Please, Jack. Don't make me beg you. You liked Jen, I know you did. You really liked her."

I pulled away. "What do you mean, 'liked'?"

"I didn't mean it that way."

"I think you did." I felt my face burn. "Sorry. I shouldn't have said that."

We stood there a moment trying not to say anything that might further fuel the fire. While we were thus engaged, or disengaged, Corliss's voice went up enough for us to hear him say, "You mean you guys haven't decided who to vote for?"

I assumed they were talking about the recall election for Rockland County Sheriff. Horace Flynn, who'd been under investigation, was facing a tough battle to keep his job.

"Jack, please?" Kristin said. "Get me out of here?"

I shook my head but found myself giving her the keys to the woody. "Go sit in the car. I'll be right there. You can play with the stereo if it'll make you feel any better."

"I'm not a child." She grasped the keys with both hands, though, the way a child would. I was getting the impression that there was a lot more to what was going on with her and Jen than I'd originally thought.

"Just wait for me in the car, okay?" I said.

"Okay," she grumped. "Hey, do you have any good CDs? You used to have the most interesting taste in music."

"No, I have some tapes you can sort through, though."

"Don't tell me you have an 8-track deck, like in that old Buick you used to drive. Remember?" She smiled, showing her slight overbite, and the one front tooth that sticks out and crosses over the other. It's one of the three reasons I used to love kissing her so much, back in the old days.

"Go sit in the car," I said, then walked back to the dock to talk to Jamie, who was showing Gretchen some specific body parts she'd missed. I tried not to look where she was pointing. Gretchen wasn't too happy about having to look there either.

She said, "I'm getting too many shadows with this light."

"Can't you use a flash?"

"Yes," she said, as if to a bothersome child, "but juries like natural light. They don't trust outdoor flash photos."

Jamie sighed. "All right. You can go."

Gretchen said, "Okay, see you tomorrow," and headed back to the parking area. Over her shoulder she said to me, as she walked away rewinding her film, "You've got my card, right?"

I politely tapped my jacket pocket and nodded.

Jamie looked back toward the ME's van and said, thinking out loud, "I guess it's time we bagged the body anyway." She took off her gloves, then said to me, "What do *you* want?"

I stood there, still burning with what Kristin had said: "You *liked* her," as if Jennifer were dead. "Nothing. I just wanted to let you know I'm leaving. Kristin needs a ride."

She gave me a sour look, then said, "So? Give her a ride. Who's stopping you?" She turned to the divers and shouted, "We're going to need some help here."

"I'm sorry, honey," I said, "but I have to. Jen is still missing, and I think Kristin has gone off her meds—"

"No kidding. If she's hanging out with Regis then—"

"I know," I said. "But someone's got to look after her. Besides, I have to find out what's up with Jennifer."

"Okay!" she griped, then she sighed, looked at me, and her tone softened. "You don't have to give me that crooked smile, Jack," she said, and touched my arm. "I know how much you like that girl." I was touched by her use of the present tense. "Now what? What does that teary-eyed look mean?"

"It means you're the only person who understands me."

"I am? Yeah?" She seemed happy and surprised.

"Yeah." I squeezed her hand. "I've got to go. Kristin needs to get away from the dead body and I have some dogs to—"

"I know. Go take care of the wicked stepmother."

I chuckled. "So, we'll talk more later?"

She gave me a pointed look. "Oh, that we will, cowboy."

I offered her another crooked smile then went back to the car to give the "wicked stepmother" a ride home.

4

The first part of the ride was quiet, except for Van Morrison singing "Angeliou." I didn't know if Kristin had put in one of my mixes or my tape of Van's *Into the Music* album. It doesn't matter. I love that song and wasn't about to get back into a fight with her while it was playing. She seemed to feel the same way—maybe that's why she'd picked it. She was slowly rocking back and forth in her seat.

Then, at some point, once we'd gotten off the back road and onto 104, we started singing along at the same time.

"In the month of May, in the city of Paree . . ."

She laughed, looked at me, then looked out the window. "Do you remember how we used to make love to that song all the time?"

I admired her laugh lines, her worry lines, and the way that life had subtly and tenderly gone about the process of aging her face. She's a year younger than I (I'm forty-one), and seven years older than Jamie (she's thirty-two), and she still looks marvelous.

I find it sad to see a beautiful woman who's had her face "worked on." They think they're retaining their youth and they just end up looking like ghouls in scarves and turtlenecks. I prefer the natural look, I guess, and I was a little proud of the way Kristin had allowed her face to take on character. I find that kind of confidence sexy and appealing in a woman.

"No," I said, "that album came out after we broke up."

"No, it didn't." She scratched her neck.

I shrugged. "I specifically remember using this song to console myself for a couple of months, right after I left New York and moved to Boston. I missed you pretty bad."

She thought it over, remembered something, then laughed. "Oh, I know what it was. It was that long weekend, remember? I came to Boston and surprised you? And we took that trip along the cape and stayed holed up in that little beach—"

"—cabin. Yeah, I remember. It poured rain for three days. Including inside—"

"—the cabin! And we borrowed those plastic buckets from the car wash. And you played me this album over and over."

"I guess you're right."

We drove along the river, singing along some more.

The sun was starting to go down and there was a bite of fall in the air and the leaves on the roadside oaks, maples, slippery elms, and sycamores were just starting to take on a fall tint, though some of the aspens and birches that grow between the train tracks and the river were more committed to the autumn dance, glittering a bright green/yellow as the late afternoon sun sparkled and reflected off the blue water.

The weather reminded me of the days in New York when we would walk through Riverside Park, holding hands. That would have been late October, as I recall. But the seasons come quicker and harder in Maine than they do in the Big Apple.

I had a huge boat of a used '66 Buick Electra then, and on

the weekends we'd take trips out of town, just motoring upstate, or through Connecticut, driving along the Housatonic River just like we were driving along the Kennebec now.

I felt both a twinge of nostalgia and a dose of remorse as I thought about this.

I turned the music down.

"So, what's with you and Regis?" I said, finally pulling my thoughts away from "Angeliou," in the city of Paris, and of the long, rainy weekend I'd once spent with Kristin Downey on Cape Cod.

"Who?" she asked.

"Randy Corliss. What the hell are you doing with him?"

"I told you, I'm worried about Jen. And he's an old friend of the family, from way back."

"Whose family, yours or Sonny's?

"Neither. Sonny's first wife's family, I think."

"I don't care whose family he's an old friend of, that guy should be locked up. And even if he weren't a dirty cop—"

"He's an *ex*-cop, just like you." There was a brief silence, then she laughed and said, "You call him Regis? . . ."

"Yeah, it fits. And he's not like *me*. He was a crooked cop and a slimy, chauvinistic—"

"I get it, Jack," she smiled. "You're jealous."

"I am not," I said a little too loudly, "*jealous!*"

Kristin touched my arm. Her eyes sparkled. "It's okay, Jack. I find it endearing, really."

I shook my head and sighed. Softer, I said, "I'm not jealous, Kristin, I'm just saying, you're a beautiful, successful, *married* woman, among other things, and Corliss is a walking single entendre."

"That's very clever. And this isn't jealousy talking? Besides, I needed someone to help me. He's a bonded private detective now, while you've been nothing but dismissive."

"I came straight to the lake when you asked, didn't I?"

"Sure, because you were worried about Jen, not me."

"And by the way," I said, "where's Sonny in all this?"

She looked away.

"He doesn't know his daughter is missing again?"

She paused. "It's, it's hard to explain."

"Give it a shot."

"They, that is, he and Jen don't talk anymore. I don't know why, really. I'm just stuck being the middle man between them." She sighed. "Plus, there are other things going on that I'm not about to discuss with you. Especially not when—"

"What other things?"

She laughed. "I guess you didn't hear what I just said."

"I heard it, I'm just not paying it any mind. What other things?"

"My god," she laughed, "you were always like this, weren't you? Self-centered and heedless of what anyone else is thinking or feeling, especially right after you got laid, as I recall."

"What things?"

"Things that are none of your business! Okay?"

The Van Morrison faded out and a Greg Brown song, "All Day Rain," came on and I realized we'd been listening to one of my mixes. I switched on the radio. You can't listen to Greg Brown and talk at the same time. At least you shouldn't.

I said, "So, what's going on with Jennifer?" John Denver was on the radio, singing about being home again.

"I don't know. She's a teenager, and she takes off in certain dangerous and unexpected directions without a moment's notice."

I said, "You know, you and I are going to have to have a long and serious discussion about this."

"There's no need, Jack. I've got someone else to help me

now. Yes, he may be a jackass and a walking single whatever, but at least he's committed to the job, not like you were."

There was no way to answer that without losing my temper. Besides I'd about reached my saturation point, Kristin-wise.

Her cell phone rang and she opened it and said, "Hello? Yes? Yes. I can hardly hear you. Where are you?" She looked over at me, saw the hope in my eyes and shook her head. It wasn't Jen. "Un-huh. I know about that, Nigel, but I—hello? You're breaking up. Let me call you back from a land line. What time is it there? Really? Jesus! Okay, I'll try you back in—what? Nigel, no, no! Shit, I lost the signal."

She clicked off the phone. "I have a show opening in London in two weeks. It's moving from the Martin Beck to the Haymarket actually, and there's a problem with the costumes. I should really be there, not here, trying to track down my goddamn *step*daughter." She scratched her throat. "Now maybe you'll understand why I need Regis to help me find her."

"I had no trouble finding her the last time."

"This is different. I just know it is." She saw me looking at her as she scratched her throat. She shrugged and said, "Some problems came up with the Depakote, so I had to change meds suddenly. I just started on this Lamictal."

I'd never heard of it and told her so.

She nodded. "It's an anticonvulsive. They've just been given approval for using it to treat bipolar, and it's giving me this awful rash. It's supposed to go away in a few weeks."

"Well, I've got some Benadryl in the glove box."

She gave me a questioning look.

"I'm allergic to dogs," I explained. "Just slightly, but still ironic, huh? Help yourself, if it's all right for you to take it."

"Yeah, it's fine," she said, then reached for the glove box, but her cell phone rang again. She shook her head and answered it, and while she spoke with Nigel again—something about the fabric for the ruffs in the second act—I just drove and thought back to those first happy days we spent together.

I first knew Kristin Downey when I was a grad student at Columbia, working on a master's degree in psychology. She was a theater major, studying set and costume design. She was a beautiful girl, 5'5", with blond hair and pretty brown eyes with long, dark lashes. Plus, she was smart. But she also had some severe emotional problems which, sad to say, I found fascinating; not because of my major but because of my *mother,* who had a similar profile, though I was unconscious of the parallels, or my fascination with them, at the time.

Those were heady weeks, full of wild nights of passionate sex. We once made love at midnight on the fifty-yard line of the football stadium. But the good times were always followed by long stretches of dark despair, marked by at least one attempted suicide. After they'd pumped her stomach and she'd regained consciousness at the Columbia Presbyterian ER, she took my hand and made me swear not to tell anyone about what happened. I dried her tears and said I wouldn't.

I broke that promise a few weeks later when my faculty advisor, Dr. Metten, began pestering me with questions about why my GPA had dipped below a 4.0 for the first time in my academic career. I stared at the ceiling for a while and then finally told him about my relationship with Kristin. It felt good to finally get it off my chest.

Then I heard something that I've heard all too often in my life: "For a smart guy, Jack," he said, looking at me over his reading glasses, "you can be pretty dumb sometimes."

"What do you mean?"

"Think about it. From what you've told me, she sounds like a textbook case of manic-depression."

Wow. I'd studied it in class, I'd even grown up around it, but I guess I had a blind spot when it showed up in the form of Kristin Downey.

So, with Dr. Metten's help, I got her into treatment, she was diagnosed properly (he'd been right), and put on lithium and valproate (Depakote), both of which she hated. This was followed by some ferocious fights, wild make-up sex, lots of apologizing, a little forgiveness, and an eventual breakup which left me feeling guilty as hell that I hadn't, I don't know, stuck it through to the end, I guess. But I was headed for Harvard Medical School, intent on becoming a psychiatrist, and she was on her way to study costume design at Carnegie-Mellon. So we split up.

We kept in touch sporadically, which I was glad of—not the sporadic part, the keeping in touch part. Sometimes, when I least expected it, and usually when I needed it most, emotionally speaking, she would go off her medication, show up in Boston, and call me from a corner bar; crazy phone calls that always led to mad, fervent reunions, which in turn almost always ended in a kind of dull and studied acrimony.

We drifted apart and she later married Jen's father. Now that I think about it, I still find myself—whenever I'm confronted with Kristin's lies and manipulations—saying mean, acrimonious things to her. I don't do it to be hurtful, just to protect myself from getting drawn into her crazy Kristin-world again. It's hard; a part of me still loves her and wants her to be happy. Just not with me.

As she finished her phone call, I remembered some of the research I'd done at the time on bipolar disorder and one of the side effects of Depakote: it can sometimes cause birth defects when taken by pregnant women. That's when it hit me why she'd had to switch medications suddenly.

I sighed and said, "So, about the Lamictal. Does Sonny know the reason you switched meds?"

"Who, the vitamin king?" she sneered. "He thinks I should stop taking *all* my medications and just up my B vitamins, and—voilà—I'll be as good as new. Like he's one to talk, with his little fascination for—"

"No, I meant does he know that you're pregnant?"

Stunned, she said, "How on earth could you—?"

"Depakote causes tetragenic birth defects, as I recall. I mean, *I* don't know, why else would you suddenly switch meds, if it's going to cause you other problems like the rash?"

She said nothing, she just stared out the side window a moment, then reached for the glove box and opened the bottle of Benadryl, popped two into her mouth and choked them down.

"So? Is he the father?"

She glared at me.

"Well, *is* he?"

"I'm not going to discuss this with you, Jack."

"Okay, so your husband isn't the father. Is it Regis?"

She roared. "You've got to be kidding."

"Well, how should I know? You have a history of—"

"Jack, I'm not discussing this with you. Period."

"And aren't you a little old to be—"

"I'm going to smack you if you don't shut up."

I shut up and drove for a while. Then I said, "So, what happened to Jennifer's mother?"

"What do you mean?"

"Jen told *me* that she was murdered."

"What?" She shook her head. "She was *not* murdered. That girl has an overactive imagination. She committed suicide. I told you as much last Christmas."

"You did?" I looked at her. She nodded and something in her eyes made me realize why she was so tied emotionally to her stepdaughter: because of her own suicide attempts, back at Columbia. The depth of feeling I saw in her sad brown eyes told me I was right. I felt my heart ache with a mixture of sorrow, guilt, and a little admiration for Kristin's maternal concern for a girl who wasn't even a blood relative.

"Okay," I said, when I felt my throat untighten, "so how did Jen's mother kill herself?"

She shook her head. "She drowned herself in a lake in Massachusetts." She gave me a look. "That's why, when the police told me about—"

"I get it." We went around a sharp curve and I said, "Okay, but why would Jennifer tell me that her mother had been— Holy crap! Aw, no."

There was a lost, dottle-colored terrier mutt trotting along on the other side of the road. His coat was the rough texture of pipe tobacco, and he was about the size of a Jack Russell. I pulled onto the shoulder and looked at him some more. He just stood there in the approaching twilight, panting and smiling at me, wagging his stubby little tail.

"Jack, what is it?" Kristin said.

"A lost dog." I turned off the ignition.

She put a hand on my arm. "You're not thinking of trying to go get him, are you?"

I stopped and looked at her. "Why wouldn't I?"

"I don't know. What if he has rabies and bites you?"

"What if he gets run over by the next car that comes by? Oh, that reminds me, I'm going to need you to get out too."

She stared at me. "And do what?"

I pointed behind me. "Go back to that curve and if you see a car coming, get them to slow down." Before she could protest I said, "Look, I don't want to cross the road and go after the dog." I explained the proper way to approach a lost or frightened dog; you always try to get the dog to come to you rather than moving toward him.

She shook her head and said, "He doesn't look lost."

She was right. He seemed tired but contented, like he'd been out doing a hard day's work chasing rats or something, and was just headed home to supper.

"It's true," I said. "He looks like he belongs to a nearby farmer or something. But what if he *doesn't*?"

She tsked at me, opened her door, and said, "I hope Jamie appreciates this aspect of your nature." She stopped. "And thirty-nine is not too old to have a baby."

"You're right. I'm sorry I said anything."

We were about to get out but stopped when we heard a car squealing around the curve behind us. A familiar red Corvette zoomed by, went about a hundred yards past us, then screeched to a stop and came roaring back in reverse. I could read the license plate: 69 VETTE. It stopped parallel to us, its engine assaulting our eardrums. Regis leaned across the seat, rolled down the window, grinned, and said, "Car trouble?"

I shook my head, looked past him to see if the dog was still there, but he was gone. All I could see was his little tail as he scampered off into the shadows.

5

I was determined to find the little critter and make sure he got home safe, but Kristin wasn't in the mood to hang around, so she got a ride home with Corliss. I think she wanted to bend his ear a little about his behavior back at the lake. Good luck.

I searched in vain for about twenty minutes, whistling and clucking my tongue, trying to find the mutt. I finally gave up when it got too dark to see anything, but made a call to animal control on the cell phone to let them know what I'd seen and where.

When she heard my location and the description of the dog, the woman on the phone said, "Oh, that's probably just Clarence. We get a lot of reports about that little rascal. He's some kind of terrier. A Patterson, I think? He belongs to a farmer who lives nearby. Don't worry, he'll probably be okay."

"A Patterson terrier?" I'd never heard of it.

"I don't know," she said, "something like that."

Once I got on the highway I was in an angry mood, so I cranked up my *Best of The Who* tape, which was cued up to

"I Can See for Miles." I probably looked like an idiot doing it; but I sang along at the top of my voice. Come to think of it, I probably *sounded* like an idiot. And as I did, I understood Leon's attraction for the braggadocio and tough-guy posturing of his favorite rap artists. They were mainly just expressing those age-old *Rebel Without a Cause* feelings, of trying to bust your way out of someone else's home, someone else's world, someone else's life, when you desperately want a life of your own. I remember how angry and embarrassed I was at my mom and dad when I was a teenager. How desperate I was to break free. How I thought I knew more about life than they ever would. What was it Dylan said? "I was so much older then, I'm younger than that now." That was me. Did I go to college in San Diego, where I grew up? No, as soon as I could leave home I lit out for Columbia University in New York City, then on to Harvard. Even now, I'm living in Maine. How much farther away from San Diego could you get, geographically speaking, and still live within the continental United States?

The Who brought those feelings back to me. They were the best of all the sixties bands at expressing teenage angst.

Maybe that was part of what was going with Jennifer, I thought. I knew she hated Kristin, she'd told me so in no uncertain terms. And I'd just been told that she wasn't on speaking terms with her father, though I had no assurance that that was really the case. Kristin was the one who'd told me that and she does tend to lie a little. Then there was the disparity in the "facts" about her mother's death. Something odd was going on in that family. Especially if Randy Corliss was an old friend from way back, as Kristin had told me he was. I wondered, briefly, how the hell he was connected.

But if Jen was still alive, I was determined to find her. Let the State Police or the FBI track down whoever killed that woman in the lake. That's their job. Yes, I felt bad for her and her family. But after all, *her* troubles were already over. And the way things looked, Jennifer's were only just beginning.

I got to the kennel, gathered up all the dogs that had to be dropped off, then drove around, dropping them off, listening to a Beach Boys tape—still in the mood for sixties music but tired of The Who. On the way home I bought some groceries: fresh shrimp, some spinach, red and yellow bell peppers, alligator pears (also known as avocados, the Hass variety), a couple of *real* pears, and a package of tortillas, along with a few sundries for James.

Frankie and Hooch greeted me at the kitchen door. Frankie was holding a toy in his mouth and wagging his tail. Hooch just stood there smiling at me with his big orange face and occasionally making a low, throaty howl of pleasure.

"Hello, boys! Nice to see you too."

Hooch glanced over at Frankie's toy. Frankie, thinking Hooch wanted to steal it, turned his head away and growled a little. I laughed. Hooch howled at me again.

"How about some dinner?" I said, putting the groceries down on the counter by the sink. Both dogs put their ears up at the word, "dinner." Frankie even dropped his toy. I laughed some more then got their dinner ready.

While they were chowing down, I put away the groceries, then I got out my address book and made a call to Sonny Vreeland at the family's apartment in New York.

I got the machine.

Next, I tried the house in Short Hills and was about to hang up after about six rings when an unsteady hand fumbled with the receiver at the other end.

"Yes, yes, hello?" a man's voice said after rattling the handset against the cradle several times.

"Mr. Vreeland? This is Jack Field, up in Maine?"

"What?"

"I'm Jennifer's employer. Or *was*. She's gone missing again. Have you—?"

I don't know if he hung up on purpose or just dropped the phone back in the cradle, but there was a click and then the line went dead. I stood there a moment, wondering whether I should call him back or just try again later.

I was getting hungry, and figured Leon would be too, so I decided to call back later and began making dinner: shrimp quesadillas, with red and yellow bell pepper slices, jack cheese, thinly sliced pears (I know, pears on a quesadilla? but for some reason it goes great with the shrimp), a chipotle sour cream sauce on the side, refried beans, Spanish rice, sautéed spinach with onions and walnuts, corn chips, and a big bowl of guacamole, made with diced Vidalias, tomatoes, a squeeze of lime juice, and fresh cilantro. Mmmm. Yummy.

"My god, Jack, that smells delicious," Jamie said, coming in the kitchen door just as I was chopping up the cilantro. Meanwhile, she didn't smell quite so delicious.

"Ooh, honey," I said, waving my hand in front of my face.

"Don't worry. I'm going right upstairs to take a shower. Oh, the sunflowers are lovely. Thanks, Jack." She put a file folder down on the big round oak kitchen table, then came over to where I stood at the counter.

"I'd kiss you, honey, but . . ."

She took a step back. "I know, I know." She pointed to the folder. "I downloaded the reports from ViCAP and ViCLAS. You were right. The first three victims were from the same area in Canada. Each of whom, my brilliant boy, had a similar set of bite marks as *our* victim, just as you suspected. The trouble is, the bodies were too decomposed to get a match."

"Really? Did you start the autopsy already?

"Hardly. I'm doing it tomorrow. I had to get a better idea on how to handle the adipocere. I've been on the phone with Dr. Liu, and on the Internet with a woman in Australia. She says that even though the saponified tissue expands, making the wounds larger than the original pattern at the time of death, we can run a computer program and make a perfect match with the photographs. Then if we can find the killer—"

"That's good." I went to the utility closet and got out a large black plastic garbage bag. I gave it to her.

"What's this for?"

"For your clothes. You can put them inside it until we can locate a toxic waste site to dump them in."

"Oh, good, that's it, Jack. Make a girl feel wanted."

"You're the one with the cactus legs, remember?"

"Hey! You're lucky I even came back here tonight. God, that smells delicious." She started to leave then turned back to me and said, "Can I ask you something?"

I said she could.

"You like enchiladas, right?"

"Yeah. So?"

"So if I'm not mistaken, every time we go out for Mexican food you almost always order the enchiladas."

"Yeah, or the chile rellenos. So?"

"So why have you never made either of your favorite Mexican foods for dinner?"

"Oh," I said. "Because then I'd have to use the oven."

She laughed. "You're afraid of the oven?"

"Sort of," I said, as she laughed some more. "See, when I'm cooking on the stove my mind is totally involved in the process. I'm right there, watching everything. But for some reason as soon as I put something into the oven, I get distracted."

She shook her head and went into the living room, laughing. Frankie and Hooch followed her, their noses glued to her clothes. (Dead flesh smell. Mmmm. Yummy.)

"I'm going to get cleaned up," she said.

"Please do," I said. "And you can laugh at me all you want,

but I don't see *you* doing any cooking around here. . . ."

She stopped by the leather sofa, turned and glared at me. "Would you like me to?"

I thought about it. "Not really."

"Good. I like your cooking just fine."

"Oh, and after dinner," I went on, "how would you feel about going up to Waterville with me?"

"Jack, I'm tired, and we have more important—"

"I know, but I want to go through the things in Jen's dorm room to see if I can find any clues."

She shook her head. "Jack, we're not breaking into anyone's dorm room. Why not just ask for permission?"

"Who said anything about breaking in?"

"Good then. Besides, we have wedding plans to take care of, remember?"

"I know. But can't we do that in the car? Though, to be honest, if I have to break into her room, I will."

"You're impossible, you know that?" She looked down at Frankie and Hooch. "Will you please stop *sniffing* me?!"

"Heyo, leave it," I told them and they came trotting back to the kitchen, though their heads were still turned Jamieward and their noses were lifted high into the wafting smell.

She parked her hip on the edge of the sofa. "And, if you insist, I'll go with you to Waterville tonight, but I can't break into the dorm with you."

"Why not?"

"Why *not*?" She came back a few steps toward the kitchen.

I put my hand up to stop her, wrinkling my nose.

"Sorry. Because, you idiot, I'm the Chief Medical Examiner now. I can't go breaking into people's houses or dorm rooms or basements or auto salvage yards anymore. I'd have to get a search warrant first and go there with at least one police officer." She sighed. "I'm starting to feel like I want to quit the ME's office."

"Why?"

"It's just, I don't know, there's a lot of administrative things to take care of, budget, and hiring and firing, and it just wears me down. Then along comes a case like this, and it makes me remember why I wanted to be a forensic pathologist in the first place, and not a bureaucrat."

"Well, quit then, if you're unhappy. But *I* can break into her room tonight if I have to, right?"

"Legally? Now that you mention it? No, you can't. You're also a law enforcement officer, remember?"

"What? Because I'm your consultant?"

She nodded.

"If *that's* the case, then—"

Before I could finish, she said, "Okay, you're fired. And I'll come along, but I'm waiting in the car." She shifted her weight. "Though I suppose . . ."

"What?"

"Well, since it's not an active case with the ME's office, and since you were asked, at one time, by her wicked stepmother to find her, I guess—"

"So, you'll come?"

"Yes." Her face got serious. "As long as you try to get permission before doing anything stupid. And you also have to promise to knuckle down with the wedding plans. We're getting married a week from Saturday, remember?"

"Really? That's big. I should have written that down."

"Jerk," she said, shaking her head at me. "Now, can I go take a shower, please?"

"Sure, but if you'd rather have a bath instead, I can keep the quesadillas warm till after you're done. I bought you some scented bath oil when I got you the flowers."

"You did?" She smiled her Christmas-morning smile, so I

knew I'd done good. She said, "The Dr. What'shisname kind?"

"Dr. Kneipp's, yep. Your choice of almond or juniper. They're both waiting for you upstairs."

"I love you, honey."

"Love you too, Stinky."

She shook her head and said, "You know, I could always rehire if you don't watch it."

"Sorry. I love you, sweetie. My sweet, delicious baby."

She smiled (or smirked) in victory. "That's better, though you don't have to go overboard."

6

While Jamie was upstairs luxuriating (not to mention, deskunkifying), I finished making dinner and got Leon fed, though I practically had to send an e-mail to get him out of the guest cottage—a renovated carriage house—where he lives with his TV, his computer, his Game Boy, and a rascally wheaten terrier mix named Magee. I buzzed him on the intercom several times, then finally went out there to roust him. He was lying on his bed—with Magee next to him—reading a school book, and listening to his stereo with the headphones on.

"Hey, Leon. Dinner's ready."

Magee jumped up, shook himself, and wagged his tail at me. Leon threw the book down, reached over and unplugged the headphones, and the room filled with rap music.

"What?" he said. Magee stretched, jumped off the bed, and came over to jump up on me.

"Good boy, Magee. Okay, off!" He jumped down. To Leon I said, "You like it loud, huh? You'll ruin your ears."

"What?" He reached over and turned it down a little.

At a respectable volume, the music didn't sound too bad, actually. "Hey, this is pretty good, Leon. Who is it?"

"Spearhead," he said. "You like it?"

"Yeah," I said surprised, "I do."

The singer, or rapper, or whatever they're called, was talking about world politics, not about roughing up some "bitches" or gang violence or killing cops. In fact, from what little I heard, it was quite intelligent and insightful.

Leon shrugged. "I can burn you a copy, if you want." He saw the blank look on my face. "It means copy it from one CD onto another, but then I forgot—you never listen to CDs."

"Not if I can help it. Anyway, dinner's ready."

"What are we having?"

"Shrimp quesadillas."

"Aw, man." He got up, reluctantly. "You ever heard of something besides seafood?"

"It's good for you. We can have spaghetti and meatballs tomorrow night, if you want."

"Tomorrow night? Yeah, right. That's what you always say. C'mon, boy."

While Magee and I watched him eat, I was also looking over the files Jamie had brought home. There were twenty-one victims that fit the profile, the first three were found west of the Algonquin Provincial Park in Ontario. I got out a map, and tried to pinpoint their exact center.

"What are you doin'?" Leon asked.

"Trying to find a serial killer's hometown."

"You can do that, just lookin' at a map?"

"Sometimes. It's called forensic geography. These types of killers start out dumping the bodies close to where they live—it's called their 'comfort zone.' " I looked at him. "You mind me telling you about things like this?"

"Nah. I see that kinda shit on TV all the time."

"Leon, you're a kid. You gotta watch your language."

"Says who?"

"Well, legally speaking, I'm your father, so says me. That's who. Okay?"

"Whatever. So, did you find him?"

"Maybe. He's either from Kearney or Huntsville in Ontario, Canada." I showed him the map.

"Huh. So, you goin' up there or somethin'?"

"No, I think he's in Maine now. After they get comfortable with their crimes, they tend to look for new locations. At least some of them do."

"So," he took a bite of food, "what's his MO?"

I laughed. "You have been watching too much TV."

Frankie and Hooch appeared in the doorway. They're not allowed in the kitchen while we're eating. I watched them a moment, making a mental bet as to which one's drool would drip down far enough to hit the floor first (the smart money was on Hooch), then got tired of waiting and told them to go lie down. They stood a moment, as if to tell me it wasn't fair that Magee got to watch Leon eat—but that's Leon's call.

"Besides," I told them, "Magee doesn't drool like you two." They gave up and trotted back to the living room.

Leon looked at me and said, "You're wack, you know that?"

"By the way," I told him, "Jen's disappeared again."

He had a fork halfway to his mouth. "You think this serial killer you're looking for got her?"

"I doubt it. His victims are all in their early thirties, close to six feet tall, and have brown hair and eyes."

"Sounds like Jamie." He chewed his food for a bit, then said, "So where's Jen gone to this time?"

"I don't know. She's missed three weeks of class and her stepmother is worried sick."

"Yeah," he laughed. "She's worried sick about being the only one left in her father's will if Jen dies."

"Is that what she told you?"

"Sort of. She doesn't like that lady very much."

I took a moment then said, "Did she ever say anything to you about her *real* mother?" I didn't want to elicit memories of his own mother's death, but wanted to know some things.

"Just that she died when she was twelve or something."

I nodded. "Did she say *how* it happened?"

He shook his head. "She seemed kinda sad about it, so I didn't ask a lot of dumb questions."

He seemed reluctant to talk, so I followed his example with Jen and didn't push it any further. I looked down at Magee. He looked back at me with his big brown eyes, partly hidden by his bushy, straw-colored fur. He wagged his tail hopefully so I scruffed his cheek. It wasn't table scraps, which is what he'd been hoping for, but he seemed to enjoy it.

Leon seemed about to say something, but then just took another bite of food. I said, "What is it?"

"Nothin'," he said.

"Look, Leon, if you know something about Jen you need to tell me what it is."

"Nah, it's nothing like that. Just some shit at school. I mean, you know, some of the kids is givin' me crap."

"You want to talk about it?"

"Nah, it's all good. The thing is," he went on, "I get the feeling she's pro'bly better off running away than staying with them."

"Why do you say that?"

"I don't know. Mostly because of the dogs, I guess."

"You mean her dad's Dalmatians?"

"Yeah," he nodded sadly. "She says all he cares about is winning at the dog shows and shit. I mean, and stuff."

"Why does she say that?"

"I don't know. She thinks they should live like regular dogs and not be explo—, I forget the word she used."

"Exploited?"

"That's it. She hardly ever gets to play with them. Except Daisy, of course. Plus, they aren't even allowed in the house."

"No kidding." Some show-dog owners are like that, I guess. I said, "Well, they do *shed* a lot, those dogs."

"Yeah, I guess."

The phone rang. I got up and went to the wall unit to answer it. It was Sonny Vreeland. He apologized for hanging up earlier, and then asked for directions to the kennel.

I told him how to find us, then asked if he was coming up.

"Yeah," he said, a bit more awake (or sober) now, "I guess it's time to put a stop to all this nonsense of hers."

I didn't exactly understand, or for that matter agree with his point of view on Jennie's behavior, but it wasn't my place to contradict him. "Well," I said, vaguely, "if there's anything I can do, let me know."

He thought for a bit. "Did Kristin ask you to look into her disappearance again?"

I explained about the situation with Corliss, letting him know my attitude about it.

"That doesn't sound good," he said. "I think I'd rather have you on the case, if you've got time. I'll pay you."

"That's not necessary. I'd be happy to do it."

"Good. Oh, and I've got three Dalmatians. I'd hate like hell to leave them behind. Have you got room for them?"

I laughed good-naturedly and told him I did, and he said that was good and that he'd see me soon, and hung up.

I went back to the table and said to Leon, "Well, it looks like we're going to get a chance to meet those dogs."

"A'ight," he said, smiling.

"You know, it seems to me that if he's going to bring his dogs up here, maybe he's not such a bad guy after all."

"What do you mean?"

I started to tell him, but didn't feel like explaining that

some, if not most, teenagers find fault with almost everything their parents do. I said, "Just that Jen may be mad at her father about something having nothing to do with the way he treats his dogs."

He thought it over. "Still, she says he won't let them run around and play like normal dogs. That's not right." He looked down at Magee. "Is it boy?" Magee wagged his tail. Leon took another bite of his dinner. "Too bad you don't know how to use the Internet, Pops." He gave me a mocking smile. This was a new mannerism of his, calling me "Pops" instead of Jack. I think it gave him a more paternal feeling for me without making him feel that he was dishonoring his father's memory. "She's got a whole blog about what's goin' on with her and her family."

"A blog?"

He explained that it was short for "weblog" and was like an online diary. I asked him if he'd read it and he said he checks it every day.

"Has she made any entries lately?"

"Nah. Not for a couple of weeks. The thing is," he went on, "she doesn't waste all the good stuff on her blog."

"What does she do with it?"

"She probably keeps it on her hard drive. So if you can find her computer, it might help you find her, I guess."

"I hope so," I said, then got up to use the phone.

I called Kristin and asked her where Jen's computer was.

"I don't know. Most of her things are still in her dorm room. The police looked through it for clues, but left all her belongings intact. Is it important?"

"It might be. Which dorm was she in?"

"Dana Hall, room 215. Are you thinking of going up there?"

"Yeah. Does she have a roommate? I need somebody who can let me in."

"She *did*. Sabrina Something. But they put her in with another girl. Jen's room is empty now, sorry. Besides, they won't let you search her room."

"Why not?"

"Like I know? They wouldn't let *Randy* do it."

"You call him Randy?"

"I'm not calling him Regis," she laughed.

"Well, I hope you fired him after the way he behaved at the lake today."

She sighed. "I tried to, but he won't quit."

I gave a surprised snort. "He's not the type to keep working for you if he isn't getting anything out of it."

"I know, but I paid him in advance for two weeks."

"So? He's the type to just take the money and run."

"Well," she admitted, "there's a reward too."

I laughed. "How much?"

"Twenty-five thousand dollars."

I sighed. "I'd have done it for twenty-five cents."

"I know. I'm sorry I've made a mess of things again."

"Don't feel too bad. I'll try to fix it for you."

"You always do, Jack. Thanks."

"Listen, you've been to her dorm. Any ideas on how I can break in, if I have to?"

"You want to break in?"

"Kristin, I've got to take a look at her computer."

"Well, I have no . . . wait. How are you at climbing trees?"

"I don't know. I could give it a shot. Why?"

"Well, there's a big oak, I think, right next to the dorm. One of the branches hangs over the roof of the dining hall, which is on the first floor. Jen's window looks out over it, which I thought was very unsafe. Anyone could get in her room. I tried to get her one in the back, but—"

"Good. Sounds like a plan, thanks."

"Jack? Don't hurt yourself."

"I'll try not to."

I hung up and called Sonny again. I asked him to call the Waterville PD and let them know I was now working the case. He said he'd do it right away. We hung up and I rejoined Leon.

"Hey, Pops," he said, smiling, "these quesadillas are pretty good after all. Aren't you going to have some?"

"I'm waiting for Jamie. You don't have a map of Colby College, do you?"

"I think there's one in the brochure Jen gave me, but I threw it out. They prob'ly have one on their website."

"Good. You can print it for me after you finish eating. You want some more rice?"

"Nah, I'm cool." He ate some more then said, "I wouldn't worry about Jen, Pops. She's got a ton of money of her own, a bunch of credit cards, and probably a dozen boyfriends to run off with. Besides, she can take care of herself, that girl."

"I hope you're right, Leon."

"Didn't you know?" He grinned. "I'm always right."

7

On the drive up to Waterville Jamie was extremely happy and relaxed. Probably from the hot bath, not to mention the quesadillas and guacamole, and the glass of wine she'd had with them.

"Aren't you supposed to be yelling at me over my lack of appreciation for my wedding responsibilities?" I asked.

She waved her hand. "Just make sure to get the marriage license this week. Do not forget. And don't forget to re-check the hotel reservations for our out-of-town guests. You should have done that two months ago."

"Why? I already made the reservations."

"Jack, just check to make sure about them."

"Okay, I'm sorry. What else?"

"Well, we need to find another wedding photographer."

This was news. "What happened to Arlen?"

"He's in the hospital. He's having a gastric bypass. What's so funny?"

"Nothing. I mean he's awfully fat, so he probably needs the surgery, but it reminded me of the fact that your malingering pal out at the lake today gave me her card."

"Gretchen? She does weddings?"

"So she said," I grumped.

"You don't think she's any good?"

"I don't know. She seemed like a pain in the ass to me. Like she'd put up an argument about whatever photos we wanted taken. But it's not like we'd want her to do it anyway."

"Why not? We need *some*body."

I was baffled "You want a forensic photographer to take our *wedding* pictures?"

She shrugged. "It might be kind of fitting to have her do it, don't you think?"

"Why? You think our relationship needs an autopsy?"

She almost hit me. "No. I just meant that you're a detective and I'm an ME . . . why? Do *you* think it does?"

"No. And I'm an *ex*-detective."

"Sure you are." She patted and stroked my arm where she'd almost hit me. "Just like Kristin Downey is your ex-girlfriend."

"Will you knock that off? I'm in love with you and only you. Although that does bring up another possibility."

"What's that?"

"Well, I have another ex-girlfriend who's a professional photographer now. I mean, I doubt if we could get her. She's always busy working for Perry Ellis and the like."

"One of your ex-girlfriends is a fashion photographer?"

I said yes, then reminded her that I lived in New York for fifteen years, and I wasn't exactly a monk during that time, but didn't mention the fact that the woman in question had been a fashion model when I'd known her. Not that that meant much to me (it was more annoying than it was appealing), but Jamie tends to get jealous over little details like that.

"No," she said, "I'd rather have Gretchen do it. I've had about enough of your ex-girlfriends, Jack." She had a point. "Have you talked to Kelso yet?"

"I can't get hold of him. Last I heard he said he'd try to

make it up for the wedding, but he just bought a new apartment and is still dealing with the legal ramifications on the ten million dollars he got from the Sebastian Video case."

"So, who'll be your best man, Leon?"

"No, I think he'd feel like I was putting him on the spot. I do have *someone* in mind, though."

I tried to figure out how to tell her my idea. It was going to be a small church wedding—just close friends and family, without a lot of pomp and fuss—but it was going to be held in the Congregational Church in New Hope, which is where Jamie grew up and where Laura Cutter, her mom, still lives.

"Okay, who?" she asked.

"Well, I have two choices. Maybe you could help me pick one of them."

"Okay," she smiled, "shoot."

"Well, I can't decide between Frankie and Hooch."

She laughed. "For your best man?"

"You hate the idea don't you?"

"You mean you're serious?" She laughed some more. "I know that dogs are man's best friend, but man's best man!" She laughed some more, then said, "Well, if you ask me, Hooch would make the better choice. He'd look awfully nice in a tuxedo. And that big orange face of his!"

"A tuxedo? I don't think so."

"Oh, yes, Jack. If the dogs are going to be part of the wedding party they both have to dress up."

"Well, okay," I griped, "but just the jacket. No pants."

She laughed again. "And Frankie will be the ring bearer."

"You mean you don't mind the idea?"

"Actually?" She looked at me tenderly. "I love it. When you didn't show any interest in taking care of your duties as the intended groom, I got worried that maybe you didn't really want to marry me. That you weren't into it as much as I was." I apologized and she said, "That's okay. Eve Arden explained that it's just a normal guy thing." She was referring to her best friends, Evelyn and Ardyth. Since they dress alike and wear their hair alike and just generally look alike, I can never tell them apart, so I always refer to them collectively as "Eve Arden" (although, in my defense, the first time I did it I was high on Demerol, after getting a bullet removed from my shoulder). The funny thing is, Jamie couldn't decide which one should be her maid of honor so they agreed to flip a coin for it and the coin landed on its side! Even a stupid quarter can't tell those two apart!

"But wanting one of your dogs to be your best man"—she went on—"that shows me that you're taking this seriously."

"How so?"

"Because, you idiot . . ." She scooted next to me and hugged my arm. "What are the two things you love most in the world?"

I nodded. "You and my dogs."

"Exactly. You may not be the most sensible man in the world, Jack, but you're definitely one of the sweetest."

"Thanks." I thought it over. "And I think you're right. Frankie and Hooch would look pretty good all dressed up."

"They'll look fabulous. Oh, and you still have to hire a band, by the way. Does that friend of yours do weddings?"

"Dennis? He's a friend of Farrell's not mine, but I could ask him. I don't know if I really *want* a band, though."

"Honey, we have to have one for the reception."

"Okay, okay. I'll call him. But they play swing and folk. I doubt if they know 'The Hokey-Pokey.'"

"All the better."

"Hey, did you hear that the guy who wrote 'The Hokey-Pokey' died? But the undertaker had a hell of a time getting him into the coffin. First he put the man's left foot in . . ."

She laughed. "Good one, Jack. Got any more?"

"As a matter of fact, I do. A new scientist showed up at the animal research lab one day, and one dog turned to the other and said, 'Hey, who's the new guy?' The second dog said, 'You mean you've never heard of Pavlov?' The first dog thought it over and said, 'Doesn't ring a bell.' "

She laughed, then the news came on and I was about to turn the radio down but stopped when the leading story was about Sheriff Flynn and the Rockland County recall election.

Jamie sat up, suddenly. "Recall?" she nearly shouted at the radio. "It's not a recall, it's a travesty."

"I know, honey."

"If the people of this county don't know how lucky they are to have Flynn as their sheriff . . ."

"I know, I know." I switched the dial to the listener-sponsored station in Blue Hill. They were playing some really cool electric blues guitar. "Hey," I said, "I think they're playing a Peter Green song."

"Jack, what are we going to do about Uncle Horace?"

"I don't know. We'll think of something. But maybe he's ready to retire anyway. He was telling me a while back that he's thinking of moving to Buffalo to be closer to Joan."

"He did?" I nodded. "He never told me that."

"Anyway, he said he was getting tired of flying up to visit her at the mental hospital all the time."

She nodded. "It's so sad, though—this whole thing."

I agreed and we drove on, thinking over the situation:

Horace Flynn's illegitimate son, Sam Kirby, had gotten into another scrape with the law. This time it was a "misunderstanding" about selling steroids to members of the health club he worked at. Some clever reporter did a lot of checking and brought to light the facts of Sam's true parentage; facts which almost everyone else in the county (except Sam) were already aware of: that Horace Flynn, not Walter Kirby, was Sam's biological father. (Flynn had an affair years ago with Walter Kirby's wife, Joan.)

There were allegations that Flynn, due to his paternal feelings for Sam, had exerted undue legal influence on a couple of occasions to keep the idiot out of jail.

An investigation was launched and there had been a huge public outcry. No indictment had been brought yet, but some powerful people in state government used an arcane election statute to try to bring Flynn down. And if you believe the polls it looked like they were going to be successful. It was a shame, too. Despite the mess he'd gotten himself into, Flynn was actually one of the last, true good guys.

Of course, it hadn't helped any that, when in a fit of drunken sarcasm, he recorded an outgoing voice mail for the Rockland County Sheriff's Department that went like this:

"Hi, this is Sheriff Horace Flynn. Please select from one of the following menu options: If you're calling to complain about us not doing anything to solve a problem that you created, press one. To inquire whether someone has to die before we'll do anything, press two. To report your dissatisfaction with the job I've been doing as sheriff, when I put my ass on the line for you people, twenty-four/seven, you ungrateful bastards, press three. If you want the sheriff's department to take over your parental responsibilities and teach your children right from wrong, when you should have done it yourself, years ago, but didn't because you're a pathetic, miserable excuse for a human being, press four. If you'd like us to fix a life you screwed up on your own, due to chemical dependency, lack of morals, or just because you're just a lazy-ass drunk, pothead or junkie, press five. To provide us with a list of state, city, or county politicians you know personally, so we'll refrain from taking legal action against you for any crimes or minor infractions you may have committed, now or in the future, press six. To tell me that you'll have my badge, or that you'll see to it that my career is over, press seven. To gloat over the upcoming recall election, press eight. To kiss my rosy, red Irish ass, press nine. Thanks, and have a nice day."

He sobered up and repented the next morning, recorded a new message, and thought nothing more about it for a few days. But some wiseacre had recorded it, then had it transcribed, and a sanitized version appeared a day or two later in the local papers, and the original was passed around via e-mail and had its own life on the Internet for a few weeks.

Jamie sighed. "If only he hadn't kept his relationship with Sam a secret all this time, none of this would have happened. It's the secrecy that people are upset about."

"Maybe," I said, thinking of something else—namely the day that Kristin had kissed me in the kennel, and the fact that because I'd kept it a secret from Jamie, she might make more of it than it really was.

"I'm serious," she said. "It's the fact that he'd kept it a secret all these years that makes him look guilty now."

"He *had* to keep it a secret, remember? Joan made him promise never to tell anybody, especially Sam."

"I know. But she's living in a mental hospital in Albany. How could she find out if he'd told anybody?"

"That doesn't make any difference to Flynn," I said. "You know how he is. He'd given her his word. That's why he's so dug in now." She smiled and stroked my arm. "Besides," I went on, "maybe some secrets are best kept hidden." I wondered if that were true or if it was just a cop out on my part.

"Well," she said, resting her head on my shoulder, "at least we don't have any secrets from each other."

I started to say something, but just kept my mouth shut and drove, listening to Peter Green play the blues.

8

We got off the turnpike at the Armstrong Road exit, then drove south along Mayflower Hill Road until I found a good place to pull over; not too far from campus that we would have to hike all night, and not too close as to arouse suspicion.

"Ready?" I asked my partner in crime.

She smiled. "Ready when you are, Columbo."

"Good." I turned off the engine, then grabbed a fifty-foot nylon training leash from the backseat.

"What's the rope for?" (It looked like a climbing rope.)

"You'll see," I said, putting it over my left shoulder.

We got out and I popped the hood, just in case any law enforcement vehicles were to drive by and see my woody. It would appear to have been parked there due to engine trouble.

It was a dark, moonless night, and we went down a low incline, wet with dew, toward a soccer field. As we made our way along, walking neither too fast nor too slow, I said, "The suspects left their vehicle on Mayflower Hill Road and proceeded toward campus on foot, coming from the north."

"Jack," Jamie laughed, "what the hell are you doing?"

"Nothing. Just imagining how the police report will sound after we get caught."

"Are you *planning* on us getting caught?"

"No, but I'm not overly optimistic about our chances."

"Well, then," she stopped, "let's go home. I'm tired."

"Me too, honey. But I've got to get inside Jennifer's dorm room. I have to find out what happened to her."

She sighed. "I know." She patted me on the back. "Lead on, Professor Holmes."

"Yes, Doctor."

We came to the soccer field and began to cross toward a thicket of trees encircling the back of Dana Hall.

Jamie said, "Did you enjoy writing police reports when you were a detective? Is that why you're suddenly engaging in this strange monologue of yours tonight?"

"Not especially. They tend to be written in a slightly turgid style, and I strive for a more limpid prose."

"Is that right?" Her eyes sparkled.

"It means clear and simple."

"Yes, darling, I know what limpid means. It also means untroubled—as in 'limpid eyes.' "

We made our way slowly toward the trees, looking carefully for any students or campus cops who might see us.

"So, knowing you," she went on, "you probably entertained yourself, much like you're doing tonight, by writing your reports in a way that was a little off-kilter."

"I wouldn't say that. Careful, watch those branches."

She glared. "You know, you *could* hold them back for me."

"Sorry. I forgot the chivalry of shrubbery."

She laughed. "Nice line."

"Thanks. I stole it, actually. From an ex-girlfriend."

"Okay, Jack, enough with the ex-girlfriends."

"Oddly enough, her name was Dana Hall."

She hit me.

We came past the last tree in the bunch and crouched our way toward a tall black oak, closest to the dorm.

I said, "This campus must be beautiful when the leaves get their full color every year. Though now that I think about it, I *did* tend to throw an arcane word or two into my police reports, like *limpid* or *dottle,* just for fun."

"I'll bet you did. And what's dottle mean?"

"It's the combination of the ash and unsmoked tobacco in the bottom of a pipe bowl."

"So glad I asked. Okay, now what?"

I pointed to the dining hall, which was only one story high and encircled the front of the building. It looked like it had been added on to the original structure. Its façade was mostly high, arched windows with white frames, and it curved around what had once been a square courtyard. The rest of the building was four stories of dark brick, with dorm windows, some of which—including Jen's—looked out over the dining hall roof.

"I'm going to throw this rope over that branch, and you're going to hold on to it from here while I climb up."

"Jack! I won't be able to hold your weight."

"Yes, you will. You're a strong girl. Anyway, the branch will act as a fulcrum. Don't worry."

"Okay, if you say so. But, listen, why don't we just go around the back and break in through the door or something? Why all the rigmarole?"

"Because, honey, it's a dormitory. It's nine-thirty, the halls will be crawling with students. We don't exactly look like we belong there."

"So? We can talk one of them into letting us in."

"Yeah, then they'd be in trouble with the administration for helping us. Besides which someone else might be antsy about seeing us there and call the campus police."

"So? Let's wait and get permission."

"I already told you—"

"I know, but we could make it into an official request."

"You want the ME's office involved? Or Sheriff Flynn? He's got enough problems these days. Besides, that would take at least another day or two and we don't have time for that. I have to find Jen's computer before Regis does."

She sighed. "Well, all right, I guess. I just wish there was an easier way to do it." She looked up at the tree. "So what am I supposed to do once you're up there playing Tarzan?"

"Then I'll hold the rope and you'll climb up after me."

"I have to climb a rope?" She shook her head. "I hated this part of PE class."

"It's not like in PE class. You don't have to shimmy up, you can use the tree trunk. Just watch how I do it."

I threw the rope over the branch, though it took three tries, then climbed up, using the tree as if I were a mountain climber. Jamie followed me while I held the rope, and we balanced precariously in the armpit of the branch.

"Now what?" she said, as I coiled the rope again.

"Now we're going to crawl over to the end of the branch, me first, then drop down to the roof of the dining hall."

She shook her head. "I'd laugh, but I'm afraid I might fall out of the tree, like a ripe apple."

For some reason, her comparing herself to a ripe apple turned me on. I shifted my weight and leaned toward her.

She said, "*Now* what are you doing?"

"Nothing."

"Did you just try to kiss me?"

"Why would I do that?"

"I have no idea, except that you're a strange man. And I can tell you just got turned on for some odd reason."

"Let's just get this over with," I griped.

"Now there's an idea. And if you're really turned on right now, I've got good news. I was so happy with the bath oil you got me tonight that I shaved my legs while I was upstairs."

I sighed. "Now you're deliberately trying to get my motor running."

"What difference does that make? As far as I can tell, your motor is *always* running." She thought a bit and laughed. "I get it. It was the line about the ripe apple, wasn't it?"

"Shut up."

"I love you, darling. And don't worry, we can make love later, as long as we don't end up in the hospital." She saw something in my eyes, laughed and said, "Okay, even if we're in the hospital. You'd kind of like that, wouldn't you?"

"Maybe."

"Okay, let's just do this before somebody sees us up here."

"Okay," I said. "You go first."

We heard voices coming toward us. Jamie huddled next to me and clutched my arm. The voices got a little louder.

"Jack, what if they *see* us?"

I looked down. It was a boy and girl, holding hands. The boy said, "Let's go to the soccer field."

The girl echoed Jamie. "But what if someone *sees* us?"

"They won't," he said, and they walked past our tree and disappeared. This reminded me of Kristin Downey and that night at the football stadium, which didn't help matters any.

"Okay," Jamie said, getting up and balancing on the limb, "now let's go."

"The thing is, honey, you're soooo sexy . . ."

"Oh, you're useless." Her eyes brightened with a clever thought. "The thing is, Jack, if we end up in the hospital, you're not going to able to make love. Want to know why?"

"No."

"Because you'll have a catheter stuck you-know-where."

I thought about it, felt a change come over me, got onto my hands and knees and said, "Okay, I'm good to go."

Jamie said, "God, men are such babies."

I crawled carefully to the end of the branch, feeling it bend slowly downward the farther out I got. Then, when I was nearly over the dining hall roof, I put my hands around it, shifted my weight over the side, held on tight, swung my legs sideways, and dropped easily, landing as softly as I could.

I called quietly to Jamie, "Okay, now it's your turn."

"Here goes nothing. You'll catch me, though, right?"

"It's not that big a drop, honey."

"Not for you, maybe." She nervously inched forward on her hands and knees but immediately lost her balance and teetered, almost falling out of the tree. "Jack!"

"Grab hold of the branch, honey. Hang on tight!"

She fell sideways, but hooked her elbow over the branch, said, "ugh," or something that sounded like "ugh," and hung on precariously twenty-five feet above the lawn. "Come help me!"

I took the rope from around my shoulder and looked up at the branch, trying to figure out a way to use it to get back up. There wasn't one. I said, "I can't get back up there from here. Just hang on with both hands and move them slowly, one at a time, toward me."

"I can't! I'll fall!"

"No you won't. You're not Jamie Cutter tonight, you're James Bond. Remember?" (She'd once told me that when we went on expeditions like this she wanted to be James Bond, not the Bond girl.) "Now's your chance."

She got into position. "Okay, but my arms are killing me. I don't think I can hold on much longer."

"Sure you can. You're very strong."

"Yeah, right. And what I mentioned earlier, about later tonight?"

"Un-huh?"

"That's definitely out of the question now."

"Fine. I don't care about that."

"Like, *unh,* fun, *unh,* you don't," she said, still inching her way over, hand over hand.

"Okay, but not as much as I care about you getting over here in one piece. Okay?"

She grunted, but it sounded like she said "okay" somewhere in the midst of the sounds she made. She got closer and closer. There was some cursing, a little taking of the Lord's name in vain, both the Father and the Son, then she got close enough to swing over and I said, "Okay, now start swinging your legs toward the roof. Okay?"

"I'll try! You promise you'll catch me *now*?"

"Don't worry."

"Shut up and promise me."

"I promise."

"Good, 'cause here, *unh,* I, *unh,* come!"

She swung her legs over to the roof and let go. Now, technically I broke my promise, but only because I didn't really catch her, per se, she landed on top of me, in a jumble of arms, legs, exclamations, and whatnot. This was followed by a lot of "Are you okay?"s and "I'm fine"s, followed by both of us getting to our feet and dusting ourselves off. Jamie had a twig caught in her hair and I gently extracted it.

She saw something in my eyes when I touched her hair, or thought she did. She said, "You hate my hair, don't you?"

"I don't hate—" I stopped and smiled. "Honey, I love your hair. It's just that the longer it is, the better I—"

"But I cut it especially for the wedding."

"I know you did. And I'm sure it'll look great."

She sighed and frowned. "If you hate it so much, then maybe we should just wait till it grows back out."

"I do not hate your hair—I love it. And do you really want to postpone our wedding just because of a stupid haircut?"

"No, although its nice to know you think it's stupid."

"That was just a figure of—"

"Anyway," she said and moved her shoulders around to get the kinks out, "we're still getting married. But you're never talking me into doing anything like *this* again."

"Fine. As long as you're not thinking about leaving me at the altar, I don't mind."

"It'll probably be the other way around. You'll probably leave me to run off with Crystal Gayle or someone."

I laughed. "I don't want you to grow it *that* long."

She looked over at the windows on the second floor. "How do you know which one is Jen's room?"

"Kristin told me it's Room 215, so it's on the second floor." I pointed to a dark window. "There's no light on and no music coming from that room over there." The others were all lit, most with desk lamps or overhead fluorescents, some with candles that flickered in the dark. We also heard a mix of musical styles floating into the night air, Norah Jones from one window, some hip-hop from another, and what sounded like Townes Van Zandt somewhere in the mix. I immediately liked whoever was playing Townes Van Zandt and could have sworn that Norah Jones was also singing one of his songs.

"Okay," I said. "You ready?"

"Ready as I'll ever be," she grumped.

"Don't worry. We got here didn't we? The rest is gonna be gravy. Trust me."

I kissed her for luck, and we crossed over to Jen's window. I dropped the rope next to it, opened it slowly and carefully, then climbed through. Jamie was right behind me.

But it turns out I was wrong: the rest of the night wasn't gravy after all.

9

It was very dark and quiet where I was resting. I slowly became aware of two things: I was lying flat on my stomach, and my hands were tied tightly, in fact, painfully, behind my back. I groaned and became aware of another detail. My head hurt like a sonovabitch whenever I tried to move.

A youngish, male voice said, "Oh, so you're awake? Okay, who are you?"

"Where's Jamie?" I mumbled into the carpet.

"Who? Oh. She's fine. I tied her up too, so don't even think of trying anything, either of you. I already called Campus Security. They'll be here any minute."

I heard a sweetly familiar voice groan, then say, "Jack?"

It was Jamie. Oh, my poor baby. She didn't *sound* fine.

I said, "Are you okay, honey? I can't see you. I can't see anything but the carpet." I strained to raise my head up.

"I told you to relax," said the male voice.

Jamie said, "Jack, what happened? Where are you?"

I wanted to explain that we'd been knocked cold as we came through the window, though I had no memory of exactly what had taken place—when you're knocked out you seldom, if ever, remember how it happened; the trauma prevents the memory center in your brain from recording events just prior to the incident—but before I had a chance to say anything, I heard muffled footsteps, then a swooshing sound, and things got dark and quiet again.

10

The kid's name was Adam. The lights were on now, and I could see he was tall and thin, and had black eyes and dank brown hair. He reminded me of a weasel. After I'd gotten over wanting to beat the crap out of him, and had rubbed some feeling back into my wrists, he introduced me to Peggy Doyle, a tall, svelte, thirtyish woman dressed in the light blue shirt, navy slacks, and dark windbreaker of the Colby College Security force. She wore white Reebok walking shoes and though most of her hair was under a hat, her green eyes and fair skin confirmed what her name had already told me—she was an Irish redhead.

Jamie and I were sitting on one of the beds, holding hands and acting remorseful. Doyle and Adam stood near the door. Adam was staring at Jamie, which is not unusual—a lot of guys do—but it reawakened my desire to belt him one.

"Thanks, Adam," she said, "you can go."

"B-But Peggy—" the weasel stuttered.

"You're already in trouble yourself, mister."

"I know, but—"

"Go back to your room. Now."

"Fine!" he said like a peevish child (or like a weasel, if a weasel could talk), then left the room.

Peggy Doyle walked past us to the desk, pulled out the chair with her right toe, keeping both hands in plain sight, then sat down. "So," she said, sitting up straight with her hands on her knees, "the famous ex-New York detective, Jack Field, and our very own Chief State Medical Examiner, Dr. Jamie Cutter. Caught breaking into a girl's dorm room."

"That's us," Jamie said brightly. "We're the Hardy boys of mid-coastal Maine."

I chuckled.

"You think this is funny, Mr. Field?"

"Well, no, not the B&E part, but what she said about us being the Hardy boys—I think that's funny. And call me Jack." I turned to Jamie. "So, who's Frank and who's Joe?"

"I'm Joe, honey. You're older, that makes you Frank."

I said, "But isn't Joe the more hotheaded of the two? Certainly I'm the one who talked you into this caper."

"Can it," said Peggy Doyle, though her eyes were smiling. "Neither *one* of you is either one of the Hardy boys. Okay?"

Contrite, we both said, "Yes, ma'am."

"And can the 'ma'am.' What are you doing here?"

We explained. Then, when I got to the part about Kristin hiring Regis, Doyle exploded. "Her stepmother actually hired *that* rat bastard?"

"You know him?" I asked.

"Oh, yeah." She knew him. She'd been a detective with the Lewiston PD, she told us, until Regis pulled some of his usual sexual harassment bullshit on her. She filed several complaints with the department that unfortunately went nowhere, so she finally took matters into her own hands. He cornered her in the police parking lot after her shift one day as she was unlocking her car door. He came up from behind and started squeezing her ass. She whirled and clocked him one.

"Nice goin'," I said.

Jamie smiled and nodded.

"Yeah, well," said Doyle glumly, "it only felt good for a minute. The knuckle on that hand still gives me trouble on rainy days." She held out her right hand, palm down, to show us a middle knuckle that was raised slightly above the others. Her hands were strong yet feminine. She wore no nail polish.

Jamie went over to examine her hand. "You know," she said, "it would only take a little minor surgery to fix that."

Doyle nodded. "Yeah, but my insurance won't cover it."

Jamie tsked. "Too bad." She sat back down next to me.

"Still," I said, "what you did was justified. The depart—"

"The department agreed on that point," Doyle said, leaning back in her chair a little now. "What they *didn't* care for was the fact that I also happened to kick him in the nuts a couple of times, just for fun, while he was out cold."

"Wait, you actually knocked him out?" I said in admiration.

She shrugged. "It wasn't that hard to do—the asshole's got a glass jaw; though I *did* have to put my back into that punch a little. Sprained my shoulder, too." She rubbed her right shoulder at the memory.

I laughed and we traded Regis war stories for a bit, then she said, "So, what am I going to do with you two?"

"Let us search the room, then let us go?" I suggested.

She shook her head. "I guess I could do that if it weren't for Adam, out there." She jerked a thumb at the door. "He knows you're here, I know you're here. By now probably everyone on campus knows you're here. Nope, I've gotta take you back to the office and call the Waterville PD."

"You could do that after we search the room," Jamie said.

"Yeah," she nodded, "I guess I could. I could even help you toss the place, if I knew exactly what you were looking for." A smile started to form in her eyes. "We could even get Adam to help us. He kinda fancies himself as Jen's protector, although she might have a different definition for him, like 'stalker.' " She looked at the door and called out, "Hey, Adam!"

"What?" the kid said through the door.

"Get your sorry ass back in here."

The door opened and Adam came in. There seemed to be three or four other students standing around out there. I couldn't see them from where I sat, but I could hear the sounds of faint, murmuring conversation and the shuffling of feet.

"Go to the library or go back to your rooms," Doyle said to the others, and the furtive noises faded down the hall.

"So," said Adam, casually taking a seat on the other bed, "are they arrested?" He said it to Doyle but he was looking at Jamie the whole time, the little creep.

"No, and it's lucky you're not, either." Doyle looked at us. "Like I said, he's been hanging around, stalking Jennifer since the first day of class."

"I wasn't stalking her. We're friends." I almost liked him after he used the present tense.

Doyle said, "Then what were you doing alone in her room when the Hardy boys showed up?"

"The Hardy boys?" he asked.

She explained.

"Oh, that. Well, I sort of come in here sometimes to think. I have an extra set of keys. And you know, I think sometimes that maybe if I wait for her, maybe she'll come back."

"That's a lot of maybes. And where'd you glom on to the extra set of keys, you little shit?"

"Jen gave them to me," he said defensively.

She looked at me. "Not likely," her eyes told me.

"Anyway," Adam said, "what are *they* doing here?"

"It's none of your business, you little punk, but that's Jack Field, the famous detective."

"Whoa," said Adam, impressed.

"Yeah," she went on, "he's here to help find Jen. And that's his wife, Dr. Jamie Cutter." Then she told Adam about Jamie's official position.

Adam whoa'd again.

"I'm his fiancée, actually," Jamie pointed out. "We're not getting married for two weeks."

"Congratulations," said Doyle, looking at me.

"What makes you think she's coming back?" I asked Adam.

"I don't know," he said, and the way he said it made me think he was hiding something, though I couldn't be sure.

"Now, here's the thing . . ." said Doyle, then she explained what we were planning on doing, and what Adam's part was going to be—to give back the illegal set of keys, butt out, and keep quiet, if he wanted to avoid trespassing and assault charges.

He agreed, then left the room to the three professionals.

I said to Doyle, "You think this Adam kid might somehow be involved in Jen's disappearance?"

"I seriously doubt it. I've busted him for pot a few times. A few times I let him slide. I got a little worried when I saw the pictures of Jen he has all over his walls."

"Uh-oh," Jamie said. "That sounds seriously creepy."

"True, that." She shrugged. "But he took them for a class assignment. He's a photography major."

"Really?" I said. "Does he do weddings?"

Jamie glared at me and shook her head.

"Hah! Who knows?" said Doyle. "The shots he took of Jen are very artistic, all telephoto, candid-camera stuff. I checked with his professor and the assignment was to capture a subject without their knowing they were being photographed."

I said, "What class was he taking, Paparazzo 101?"

Doyle shrugged. "It's more like photojournalism. And his

professor said he had to redo the assignment. Said he'd kind of crossed the line into invasion of privacy territory. I can show you what he's got on his walls, if you want to see them."

"Thanks," I said, then joked, "but we can always just break into his room later if we have to."

She chuckled and shook her head. "Look, I know it sounds kinky, and he *is* a little obsessed with her, but he's mostly harmless; not a bad kid, really—just a lonely little shit."

Jamie said, "Why do you have to be so hard on him?"

Doyle tilted her hat back and looked sideways at Jamie. "I guess bein' a female medical examiner is different from bein' a female cop—or even working campus security—so you wouldn't know what it's like. Long story short, you gotta take an attitude with some people or they don't respect you."

Jamie smiled and said, "I'll have to remember that."

"Remember it?" I said. "You do it with *me* all the time."

She gave me a backhand swat then said, "So, are you married? Do you have any kids?"

"Easy, Doc," Doyle said. "There'll be plenty of time for female bonding once you're done here and I take you back to the office. We can even share recipe secrets if you want."

Jamie laughed. "Jack's the one to talk to about that." She stroked my shoulder. "He's an excellent cook."

"Just stovetop stuff, really," I said. "Nothing fancy."

"Great," she said. "Now can we get this show on the road?"

11

Doyle watched while Jamie and I went through Jen's dorm room, but the only things we found that might be of any use were some school notebooks, a couple of CDs, and a laptop. I hoped it contained the hard drive that Leon had told me about.

Jamie turned it on but couldn't access any of the files. She said, "I'll have one of my computer geeks try it tomorrow."

"No," I said, "I'll call Tulips," referring to a computer expert who was writing a set of algorithms for me to prove that the canine pack is a self-emergent system. "That way we can keep it under the official radar."

"Good idea."

Doyle said, "So, are you two done here?"

I looked around. "Well, I think we've looked everywhere."

She shook her head, went to the bed, pulled it away from the wall, reached down and drew back a corner of the carpet.

"A lot of kids hide drugs in their rooms. You gotta know how they think." She reached down and retrieved a small stack of letters and photographs, tied with frayed pink and green ribbons. Pink and green were Jennifer's favorite colors. "Luckily, Jen's a good girl. She's only hiding *these*."

Jamie said, "Nice work."

She nodded, politely. "Like I said, I used to be a detective. And a pretty good one, if I do say so."

I said, "Seems like you're wasting your talent here."

She shrugged a "Yeah, but what are you gonna do?" kind of shrug. She went to the closet, found a nylon backpack, dumped out its contents, and put the items we'd found inside. Then she sighed and said, "Sorry, but I'm still going to have to take you back to Roberts Hall, just for the official record. But don't worry. Once I've written it up, I'll kick you." She went to the door. "Now, if we can only get you out of here without too much hoo-hah from the kids . . ." She opened the door.

There were about thirty students, queued up in the hall, with Adam policing the line. Some were waiting to see if they could be of any help in finding Jennifer, some were waiting just to see me. That's one of the drawbacks of solving a couple of high-profile murders, as I'd done recently. One of the cases had even been captured live, on camera, with a worldwide satellite feed. As far as I was concerned, I was just a kennel owner and a dog trainer. But as far as some of these kids were concerned, I was a celebrity. They all began crowding around me and calling out, "Mr. Field, Mr. Field."

Jamie loved seeing me squirm. And, as I tried to get through the crowd, I caught Peggy Doyle out of the corner of my eye. She was also grinning at my discomfort.

"You *could* help out here a little, you know," I told her.

"You're damn right I could. I'm just having too much fun, watching the great detective at work."

"Well, that's just swell."

"Oh, all right," she grumped good-naturedly, then addressed the students. "Okay, people, now listen up! Don't speak unless you're spoken to. Gimme a show of hands—how many of you knew Jen Vreeland?"

Everybody raised their hands.

"No, no." She shook her head in annoyance "I'm serious. I don't want you raising your hands just because you might've borrowed her shampoo once or copied her English homework. Raise your hands only if you really *knew* her."

Everybody raised their hands.

Doyle shook her head. "Okay, let's make it real easy: gimme a show of hands . . ."

Everyone got their hands in position.

". . . of anyone who has Jen's cell number."

A few hands shot up then came back down. A few hesitated, then raised, then lowered their hands. We were left with three students; all girls. They looked at the others with a kind of superior, yet politely apologetic attitude.

Doyle introduced them: Sabrina, a pert, petite brunette with big hips and an anxious smile; Darcelle, a tall, relaxed, black girl in sweatpants and T-shirt; and Lorrie, a dishwater blonde of medium height, who wore men's khakis, a white button-down shirt under a navy V-neck sweater, and had on glasses and a backpack, both of which she kept playing with.

Doyle put them at the front of the line, then did a triage with the rest, asking who'd talked to Jen or had heard something definite—not just a rumor (several hands came down when she made that distinction)—that might help us find her, etc. She put each category in different parts of the line.

While she was thus engaged, Jamie's cell phone rang.

"This is Dr. Cutter," she said, then gave me a meaningful look. "They did? That's great." She listened, looked at me some more and said, "I don't know. I'll ask him." She cupped the phone and said, "It's Greg Sinclair. They found the guy."

"No kidding. The one watching us across the lake?"

She nodded. "Greg doesn't think he's the doer and wants to know the killer's profile before they release him."

I shrugged. "Middle-aged, white male, with an advanced college degree in some kind of scientific discipline. He probably has a reasonable explanation for being at the lake. Oh, and he grew up in Ontario, Canada. That's definite."

She told Sinclair what I'd just said, then listened to his reply and beamed at me. "No kidding. To a tee?"

"Has he asked for a lawyer?" I asked.

She put a finger up, telling me to wait. "I don't know," she said into the phone, "maybe you should talk to Jack."

Doyle came over. "We might as well get this over with. We'll hold short interviews in Jen's room. Short ones."

"Then we can go home?" I said.

"No, I still have to write this up. And make it quick. They have classes tomorrow. There's a lot of rumors flying around about a girl's body being found in a lake."

"Oh, I can straighten that out." I addressed the students: "Okay, everybody—I know some of you heard about a girl's body that was found in Potter's Pond this afternoon."

Jamie handed me her phone. "He wants to talk to you."

Into the phone I said, "Hang on a sec." Then said to the students, "It wasn't Jen's body. The dead woman wasn't a college student, she was in her early thirties."

"Jack," Jamie said, "that hasn't been determined yet."

"I know," I said, "but that's the profile." To the kids I said, "And the police already have a man in custody." Into the phone I said, "You *do* have him in custody, don't you?"

Pissed, Sinclair said, "Yes, but thanks for announcing it to the world. And he may not be the killer. He says he has a perfectly legit—"

"Of course he does. What are you holding him on?"

"It *was* trespassing. Now it's suspicion of murder, I guess." That was good. They could hold him for seventy-two hours on that.

"Did he ask for a lawyer yet?"

"No, actually. Hang on a sec." There was some murmured conversation. "He says he wants *you* to interview him."

I expressed my surprise and curiosity.

"He says he's confident that you can clear him. I think he recognized you when he saw you at the lake, though he denies looking at the scene through his telescope."

"Of course he does. You said he had a legitimate reason for being at the lake?"

"He's a botanist. He was studying kettle bog vegetation."

"What the hell is kettle bog vegetation?"

"Yeah, I never heard of it, either."

Doyle said, "The college owns a kettle bog complex northwest of here. Wasn't she found in Potter's Pond?"

I confirmed that fact.

"That's not part of the Colby complex. Now, can we get on with this?"

"Sure," I told her. To Sinclair I said, "Keep him on ice. He may be the guy. Here's Jamie," and handed her back the phone. To Doyle I said, "You know what a kettle bog is?

"I'll explain it later." She gave a nod to the kids.

I shrugged, then to the students I said, "So, if any of you are here because you're worried about that body in the lake, you can all go study or watch TV or smoke pot"—this got a laugh—"or whatever you were going to do tonight anyway."

Half the group began to wander off, still discussing things and making up more rumors. Even Adam went back to his room, which was right next door to Jen's.

Doyle said, "You're encouraging them to smoke pot? That's real nice, Mr. Field."

"It was a joke. And call me Jack."

One of the kids raised a hand and said, "I have a question about my dog."

"They let you keep dogs at the dorm?"

"No, it's my parents' dog."

"What kind of dog is it?"

"No!" Doyle said, emphatically. "No dog questions, no questions about the body in the lake, and *no* smoking pot in your dorm rooms. You either have information to offer about Jen Vreeland's disappearance, or you need to get your butts out of the hall. Now! Everybody got that?"

There were some murmured "Yes, ma'am"s and "Okay, Peggy"s and "Thank you, Officer Doyle"s, and most of the rest of the group began to disperse. The girl with the dog question hung back, shooting me a question with her eyes.

Doyle made a gesture toward Jen's dorm-room door.

"Hang on a sec," I said to Doyle. "And call me Jack."

I went over to the girl with the dog question. She was shortish, had an angular, lightly freckled face and long light brown, kinky hair, pulled back. "What's your name, sweetheart?"

"Julie. Julie Zimmerman."

"Hi, Julie. What kind of dog did you say it was?"

"He's a Patterdale terrier, and he has this habit of—"

"You mean Clarence?" (Of *course*—that was the name of the breed that the woman at Animal Control didn't get quite right: he was a "Patterdale," not a "Patterson" terrier.)

"You know him?" Julie asked, surprised.

"No, but I think I sort of met him this afternoon. He was wandering by himself on the road by Potter's Pond."

"That's Clarence. He likes to roam. That's one of the—"

"Has he been neutered?"

"Mr. Field," said Doyle.

"No," said Julie. "And my father absolutely refuses to—"

I said, "Well, that's good. He *shouldn't* be. On the other hand, he does need to be taught how to enjoy staying home. Unless we want to create a new breed around these parts, the Clarencedale."

She laughed. "Don't give him any ideas. He already thinks he's pretty hot stuff."

"Mr. Field," said Doyle, "what have I been telling you? We need to get moving."

"Fine, and what have I been telling *you*?"

"Okay, fine, *Jack* . . . let's get this over with before the chief hears about what's going on around here, do you mind?"

"No, that's a good idea." I gave Julie my card and told her to call me, anytime—that I'd like to meet Clarence in person to try and talk some sense into him. She laughed at the thought, then said she'd like to see me try.

I turned to Doyle and said, "Can we just have a quick look at Adam's photo gallery before we do the interviews?"

"Fine," she huffed, then to the three girls she said, "You go on inside. We'll be in to talk to you in a minute."

They all went toward Jennifer's door, Sabrina last. She saw Doyle knock on Adam's door and said, "Adam doesn't know anything. Why are you going to talk to him?"

"Get inside! Now!"

Sabrina stamped her foot but quickly obeyed.

12

Adam opened his door a crack and said, "What?"

I said, "I heard you've got a few pictures of Jennifer on your walls. I'd like to see them."

He stood there with his head poking through. "I took them all down. Anyway, they were for class."

"So, let's have a look," I said and pushed past him. Doyle and Jamie followed me inside.

I was expecting to see all the walls covered with pictures of Jennifer, but they were only on one—the one opposite his bed, probably put there so he could lean back on his pillows and stare at them.

I said, "You took them all down, huh?"

He shrugged. "Most of them, I did."

There must have been at least fifty black-and-white photos, of all shapes and sizes, including a couple of poster-size blowups. He had two standing lamps set up to shine on them. There was nothing particularly salacious about them. They were just shots of Jen doing her everyday activities: studying at a carrel in the library, reading under a tree on campus, eating at the dining hall, talking with friends before class, sitting on the bench at basketball practice, and the like. I'm no expert—my appreciation for this so-called art starts and ends with Ansel Adams—but from what I could tell, they were really good. Each one was framed in such a way as to draw your eye easily and inevitably to the main subject. And each one caught her in a different mood and seemed to catch that mood perfectly.

I was also struck by another thing about them: I had never thought of Jen as being particularly pretty, probably because of the way she dressed and did her hair, but Adam had found a way to capture something I hadn't seen in her before. The girl was quite beautiful in a simple, unassuming way.

By now Adam had thrown himself onto the bed and was glowering at our intrusion into his private world. He was wearing nothing but gym shorts, athletic socks, and a Colby College T-shirt.

"Some mural you've got," I said.

"I told you, it's a class project," he said defensively.

"Un-huh." I took a seat at his desk, the top of which was covered with proof sheets. Jen was the focus of these photos as well. There was also an empty CD case for a Townes Van Zandt album. On the cover was a photo of the singer sitting at a table in a blue kitchen. It just happened to be my favorite Townes Van Zandt album.

Jamie, who was still scrutinizing the wall, said, "These are really good. I never knew how pretty she was."

"She'd hate it if you said that to her. She says physical beauty is a trap."

Jamie turned to look at him. "You need to expand your subject matter a little, but you're a pretty good photographer, mister."

"Thanks. So? What do you want?"

I looked at the other bed, which was unmade and had clothes piled on top of it. I said, "Where's your dorm-mate?"

Adam shrugged. "He hooked up with someone from another dorm. He's probably with her, I guess."

"Yeah? Did you ever try to hook up with Jennifer?"

"No. It wasn't like that. I told you, we were friends. Besides," he added sadly, "girls don't like messing around with guys in their own dorm. They call it dorm-cest."

That sounded reasonable. I riffed through the proof sheets a little. "When were these taken?"

"I don't know. The same week she ran off."

"How do you know she ran off? How do you know something didn't happen—"

"No, nothing happened to her. She just ran off, I'm telling you. She was freaking out because she thought someone was after her."

I felt my spine itch. "How do you know that?"

"She told me. Plus, she wrote a note before she left."

"Okay. Let's see it."

"I didn't . . . I didn't keep it," he lied.

"Like fun you didn't." I looked at his nightstand. It was within arm's reach. "So if we look through that little drawer of yours, we won't find it?"

"I told you, I don't have it anymore." He seemed less angry than just depressed or even despondent.

I stood up. "I think you do."

"It's private," he said, and stood up in front of the nightstand. "You can't—"

I was getting in the mood to beat it out of him if I had to, but Doyle asked, "You want to help us find Jen or not?"

His face contorted. "Please. It's private. I can tell you part of what she said. I've got it memorized."

I looked at Doyle. She shrugged. I took a deep breath.

"Okay," I said to Adam, "what'd she say?"

"She said, 'Dear Adam, I have to leave school and go somewhere. I don't know where yet, but don't try to find me.

He's back again, the man I told you was after me.' Then she said some other things I can't tell you about—"

"What things?" I said.

"I told you, they're private."

"Okay, then give us the gist of it."

"She . . . she thanked me for trying to do something to help her, even though I wasn't able to. Then she said, 'We'll always be friends,' and then she signed it, 'love, Jen.' "

Jamie said, "Who was after her?"

"I don't know. She said her mother was murdered when she was twelve and that the man who did it was after her now too."

I said, "Did she tell you anything about him?"

"No."

I thought it over. "What'd you try to do for her?"

"It's nothing, really."

"If it's nothing then tell us what it was."

"But I *can't* tell you. It might get her in trouble."

"Like she's not in trouble now?"

"This is different. It's secret. It's private. Please don't make me show you the note. Please?"

Doyle said, "Maybe one of her other friends can tell us more about this mystery man."

"Then let's go talk to them. I want to find out who was after her." I stopped, looked back at Adam, and pointed to the CD case. "I like your taste in music, by the way."

"What? You like Townes Van Zandt?" He smiled.

"Hah!" Jamie said, "he's Jack's favorite songwriter."

Adam said, "Well, that's because he's only the greatest songwriter who ever lived."

"That's enough of that," Doyle said, and opened the door, holding it for Jamie.

We left Adam alone and went into the hall.

Jamie said, "What do you think?"

I shook my head. "He's in love with her, or thinks he is, no question. But I don't think he'd hurt her."

"I agree. He *is* creepy, though."

"Yeah, but he has no idea where she is."

"How can you be sure?"

"If he did know where she was, he'd probably be there, hiding in the bushes, taking pictures of her."

She chuckled and nodded.

Doyle opened the door to Jen's room and we went inside to start our interviews, but there were two men with the three girls. One of them was a complete stranger to me. The other I knew all too well. The one I didn't know was a campus cop—a scrawny kid with pimples, probably not much older than the students he was paid to protect.

The one I knew was Randall Corliss.

"So, Field," he turned and said with a smirk, "you trying to horn in on my case again?"

"Okay, that's it," said Doyle. "No more hanging around the dormitory. We're taking this back to the office, *now*."

Doyle sent the other campus cop, whose name was Hupfnagel or Hopfangle or something, back out on rounds and escorted the rest of us, including Regis and the three girls, to Roberts Hall, which was clear across campus. She easily fielded the questions from curious students we passed along the way.

"Shouldn't you be studying?" . . . "None of your business, that's what." . . . "Go back to your dorm room or go to the library."

"The library is closed," someone said.

"Then shut up."

At one point Sabrina, the talkative one, said to some kids we passed, "That's Jack Field, the famous detective."

Darcelle said, "He's gonna help find Jen Vreeland."

The other students started to clump together and began to

follow us at a safe distance. Doyle turned and stopped them with a look. They scattered.

Then she turned to the three girls. "That's enough of that. And no talking about Jen until we get to the office."

They nodded in compliance.

13

"I'm working for the girl's family," Regis said as Doyle pulled out a couple of chairs for me and Jamie, across from her desk in the security office. It was almost eleven. "I want that computer," he went on, "and anything else you found."

"Tough shit," said Doyle. She poked her head through the door and said to the three girls, who were in the waiting room. "I thought I told you, no sharing stories, no making things up."

Someone—I think Sabrina—said, "But we were just—"

"I know what you were just. Now, knock it off. Keep your yaps shut until the great detective can talk to you. You got it?"

"Okay!" said one.

"Yes, ma'am," said another.

She gave them an emphatic nod, then took a seat behind a desk, where she'd put the laptop, the letters and photographs, and the rest of the things we'd taken from Jen's room.

" 'The great detective,' " Regis said with a sneer.

"Who did you say you were working for?" Jamie asked him.

"The girl's family."

She nodded and said, "You mean her stepmother."

"That's right. So?"

"So," she put a hand on my shoulder, "Jack was hired earlier tonight by the girl's father."

Doyle sat back in her chair and tilted her chin at Regis. "I guess the old man trumps the stepmother. Take a seat."

He looked around for a chair.

"Grab one from the waiting room. We're gonna be here a while," she said, making a fake apologetic face. "We've gotta wait for the Waterville PD to show up and write a report."

He shook his head. "I don't have time for this." He chewed on his cheek, looked at the computer and the rest of the stuff, took a card from the pocket of his jacket, tossed it on the desk next to them, and said, "I'll see ya later."

Doyle watched him go, then sighed and shook her head. She seemed unhappy with herself about something. She saw me looking at her and said, "You know, it's too bad he's such a jerk. He's got a really nice butt."

Jamie and I laughed. Doyle picked up the phone and pushed the stack of letters and photos toward me. While she talked to the Waterville PD, I riffed through the pictures. I found a color shot of a young Jen and her mother, taken at a vacation cabin by a lake. Her mother was wearing a pink and green summer dress.

I showed it to Jamie. "Jen's favorite colors."

Doyle got off the phone, pulled the computer toward her and said to the door, "Sabrina, you're first."

The girl came inside. I got up to give her my chair, and then parked one hip on the corner of the desk as she sat next to Jamie. Doyle opened a desk drawer and got out a set of miniature tools—a couple of screwdrivers and a pair of needle nose pliers—and began taking the computer apart.

While she was doing that, I interviewed the three girls, and showed them all the photo of Jen's mother, but didn't learn anything new about her disappearance; just that Jen had told them that she was afraid someone was after her—someone who wanted her dead. Sabrina suggested several times that we take a hard look at Adam, though those weren't the words she used. She called him a slimy little creep. Repeatedly.

They'd all seen the picture of her mother. Jen had showed it to each of them in a private moment and had told them it was taken on the morning of the day her mother was murdered. I told each one what Kristin had told me, that her mother's death had been ruled a suicide, and got the same cynical reaction. "Of course it was *ruled* a suicide," they said. "But look at their faces in the picture. They look so happy. Why would she kill herself?" Or words to that effect.

"Okay, how about this?" I finally told Lorrie, who was the last one I talked to. "Did Jen tell you how old she was when her mother died?"

"Yes. She was twelve."

"And she told you that specifically? That she was twelve years old? And that this picture was taken the day of her mother's death?"

"Yes," she said with a questioning look in her eye.

"Okay. Thanks for helping out."

Doyle, who'd finished taking apart the laptop, told them they could go back to the dorm. Then, after they'd gone, she put her hand out for the photograph. I gave it to her.

She looked at it and said, "The mother looks happy to me. Not that that means anything. She coulda gone nuts later that day. Or she could just be smiling for the camera."

She handed it to Jamie, who looked at it again, then at me. "How old do you think she *was* when this was taken?"

"Five or six," I said. "Definitely not twelve."

"Let me see that again," Doyle said, taking the photo from James. She looked at it, then looked at me. "So that's what you were gettin' at with those questions."

"That's right. Either Jen's got things mixed up in her head or else she's created some kind of dramatic story for herself to help her cope with her mother's death."

Jamie said, "It had to have been a defining moment."

"I know. And we still don't know which is true: that the picture was taken on the day her mother died, meaning Jen was five or six, or that her mother died when she was twelve . . ."

Doyle didn't seem to be listening. She was holding the needle nose pliers and peering at the laptop's motherboard.

"Ah-hah," she said finally, "I found you, you little sucker." She pulled off a piece of the circuitry that looked to me like nothing more than a fat staple.

She plugged the computer in, even though it still seemed to be in pieces. She turned it on, waited for it to warm up, did a few things on the keyboard, then twisted it around so we could see the lit screen and said, "I just disabled the security system. We can download any files we want to now."

"Wow," I said in admiration. "Nice work."

She made a self-deprecating shrug, then stretched her arms back and put her Reeboks up on her desk, while I downloaded the files to a zip disk.

I was almost finished when an officer from the Waterville PD—a crusty veteran named Zeke Evans—showed up. He seemed peeved about it all, but he took our statements, and Doyle's, and asked her what she wanted him to do with us.

"That's your call, Zeke. We've got no beef here."

"Colby won't press charges?"

"Nope."

"Then why'd you call me? Just to ruin my evening?"

"I haven't ruined your evening, Zeke, I've enhanced it."

He smiled at her then he looked at me. "I thought you were a dog trainer now, not a detective."

"Tell me about it," I said.

Jamie stroked my back and said. "He may have helped catch a serial killer earlier today."

"Maybe," I said.

Evans nodded. "You mean the body in the lake?"

We told him yes.

"This have anything to do with the girl's disappearance?"

I shrugged. "Probably not, but who knows at this point?"

He nodded. "Well, I hope you nail him," he said. "And I hope you find that missing girl." Then he told us not to break into any more dorm rooms, gave a secret look to Doyle, who nodded, and told us he'd be waiting out front to "escort us off campus."

Doyle gave us the stack of letters and photos, along with the zip disk and told us we were free to go.

We thanked her and I said, "Can I get my leash back?"

"Your leash? Where is it?"

"On the roof of the dining hall."

"Jack!" Jamie smacked me with the back of one hand. "That was a *dog* training leash, not a mountain-climbing rope?"

I shrugged. "It's made of the same material."

"And you didn't tell me?"

"Would you have climbed the tree with me if I had?"

"What do you think?"

Doyle interrupted us. "I'll have maintenance look for it tomorrow. Now, get out of here. I've got work to do."

We got to the door and she said, "Hang on." She opened a campus directory, looked something up, wrote a name and phone number on a scrap of paper, came over and gave it to me.

"What's this?"

"You're interviewing that serial killer tomorrow, right?"

"Yeah?"

"That's the number for Dr. Petersen. She's head of the botany department. Since your suspect claims he was at the lake to study kettle bogs, I figure you're gonna want to know a little about the subject before you talk to him."

"Good thinking," I said, then remembered the look that had passed between her and Zeke Evans. "I guess having your pal Evans escort us off campus was your idea too?"

She shrugged. "I figure, why not? It's a bit of a hike back to your car."

Jamie and I exchanged glances.

Doyle said, "You own a cream-colored '38 Ford station wagon with oak and mahogany trim, vanity license plate says: DOG HILL, am I right?"

"That's right. It's the name of my kennel."

Amazed, Jamie said, "You know everything, don't you?"

"Everything except how to get you two out of here. Now beat it. I've got students to look after."

On the ride home Jamie curled up on the seat next to me, with her head in my lap. I sometimes think about selling the woody. It's a great car, it reminds me of California and the beach, and it looks zippy when I drive up to a client's house to pick up a dog, but it's not very practical; especially during the Maine winters—which seem to last about six months. But it does have one advantage: the wide front bench seat where Jamie can curl up next to me on long drives and sleep with her head in my lap.

As I stroked her hair with one hand, and held the steering wheel with the other, I couldn't take my mind off that photograph—the one of Jen and her mother, taken at the lake. Something about the way they stood together, Jen beaming brightly at her father, who I assumed was behind the camera, and her mother in the pink and green dress, with one arm draped easily around her daughter's young shoulders. They looked so happy. But now the mother was dead, the girl was missing, and there was a serial killer waiting for me at the state police lockup in Augusta.

While I was thinking about this Jamie yawned and said, "Jack, I think I really like her."

"Who's that, honey?"

"*You* know . . . Peggy Doyle."

"Yeah," I smiled, "so do I."

"You think it's too late to invite her to the wedding?"

"It might be a little awkward, but I can ask her."

"Good. We need more people on your side of the church."

14

I spent most of the next morning on the phone, taking care of my bridegroomly duties, among other things. Then I had a conversation with Dr. Carla Petersen—the head of Colby's botany department—to get the background info on kettle bog vegetation and whatnot.

I also got a call from Tulips, also known as Amy Beckwith, PhD. She was teaching math now at Bates College and was working on a computer model to help prove my theory that the pack is an emergent heterarchy, not a dominance hierarchy. She called to tell me that there can't be three types of dogs: assertive, cooperative, and tentative; but it's true—there are. Every dog comes into the world with a genetic predisposition to one of those three behavioral tendencies.

"But the computer doesn't work that way, Jack. You can't give it three choices, only two. Maybe we should go back to what you told me was the traditional model; that dogs are either dominant or submissive."

"No, that's wrong. Besides, it's too complicated."

"No, it isn't. It's totally binary."

"Yeah, but it's too complicated for the way dogs operate. Dominant and submissive behaviors require a higher level of thinking than a dog's brain is capable of. Besides, the instinct for cooperation while hunting is what makes dogs and wolves sociable. That's the whole point."

The phone was silent for a moment, then she said, "Well, that's easy, then. I'll write the program to show that they can either be cooperative or uncooperative."

"But you're still missing—"

"Let me finish. If a dog is in the cooperative category, the computer goes from there, using the two polarities you already gave me of taking either the most direct action or the most indirect. It's still binary. And if they're in the uncooperative category, we program two choices for that—uncooperative/assertive or uncooperative/tentative. Then you break it down to uncooperative/assertive/direct, and so on."

"That'd work. But you're adding a lot more steps."

She laughed and said, "That's because computers are dumb. You have to break things down for them."

"If they're so dumb, then—"

"Good. I know just what to do now, thanks."

"Uh, you're welcome," I said, but she'd already hung up.

Then I called Kelso to see if he could find out anything for me about the death of Jen's mother, but he was still incommunicado. It was important, so I figured I'd just have to do the research on my own.

I took Frankie and Hooch with me to Leon's room, and was going through Jen's electronic diaries on Leon's computer (with my dogs and Magee fast asleep on the bed) when I got a call from Peggy Doyle. She'd located the official files on Rose Vreeland's suicide, and wanted to fax the copies to me.

"That's very industrious of you, thanks. But I'm afraid I don't have a fax machine."

"I'm sorry. Could you say that again?" I repeated it and she laughed. "How do you expect to find her if you don't . . . never mind. Exactly what century do you live in, Jack?"

I started to explain my desire to live a quiet life in the country, training my dogs, and not being bothered by modern technology and murder cases, but she interrupted me:

"Look, you studied psychology, right?"

"Yeah, why?"

"What's ideation mean?"

"Having certain kinds of thoughts."

"Why don't they just say that? Jesus. Anyway, it seems that the mother's death was attributed to suicidal ideation, which was a side effect of the Prozac she was taking."

It made sense. Prozac has been linked to suicides in a percentage of the people taking it. I asked why the wife of "the vitamin king" would be taking Prozac in the first place.

"You're not gonna believe this. Jennifer had two younger brothers who both died of SIDS. If I was a mother and lost two of my kids like that, I'd be on Prozac and Elavil and anything else I could think of, including straight bourbon."

"No kidding."

"I'm telling you, this family's got some kind of dark cloud hanging over them, like the Kennedys or something."

I thought of Sonny's apparent drunkenness when I'd called him the night before. Maybe he and his wife had both been drunks. "Had the mother been drinking that day?"

"Have I got to sit here and read you the whole goddamn file, over the goddamn phone?"

"No, you're right. I should come get it from you. Where are you located? Let me grab a pen."

"Skip it. I could use a drive in the country."

I started to give her directions but she interrupted me.

"You think I can't find you? Look, you gonna be around for a while, or is a telegram more your speed?" Then she hung up, laughing at me.

I went back to the computer and found an interesting passage in Jen's diary. I tried to print it out but I couldn't get the damn printer to work. I kept pressing Command-P but each time I did I got a box saying the computer couldn't find the printer. I began talking to the computer (yelling at it, if you must know), saying things like, "What do you mean, you can't find the printer? It's sitting right next to you?" Finally, I realized the damn thing wasn't turned on. Tulips was right: computers *are* dumb.

At any rate, this is what I printed out:

Adam's a little turd, I finally realized. He said he could get me a gun, but it was all just talk. He. just wants to get with me. What a weasel. Like I would have dorm-cest with him? No freakin' way. I should have listened to Sabrina.

Now what am I going to do? I saw the man who killed my mother yesterday on campus. I know it was him, I'll never forget that face. But no one will believe me. I wish I could just go away and disappear somewhere he can never find me. But where can I go?

I could call Jack. I know he helped Leon escape the drug dealers who killed his family. But I can never look him in the face again. God, what is wrong with me? Why did I have to kiss him that day? He must think I'm terrible. Well, he's right. I am terrible and I probably deserve to be murdered. That's my destiny.

So what, Jen? Just close your eyes and accept it.

The thing is, though, I miss Frankie *so much.* I'd hate it if I never saw him again. I know he misses me too. *I can just feel it.* Maybe I could sneak into the kennel late at night and see him one last time before I go.

I do have to go, don't I? I have to go somewhere and become a different person. That's the only way I'll ever be safe. But I can't go without saying goodbye to Frankie, can I? It's stupid—he's just a dog—but I have to see him again.

Crazy me.

That was the last thing she wrote. It brought a tear to my eye—her love for that dog. Hell, I felt the same way about him myself. But it made me a little hopeful that Jen was still alive somewhere, waiting for a chance to come say goodbye to him before she disappeared forever. I knew she hadn't done it yet. If she had, Frankie would have let me know.

My cell phone rang and I clicked it open. It was Sinclair. He told me they'd set up the interview with the suspect for eight o'clock that night, if that was all right with me. I asked why so late and he said they wanted to wait until after Jamie had the initial autopsy results squared away so they'd have *some* evidence at least to use as leverage, if we needed it.

I said that was fine with me, then asked if it was all right with the department to have a civilian doing the interview.

"Technically you're an employee of the ME's office, so we're good on the legal angle."

I said eight was fine and that I'd see him then.

I closed the phone and looked over at Frankie, who was snoring, fast asleep, next to Hooch and Magee.

I said to his sleeping form, "You'd let me know if Jen came by to see you, wouldn't you, Frankie?"

He lifted his head and wagged his tail once. It hit Hooch in the face and woke him up. Hooch wagged *his* tail, which hit Magee in the face. In one quick motion Magee jumped off the bed and lay next to it. Then he tucked himself into a safe ball and closed his eyes again.

It may sound strange but some dogs are telepathic: Hooch, for example. He became my dog when he escaped from a junkyard near Belfast and trotted the thirty miles to my kennel. He'd never been there before, so how else could he have known how to find it except through some kind of emotional connection he had with me, a connection he'd developed just because I played fetch with him for a few minutes (while Jamie was examining a wrecked car for a case we were working on).

Frankie, on the other hand, has never shown any such abilities. He's an amazing dog yet there's something hidden about him. Sometimes he'll lie on his bed with his head erect and stare off into space, as if thinking. Sometimes when he goes to his water bowl he'll just stand there, not looking at the bowl, just staring at the wall, again as if thinking.

He stared at me now with his doleful droopy eyes, waiting to hear what I wanted him to do. But he didn't say anything about Jen, or about anything else. How could he, he's just a dog. But I knew he'd find some way to let me know if she came to see him. I could just feel it.

Crazy me.

15

I took the dogs out for a play session in the bright autumn air, then about an hour later Farrell Woods yelled down from the front door of the kennel building. He said there was a call from Leon's school; the kid had gotten into a fight with some other students and was waiting in the principal's office for me to come take him home.

Peggy Doyle arrived just as I was about to leave. I told her what was up and she agreed to drive down to Camden with me so we could go over Jen's case together on the way.

"There's more of a cloud over this family than we thought," she said, as I pulled the Suburban onto the county road. "Rose Vreeland had a twin sister, Lilly, who also died by drowning, though *this* one was a definite homicide."

"You're kidding. It happened around the same time?"

She looked through her stack of fax sheets. "Um, nope. This was seven years later. She and Jen were staying at the same lake cabin—it's in Massachusetts, by the way—it belongs to the mother's family. And guess who witnessed the crime?"

"Ah, the poor kid. She saw it happen?" No wonder Jen had got things mixed up—she'd seen her mother's twin sister get killed at the same lake her mother had drowned herself in.

Then I thought about what Jen had written in her diary—that her mother's killer was still out there, and was after her. I said, "Was Jennifer attacked too?"

"No, she watched it happen through the kitchen window. The poor woman was brutally raped right in front of her eyes. Jen didn't see the whole thing, though. She passed out. And when she came to, it was over, and the aunt was gone."

Doyle filled in the details. Jennifer had been down at the lake, a little before sunset, throwing wildflowers onto the water as a remembrance for her mother. When she got back, there was a dark blue car parked in front of the cabin and the front door was standing wide open. She heard cries for help coming from inside, started to go in, but heard a man's voice making threats to kill her aunt.

She described the voice as harsh, wild, and dangerous. She stood there fearful and trembling, unable to go inside and help her aunt. She went around the cabin to the back door, walking slowly and carefully so as not to make any noise, and saw movement through the kitchen window. She stopped to look.

The lights were on and the man seemed big and powerful and held her aunt's neck in one hand while he used the other to rip her clothes off. Jen looked around for an axe or a big stick to try and stop him, but she couldn't find anything.

Meanwhile, the aunt was clutching her attacker's arms with both hands, crying, pleading for her life. That's when Jen passed out.

"Jesus," I said, then drove awhile, not saying anything.

After a bit, Doyle rolled down her window and said, "It's kind of stuffy in here."

"Yeah," I agreed, and rolled my window down a little too. Finally, I said, "So, then what? He drowned her in the lake?"

"No, the body was found tied under the dock in a nearby lake, in early November. She'd been raped in late July."

It took me a moment to notice that I wasn't breathing and that my knuckles were white on the steering wheel. I took a deep breath, unclenched my fingers, and said, "And some kid was swimming under there, looking for something valuable, like a diamond necklace, and he found the body and reported it?"

Her eyes got wide. "Uh-oh. It was the same guy they got in custody now?"

I said it was, then went over the timeline in my mind:

- *Twin sisters Rose and Lilly Blythe grow up in New Jersey where Rose meets and marries Sonny Vreeland.*
- *Lilly??? (I don't know anything about her yet.)*
- *Rose and Sonny have twins that die in infancy.*
- *Rose soon has another child, Jennifer.*
- *Over the next five years Rose sinks into a depression and eventually drowns herself in a lake.*
- *Seven years later, Lilly Blythe is attacked and murdered near the same lake where Rose drowned herself. Jen Vreeland witnesses the attack and believes that her mother was killed, not her Aunt Lilly.*

"What are you thinking?" asked Doyle after a bit. "That it's too much of a coincidence that these twin sisters died seven years apart near the same lake cabin?"

I said, "No, actually. People have a natural tendency to die wherever they happen to be at the time they die." She chuckled. "If they both spent time at the lake then it's not much of a coincidence that they'd both die there. Plus, twins—I don't know the statistics, exactly, but there's something about twins and coincidence; it seems to follow them around. No, I think the only real coincidence is the drowning angle. I'll tell you what *does* puzzle me, though."

"What?"

"Well, Jen definitely saw the man who raped her aunt. But the killer didn't see *her,* right? Not unless he came out back and found her where she'd passed out on the porch."

"Which he could've done. But his car was out front."

"Right. And if he'd seen her, he probably would have killed her too. But here's the thing. Jen is sure that her mother's killer is after her. It's in her diary, she told her friends about it. In fact, it's so real for her that she says she saw him on campus the day before she disappeared."

"No kidding. Maybe there was a visiting professor on campus that day. The suspect is a botany professor, right?"

"So I'm told, but, yeah, if you could look into it for me, that would be great.

"Anyway," I went on, "I think her belief that her mother was murdered is a fantasy she'd built around the shock of seeing her aunt being attacked, which took place right after she'd thrown the flowers in the lake for her mother's memory. Then there's the guilt about not being able to do anything to stop her aunt's attacker. In reality, she *couldn't* have done anything. She was just twelve, and he was a lot stronger than she was. But clearly the two events are linked in her mind."

"And since she was around five when her mother died . . ."

". . . her mind has switched gears and the man she *thinks* killed her mother is the man who actually *did* kill her aunt."

"That makes sense."

"Yeah. And my feeling is that he's really been after her. That's not a paranoid fantasy on her part."

"How do you know?"

I shook my head. "I can't put my finger on it. The guilt would be strong enough for her to need to punish herself for not saving her aunt. That feeling is certainly there in her diary. She even said that she deserves to be murdered."

"Well, there's your answer. She's imagining him as a way to atone for not preventing her aunt's death. That's all."

"Maybe. The only thing that points in that direction is the fact that the killer probably didn't see her. She was hiding outside. And when he took the aunt with him, he probably wouldn't have gone out the back way and seen Jen there, passed out. His car was out front, right?"

"That's right."

"So, you're right: if he never saw her, how could he know who she is, let alone be after her?"

She thought it over. "Good point. It either has to be someone with access to the police reports, or else her name or her picture was in the paper or on the news."

I gave her a look. "They don't usually publish names and photographs of twelve-year-old murder witnesses."

"True. I think I should check it out, though, just to be sure."

We pulled into the parking lot of Camden Hills High.

"Good idea," I said.

She said, "Do you really think he's been after her all these years? Maybe she imagined that, too."

"Maybe. But she saw his face that day. It has to be etched in her brain. I don't think she'd mistake that face for someone else's or make up a fantasy version of it."

She said, "Well, all I can say is, it's a good thing they finally got the guy in custody."

"Not so good for me." I parked and switched the engine off. "I have to sit in a room with this sick bastard tonight and get him to confess. And I have to do it while stifling an overwhelming impulse to beat the confession out of him."

Her eyes sparkled. "You really like Jen, don't you?"

"Yeah, I do. Meanwhile"—I laughed a sour laugh—"here I am with all these violent feelings for the guy who did this to Jen's aunt and who's been after her all these years, but I also have to take Leon home and teach him that violence is not the solution to your problems."

I started to open my door but she put a hand on my arm.

"It's true, though," she said. "Look at me. If I hadn't kicked Regis in the nuts that day, I'd still be a detective."

I nodded, then looked at the fax papers and said, "Seems to me like you still are, partner. And a damn good one."

"Partner?" she groused. "Gimme a break." But I caught the glimmer of a smile in her eyes as I opened the door.

16

The principal, Mr. Van Noy, met me outside his office and said that Leon had to be suspended for two days. That's all.

"That's all?" I said too loudly. The school secretary, who was sitting at a computer, turned her head and looked over her glasses at me. In a softer tone I said, "It's summer school. He can't afford to be out of class that long."

He shook his head. "He can make up the work," he said, then told me what happened: a few of the seniors—three of them, to be exact—had taken to calling Leon (who was a junior) the "n" word whenever they'd pass him in the halls, and he'd finally had enough. He took a swing at one of them, broke the kid's nose, and got beat up pretty bad by the other two.

"How bad is he? Is he okay?"

"Just a black eye," he said. In their "defense," he told me, these seniors had told him that they hadn't meant to insult Leon, exactly. They would say things like "Hey, niggah! Wha's up?" the way rap artists do.

"And that's an excuse?"

"No, but—"

"These were white kids?"

He shrugged. "Leon's our only African-American student."

"Have *they* been suspended?"

"Well, no. Since Leon started it—"

"He didn't start it, they did." I went on to lecture him that the other kids hadn't even started it, that it had started four hundred years ago. I think I may have sworn a little when I said it.

He shook his head. The secretary glared at me. "Keep your voice down. And we don't tolerate that kind of lang—"

"I will not keep my voice down. And what kind of language *do* you tolerate, you little futtshicker?"

His cheeks turned red. "What did you just call me?"

I snorted. "I called you a futtshicker."

Now he was confused. "But that's not even . . . a *word*."

"Yeah, but it pissed you off, didn't it? Made your blood boil? Mostly because of my attitude when I said it. Now just think of what a *real* word, like the one these kids have been using on Leon, can do to a sweet, gentle kid like him."

He sighed. "I still have to suspend him for fighting."

"Fine, but I want those other kids suspended, too. And I want it explained to them that certain words and behaviors are not acceptable in your school or they'll be expelled entirely. You got that? If you don't, I'll sue your ass."

"For what?" he whined.

"For fostering a racially hostile learning environment."

The school secretary tsked at me. I probably would've tsked at me myself if I'd been her. It was a silly threat, based on political correctness, which wouldn't necessarily solve the problem. But I was Leon's father and I was pissed.

"Okay, okay, look. This is getting out of hand. I think maybe we need to set up some sort of sensitivity seminar or—"

Leon popped his head out the door. His left eye was a little puffed up. "Yo, Pops. Can you just take me home?"

"No. I want to get this settled."

"It's settled, a'ight?" He came through the door and just stood there. His face was relaxed and calm. "It's over with. I shouldn'ta hit 'em, but I did and I'm sorry. Okay? I don't want no seminars and shit like that."

I gave him a hard look.

"I mean, no seminars and 'stuff,' a'ight? It's over."

I looked at Mr. Van Noy. He said, "Okay, I'll suspend the other students. They'll all spend the day tomorrow in detention in study hall." He looked at Leon. "Okay?"

"Okay with me. Where'd they take Jason?"

Mr. Van Noy asked him why he wanted to know.

"I want to apologize."

"That's not necessary," Van Noy said.

"Yeah, it is. I shouldn'ta hit him, you know? Something just came over me and I lost my temper and I want to tell him I'm sorry for breakin' his nose and shi . . . and stuff."

Mr. Van Noy tilted his head toward the door and said, "He's still in the nurse's office, I believe."

"Good. I'll be right back."

After he left, Mr. Van Noy smiled and said, "You know, I think you've got a pretty good kid, there, Mr. Field."

"You have no idea." I looked at the secretary, who was about to sip from a cup marked, World's Greatest Secretary. "Futtshicker," I said, hoping to get her to do a spit take. She just choked a little. "It's not a real word, you know."

After Leon was done apologizing we went to the parking lot and I introduced him to Doyle, telling him she was helping me find Jen ("That's cool," he said as he got in back), and we chatted a bit about baseball. He buckled his seat belt and listened to his iPod while Doyle and I discussed the upcoming recall election.

"It's a damn shame," she said. "Flynn's a good officer. He just made a couple of dumb mistakes."

"And pissed the wrong people off."

"True, that," she smiled.

"Listen, I don't mean to put you on the spot, but Jamie and I were talking, and we really like you a lot . . ."

"Is there a point here?"

I chuckled. "Well, we were thinking of inviting you to our wedding, if you don't have anything else—"

"Well, that's nice, and I'm flattered but I think I'll pass on the big ceremony and all. Long story short, I'm not that crazy about sitting in church, but I'd be happy to come to the reception, if that's all right."

"Sure, that's fine."

"Good. I can avoid church *and* get something to eat."

When we got back to the kennel we said goodbye to Doyle, and I thanked her again for her help, then Leon and I went to the kitchen to have lunch together. I made tuna-melts and cut up some carrots and celery to crunch on.

"Yo, Pops," he said, while dipping a carrot stick in a bowl of bleu cheese dressing.

"What?"

"Where'd you get that word from? You know, the one you used on Van Noy?"

"Oh, that." I laughed. "I don't know, Leon. Something came over me and I just made it up."

"Pretty cool." He nodded. "So, you any closer to finding out what happened to Jen?"

I told him I thought so, or hoped so. "At least I know now why she disappeared. I just don't know how to find her yet. Are you sure she hasn't been in contact with you?"

"Course I'm sure," he said. "I woulda told you."

"Even if she made you promise not to?"

"I guess." He looked at me, wanting to know more. "Is it really serious this time?"

"Maybe. She could be in danger, Leon. So you have to let

me know if she calls." He agreed, then I said, "You sure you're all right with everything that happened?"

"Yeah. I'm cool." He explained that while he was in Mr. Van Noy's office he'd had a chance to think things over, and he'd remembered something I'd told him when he was struggling to teach Magee the stay command—that the dog just needed to learn better impulse control. "So, I was thinkin', that's why I hit Jason today. I didn't have no impulse control. So then I thought, how can I teach that to Magee if I can't even do it myself with these stupid kids? So that's my new goal."

"Teaching Magee to stay?"

"Nah. Controlling my temper, you know what I'm sayin'?"

Van Noy was right. I had a really good kid.

"I'm proud of you, Leon." I grabbed his neck. "You want to help me rake the leaves out front when we're done eating?"

"Nah, I don't think so." He gave me a mischievous smile, then shrugged. "I got a ton of homework."

17

I made a few phone calls to the press. I'm lucky to have a pretty good relationship with most of the news outlets in the state, and not just the TV station in Portland where I do a bimonthly segment on dogs for the Saturday morning show. The body in the lake was a big story, and the fact that the State Police now had a suspect in custody made it even bigger. I suggested that they put up a picture of Jen whenever they ran the story, saying that her disappearance may be related to the suspect, who was now safely behind bars. My hope was that Jen would see the broadcasts and come out of hiding.

After that was taken care of, I was out raking leaves—this was around one—with little or no help from Frankie and Hooch, and none from Leon, when a dark green Land Rover with Maine license plates pulled into the gravel drive. A slender white-haired man, wearing a safari jacket and a pair of desert boots, got out, followed by three wild-eyed Dalmatians.

They shook themselves in unison, then looked around the place. "Not bad," they thought, then began tearing through the front yard, frolicking in the piles of leaves I'd just made, tearing them all to pieces.

Frankie and Hooch woke up and barked at them.

"Rorschach, Seurat, Daisy!" the man called out. "Knock it off. Come! Come here now!"

They were too intent on frolicking so they ignored him.

"What are you gonna do," I called out to him with a shrug. "They're Dalmatians."

"What's that supposed to mean?"

I leaned on my rake. "*You* know—twenty percent are born deaf and the other eighty percent don't listen."

He took a moment, then laughed. "That's good. I'll have to remember that one." He came over and introduced himself. "Sonny Vreeland," he said, extending a long, slender hand.

We got the introductions out of the way, including the names of all the dogs, then there was the "how was your trip," followed by the words, "fine, private jet, rental car, though I got a little lost," and then "where are you staying," "I guess at a motel, if there's one nearby," and me giving him the names and numbers of a few places in Camden, and the rest.

Then I took him on a tour of the kennel, with his three spotted dogs running through the place, barking at the cages and causing a ruckus with the other dogs, and the two males lifting their legs and marking all the walls.

I introduced him to Farrell Woods and Mrs. Murtaugh, then asked him if he'd like to come into the house for a bit and have a drink or a bite to eat, and talk about his daughter.

"What? Oh, yes," he said, as if he'd forgotten the purpose of his visit. "Have you found out anything?"

"Not about where she is now, but I dug up a few things about her past that might be helpful."

"Uh-oh. What kinds of things?"

"Let's get your dogs settled, then we'll talk." I didn't want those two males running around the house, marking my living room furniture. Maybe he had the same problem at home, and that was why he didn't let them inside his house.

"Fine. While you're doing that, have you got a restroom?"

"You've certainly been thorough," said Vreeland, after I'd told him what I knew about Jen so far.

"Well, I had some help."

He was holding a glass of cranberry juice in one hand and was tapping the fingers of the other on the arm of the big leather chair. I was on the leather sofa. Frankie and Hooch were settled in their usual spots by the fireplace. The leaves were still outside, still scattered across the lawn.

"So," I went on, "after all that's happened to her, did you ever get her into therapy?"

He stared at his glass, a little distractedly. "I can see now that we should have. I just thought, I don't know, that she'd grow out of it." There was something odd about his response, like he knew he was supposed to act that way and was just going through the motions.

"Well, she hasn't. And your sister-in-law's killer has been after her all this time. Or so she says."

"But, how could that be? She doesn't even remember what happened that day."

"Well . . ." I explained it again.

"She's confused the two events? Really?" He stared into space. "Sorry, I guess I'm a little worn out from the trip." He explained. "I rented a private jet, then rented a car at the Portland airport. Then we got lost looking for . . ."

"So you said." I was beginning to wonder if he had early Alzheimer's or something.

"Did I? Sorry."

"Anyway, I think her life's been in danger since then."

"But they've got the killer in custody now?"

"If he's guilty, yeah. Hopefully I can get him to confess tonight." I told him about the upcoming interview.

"Can you find her? Help her somehow?"

"I can try."

"I still want to pay you."

"I won't take your money. Except the boarding fee for your dogs, of course." I smiled.

He went for his wallet.

"Later," I said. "Right now you're a little tired. You should check into a motel. We can talk more tomorrow."

He put his drink on the side table and started to get up but stopped. "Can I look at those diaries you mentioned?"

"From her computer?"

He nodded.

"I don't think so."

He gave me a blank look. "But I'm her father."

"I know, but they contain her private thoughts. I think she'd be uncomfortable about having you read them. She'll be upset when she finds out that *I* read them. We don't want to make it any worse for her emotionally than we have to."

"No, you're right." He just sat there. "This has been hard for me too, you know. Losing my wife, then dealing with her sister's murder. Kris has been great, but . . . ," He looked me in the eye. "About your phone call last night."

"What about it?"

"I was . . . I was sort of asleep the first time you called."

"Sort of?"

He sighed. "I take a natural supplement to relax. It also stimulates growth hormone. And it's supposed to reverse the aging process, improve memory, among other things."

Kristin had said something about Sonny having a fascination with something or other, though she hadn't finished the thought. I finished it for her:

"You're taking GHB?" I said.

He nodded. "I just thought I should explain. It's not like taking drugs. It's a natural component of metabolism. I try not to overdo it like some people."

I could have cared less what he did, but said nothing one way or the other.

He said, "Have you ever tried it?"

"Me? No. I tend to avoid illegal drugs."

"But it shouldn't *be* illegal. And it's not a drug. It's a short-chain fatty acid found in meat and some vegetables."

I told him that I went to Harvard Medical School, though I dropped out in my second year, and that I was aware of the origin as well as the medical and psychiatric benefits of the stuff: that it's used in Europe as an anesthetic, especially during childbirth, and has been helpful in the treatment of alcoholism. "It's also been used by psychiatrists," I said, "to assist in the process of abreaction."

He nodded. "So you know its benefits." He stopped a moment. "Abreaction?"

"Sorry. I studied psychiatry. It means the release of hidden or repressed emotion through verbalization."

"Interesting. I didn't know that; but I can see why—"

"But it's also used as a date-rape drug. And some people can develop a strong psychological dependency to it. Especially since there's no hangover like with alcohol."

"I just use it for anxiety and to help me stay young."

"Look, after you find a motel you can knock yourself out, for all I care. Take your GABA to your heart's content. But for now, let's focus on Jen's disappearance."

He just sat there. "You don't like me, do you?"

"I don't know," I said. "I hadn't thought about it one way or the other, though I'm starting to seriously head in that direction." He was getting under my skin with this weird act of his. "Look, your daughter's missing, her life may be in serious danger, and you act like you're concerned but I get the funny feeling that that's all it is, just an act."

"I *am* concerned. Believe me. It's just that I don't . . . process or express my emotions very well. That's one of the things the GABA's supposed to help with."

Well, it ain't working, I wanted to say.

He looked around. "Where are my dogs?"

"In the kennel."

"Oh," he said, but it was just his mouth moving.

"Look, Vreeland, thanks for sharing your predilections with me. It's been lovely. Now listen, does Jennifer have a favorite spot, someplace she'd go to feel safe?"

"And you'll take good care of my dogs?" he reached into a pocket of his safari jacket and took out a clear glass bottle.

"What are you doing? Don't do that."

He opened the bottle and poured a dose of blue liquid into his cranberry juice. "I think I need a little more to settle my brain."

I just stood there. "You already took some while you were in the bathroom earlier, didn't you?"

"Yes, but it doesn't seem to have taken effect like it should." He drank the mixture.

"Look, Vreeland—"

"I just need to sit here for a moment, do you mind?" Then he closed his eyes and fell asleep.

I just stood there staring at him. "Hello? Vreeland?" He didn't respond so I went over and tried to wake him up. "Hey!" I shook him. "You can't sleep here. Come on, wake up!" I shook him some more, pretty hard. All that happened was that his chin fell onto his chest and he began to drool.

It was no use; he was out cold.

I went over to the coffee table to use the phone to call Kristin and thought, Leon was right, Jen would be a lot better off without Kristin and Sonny as parents. "You know what," I said to Frankie and Hooch, "maybe I ought to adopt her too."

They opened their eyes and wagged their tails. There had been no mention of the words dinner, ball, or wanna go play, but they were hoping they might spill out at any moment. They didn't, though. All I said was, "Kristin? It's Jack. Your husband just fell asleep in my easy chair."

"What is he doing there?"

I told her everything, including the drooling.

"Jack, didn't I tell you not to call him? Jesus. You don't listen, do you? He can't handle this kind of stress."

"Tell me about it. I tried to wake him up, but—"

"There's no point in doing that. He won't wake up, in fact he *can't* wake up until after the damn stuff wears off."

"Is he all right? Should I call the hospital?"

"No, he'll be fine in a little while. And I'll be there as soon as I can. Just don't let him leave on his own."

After I hung up I began to have a little more sympathy for Kristin. Apparently she had a lot to deal with. And she'd really stepped up to the plate, as far as trying to take care of Jennifer was concerned.

I also had a ton more sympathy for Jen. Jesus, the things some people go through with their parents, which reminded me of where the pathology of most serial killers comes from—directly from good old mom and dad, or whatever sick uncle or grandparent abused them as children. But I didn't want to think about that, so I put a pillow behind Sonny's head, found the bottle of GHB in his jacket, confiscated it, put it in the pocket of my yard coat, then said to the dogs, "Hey! Who wants to help me rake some leaves?"

They got up, shook themselves, and followed me outside.

I love dogs. Sure they have some weird predilections: licking themselves for one thing, sniffing one another's butts for another. But those are natural, instinctive behaviors.

Dogs aren't in the habit of sitting alone in dark rooms at night, getting high, withdrawing from the world and avoiding their problems, all the while convincing themselves that they're only doing it for positive, health reasons.

18

It was a nice feeling, pulling the rake through the grass, catching the stems of the fallen leaves in the tines, and then pulling them together into a pile. It's funny how doing a simple chore can be so therapeutic. It's also a good way to find the solution to a mental puzzle. Once you stop thinking about it, the answer sometimes just comes to you. I had gotten quite a few piles made when I suddenly realized where Jen had gone. Or that if she hadn't gone there yet, she was going to, after she came and said goodbye to Frankie.

While I was thinking this over, a beat-up, white Toyota pulled into the drive and parked, and the kid, Adam, got out.

I leaned on my rake. "Hey, Adam. What's up?"

"I . . . I wanted to show you Jen's note. You said . . ."

I put down the rake and motioned him over to the porch. He came walking over, his head hanging down. He was holding a piece of paper in his hand. I sat on the stoop and he took a seat next to me and said, "I didn't want Officer Doyle to see it, but since you're not the police . . ." He handed it to me.

I read it but didn't learn anything new. The part he was afraid to show Doyle was where she thanked him for trying to get her a gun. The rest was pretty much the same as he'd recited it to us in his dorm room, except there was a reference to the pictures he'd been taking of her. She wasn't happy about that. As I handed him back the note he said:

"You won't tell her, will you?"

"Who, Doyle? No, I don't see why I should, unless you know of some other way Jen could have gotten the gun."

He shook his head. "I told her I was going to find one for her, but I only said it because I was trying to . . ."

Get in her pants, I thought, but said, "Impress her?"

"Yeah," he said sadly. "And I took all her pictures down after you left last night. I guess I'm just a loser."

"You took *all* of them down?"

He shrugged. "All but one, you know. I had to kind of leave that one up just to let her know . . . I mean, just as a kind of symbol that she's coming back or something."

"When did she tell you about the man she was afraid of? I found out she'd seen him on campus the day before she left."

He shrugged. "She was kind of mad at me that day."

"Why?"

" 'Cause I couldn't get her the gun, and . . ."

"She found out about the pictures?"

"Yeah. She was pretty furious about that." He smiled a sad smile. "It was really cool of her to kind of forgive me for that in her note. I—I tried to explain to her that—"

"That doesn't matter now, Adam. What matters is that you showed me the note. And maybe now you can help out with the investigation."

"I can?" He seemed hopeful and happy. "How?"

"First of all, do you know if Jennifer was using any drugs? Maybe something to relax, like GHB?"

"Hah! She was really down on that stuff. She said her father was like a junkie with it."

She was right about that. "That's good to know. And I want you to print up every photo you took of her that day."

"The day before she disappeared?"

I nodded.

He hung his head. "That's a lot of pictures."

"Well, just the print the ones where you can clearly see someone in the background."

He looked up at me. "I mean, I could do it, but I don't think I have enough money for that much paper. Plus I have to put in for all the chemicals I use at the darkroom."

I stood up and he did the same. I reached in my pocket. "How much do you need?"

"A box of paper costs twenty dollars. I'd probably need two boxes."

"That *is* a lot of pictures," I said, shaking my head. "But it might help us find her." I gave him a fifty. "And print the whole frame. Don't crop anything."

"You think this guy might be in one of the shots?"

"Never mind what I think," I said. I didn't want Adam getting any big ideas about getting involved in the case or going after anybody. "Just print the pictures for me."

"Okay," he nodded. "I'll get on it right away." He walked or, rather, almost sprinted back to his car. When he got there he turned. "So, what's your favorite Townes Van Zandt song?"

"You mean besides 'Pancho and Lefty'? I don't know."

"Mine's 'Come Tomorrow,' " he said.

"Yeah, that's a good one."

He smiled, got in his car, and drove off.

I went back to the leaves and picked up the rake, with "Come Tomorrow" running through my head.

After a while, Sonny appeared on the front porch, looking spry and rarin' to go. "Sorry about that," he said. "I think I'll go check into a motel now." He danced down the steps.

"Are you sure you're feeling up to—"

"I'm fine. Never better. That's what's so great about the GABA. It really rejuvenates you."

"Okay," I said, putting down the rake. "Let me write down the directions."

"No need. I think I'll take up your suggestion on The Samoset. It sounds like a good spot."

"It's kind of hard to find if you've never—"

"Nonsense." He repeated the directions I'd given him, just in passing earlier, word for word.

"Well, okay then," I said, kind of amazed at his sudden transformation. "But Kristin should be here any minute."

"You called Kris?" His face got small.

"Yeah."

"What'd she say?"

"She said she'd be right here. And not to let you leave until she got here."

"She's coming? That's good," he said but didn't mean it. He looked up at the county road, which runs behind the back of the house. His hand went to the pocket of his safari jacket. He was feeling around for his missing bottle of GHB.

"Lose something?" I said.

He shook his head. "It doesn't matter. Let me just look in on the dogs before I take off."

"Don't you want to wait for your wife? She told me—"

"No, she's going to be upset that I came to see you. Just tell her where I'll be," he said and went into the kennel to say goodbye to the dogs. I could hear them all barking the minute he went inside. Then he came out, got into the car, and drove off without saying goodbye.

A few minutes later, Kristin arrived.

"Where is he?" she said as she got out of her car.

I told her, then said, "Don't worry." I reached into my pocket and produced the glass bottle. "I got his stuff."

She shook her head. "I'm sure he's got plenty more stashed somewhere. How do I get there?" I told her and she said, "Thanks, I'll call you later," and took off.

19

While my attention was diverted, Frankie and Hooch had decided to re-scatter the leaves in the biggest pile I'd made.

"Hey!" I said and they turned to look at me.

"What'd we do?" their eyes seemed to say. "This is fun."

"Just knock it off, okay?"

Frankie shook himself and Hooch came trotting over to me and pushed his big head against my hip, looking up at me with his mournful eyes. "Ah, good boy, Hooch," I said, even though he'd just slimed my pants.

I wiped his drool off with a bandana, got back to the leaves, finished the raking, scooped them into a couple of plastic garbage bags, and had just gone into the house to call Doyle, to see if she could get me the location of the Blythe family's cabin in Massachusetts, when she called me.

"That's funny," I said. "I was just going to call you."

"Isn't that nice," she said sarcastically. "What about?"

I took out the bottle of GHB and put it on the coffee table and looked at the label. "I was wondering if you could find out the location of that lake cabin in Massachusetts."

"Sure. Why? You think Jennifer might go back there?"

"The thought did occur to me."

"Interesting. I'll get right on it."

"So, what's up? Why'd you call?"

She told me she'd looked into the idea that Jennifer had seen her aunt's killer on campus the day before she disappeared, but if it was Clay Henry, there was no record of him being on campus that day or any other. "But get this," she said, "Randy Corliss *was* here that afternoon."

"Well, he'd been hired to find her."

"Hello? Jack? The day before she disappeared?"

"Oh, right." I laughed. "Sorry. I'm not thinking clearly. It's probably a side effect of the GHB."

"What?"

"Nothing." I thought about it. "So what was Regis doing on campus?"

"Two reasons I can think of. He's been bangin' a student is one."

"Yeah, that sounds like him. And what's the other?"

"The other is I have no idea. Just up to no good."

"That sounds about right. Well, good work, as usual."

"Thanks. After I get the location of the cabin, you need me to check out this perp's background for you too?"

"Who, Clay Henry? No, the State Police have a full file on the guy. I'm going to look at it tonight before I interview him." I thought of something. "Maybe you could talk to those three girls again. She might have given them a description of the man she saw on campus. It wasn't in the police file."

"I know. They kind of glossed over that, didn't they?"

"And Adam was just here." I didn't mention the gun. "He said he took a lot of shots of Jen that day. I'm having him print them all up. Maybe we'll get lucky and our perp will be in the background of one of his pictures. It's a long shot. He doesn't focus much on the background when she's in the frame."

"Still, there's a chance. Why did he come see you?"

"He wanted to show me Jen's note while you weren't around."

"Oh, yeah? What was in it?"

"Just what he said last night. And that Jennifer wanted him to get her a gun for protection."

"So that's what it was."

"I promised him I wouldn't tell you, so—"

"I won't mention it if I see him. Don't worry."

"He probably only said it so—"

"—she'd go to bed with him. True, that."

"Okay. Call me again if you find out anything. If I'm not here, I'll be on my cell phone."

She laughed. "You actually have a cell phone, huh? Who bought it for you, your lovely fiancée?"

"Lucky guess," I said and gave her the number.

"I'm not lucky, just smart. Okay, talk to ya later."

I got two more calls, right in a row. The first was from Jamie. She'd finished the preliminary autopsy. The woman in the lake was named MerryAnne Moore: thirty-two, from Belgrade, and was married with two kids. "I'm going up there to make the notification now."

"That's never fun," I said, then I caught her up on the Vreeland family's strange behaviors and again mentioned my idea about where Jennifer might go.

"But wouldn't she feel safer somewhere far away from there, the farther the better?"

"Maybe not. Maybe it's the last place this guy would look for her. Or that's what her mixed-up brain is telling her."

She sighed. "I hate making family notifications."

"Yeah, I know, honey."

"On the bright side, I got my gown back from the tailor's. *Finally*. And it fits perfectly."

I laughed. "You tried it on in the morgue?"

"No," she laughed, "in my office."

"I can't wait to see you in it."

"Really? You have to wait, you know. Now I just have to decide which shoes to wear."

"Really? What's the problem?"

"Well, they both match the dress, which is a soft cream, but I can't decide between the heels or the flats."

I hate when she starts talking wardrobe options with me, but for some reason I said, "Which pair do you like better?"

"The heels."

"Well, wear *them*."

"But, honey, then I'll be taller than you."

"So? You're already taller than me."

"No, I'm not. I'm almost two inches shorter."

"I didn't mean physically."

"What a lovely thing to say! So, you wouldn't mind?"

"Heck no. I think you should be the tallest and prettiest one in the entire church."

"Even if I'm prettier than you?" she laughed.

"Well, that *is* a bit of a stretch but with enough makeup . . ."

She laughed some more, then sighed and said, "I'm being tag-teamed by my mother and Eve Arden. One of them calls me every half hour to talk about the wedding."

I laughed. "That's kind of nice, in a way."

"I guess, but I'm starting to wish we could just go to the courthouse and get it over with. Did you get the license?"

"Of course," I lied. "But much as I'd like to avoid all the people and the folderol, I'm still really looking forward to the big moment, you know, when the music starts and I turn and see you, holding your father's arm, and walking down the aisle toward me in your beautiful gown."

"You do? And don't you mean toward you and your dogs?" She laughed. "I really do look good in it. And my hair is just the right length for the veil, by the way." There was a pause. "You still hate my hair, don't you?"

"No, I was just picturing how you'd look in your veil."

"Really?"

"Do you think we could take it with us on the honeymoon? I explained, "It's just that the idea of you in bed, wearing nothing but a veil, is very appealing to me all of a sudden."

"Fine," she laughed. "I'll wear the veil to bed for you on our first night, if that's what you want. Just don't forget the marriage license."

"Honey, I just told you—"

"I know what you *told* me. And I know you haven't done it yet. You have to apply at the Rockland City Clerk's Office. It costs twenty dollars."

"What about the blood test?"

"That's easy. In Maine, there isn't one."

"Okay," I said, "I'll drive down there now. Can you do me just one little favor, though?"

"What's that?"

"I know I'm not supposed to see you in the dress until the wedding, but could you bring the veil home tonight?"

When she was done laughing she said, "We'll see. Anyway, I have to go. Wish me luck with the victim's husband."

"Good luck. Sorry you have to tell him."

The next call was from Julie Zimmerman, who'd asked me about her dog Clarence the night before. Her father, Oscar, had agreed to let me talk to them about training Clarence not to wander off so much, and maybe a few other things, like not pestering the cat and so forth.

"Could you come over this evening, do you think?"

"Well, I have to drive down to Rockland now, then to Augusta around eight. So I guess I could drop by after six."

"That would be perfect." She gave me directions.

"Will Clarence actually *be* there?" I said.

"Hah! Good question. It's around his dinnertime, so he should come wandering back sometime around then."

I hung up and called Flynn and suggested we meet for dinner after I registered for the marriage license.

"Dinner? Are you buyin'?" he said, in his gruff voice, though with his Down East inflection it sounded like, "Dinnah? Ah you buyin'?"

"Yes, and you do like to eat, don't you? Or are you too busy packing up your office to help me find a missing girl?"

"Jennifer Vreeland? Colby's not in my jurisdiction."

"That never stopped you before. So, are you in or out?"

"I'm in, if you need my help. Do you really think I'm going to lose the election?"

"With your current approval rating? What do you think? Though finding a missing teenager couldn't hurt your chances."

"I suppose. Just no spicy food, okay? I know you like that Mexican place, but my system can't handle it."

"Fine, we'll have Italian."

"Okay," he said. "There's Da Napoli. They make a good linguini carbonara."

"Da Napoli it is, then." This reminded me I'd promised to make spaghetti and meatballs for Leon, and it looked like I wasn't going to have time. It was almost three and I didn't know if the city clerk's office closed at four or was open till five, so I went out to the kennel to find Mrs. Murtaugh.

She was finishing the grooming on a couple of cats.

"I have to go do some things—getting a marriage license, for one—and won't have time to make Leon dinner. Could you—?"

"Of course! I'd love to."

I knew she wasn't just being nice. She loves to cook for us and rarely gets the chance. "Thanks. I promised I'd make him spaghetti and meatballs, if that's okay. What's wrong?"

"Nothing's wrong, dear boy. I'm just trying to remember if I have any bread crumbs up at the house."

"That's all right," I said. "I've got everything you need except for the ground pork and the ground veal."

She tsked. "I don't approve of veal. The way they treat those animals."

"Yeah, me neither," I said.

She went on in detail about the way veal calves are treated.

"Anyway, Leon won't know the difference. Straight hamburger will be fine for him."

I told Farrell Woods what I'd be doing—he was just leaving to do the pickups and drop-offs—and he reminded me that he and Tulips had an NA meeting later that night. He'd been helping her with a drug addiction.

"Yeah? How's that going?"

He gave a casual shrug. "It works if you work it."

I had no idea what that meant. "Is she still singing?"

"Yeah," he groused. "One of the other professors plays jazz piano on the side. She's been rehearsing with him."

"That's good. She loves singing Billie Holiday."

"Yeah, and Billie Holiday was a junkie, just like her."

"Former junkie," I said, but he didn't hear me.

"Plus, he's married. And I think he's just stringing her along, telling her she could be the next Tierney Sutton."

I said, "Well, that's aiming pretty high." Then I mentioned the need for a band at the reception. He told me he'd call his friend Dennis later that night and try to set it up. "Though," he said, "Tulips and her trio could probably do it if they're not available."

I thanked him then went to the carriage house and told Leon what I was up to and told him to keep an eye on things till I got back. He said okay, then I got some training gear together for my session with Clarence, hopped in the woody, put in a Townes Van Zandt tape, and drove as fast as I could to get to the Rockland City Clerk's Office before they closed.

All I thought about, the whole way down, was seeing Jamie later in bed that night, wearing nothing but her wedding veil. I guess I wasn't that much different from Adam, in a way. I was just luckier than he was because Jamie loved me back.

20

I met Flynn at Da Napoli's a little after five. He was waiting for me at a little table with red-and-white tablecloth and a candle stuck in an empty bottle of Chianti, wrapped in straw. He was eating breadsticks and sipping wine. He was in uniform, which caused some of the other diners scattered around the place to stare and point. I wondered briefly how many of them would vote, and what their votes would be.

We said hello, I sat down, and we looked at our menus while the waiter tapped a pencil against his order book.

Flynn ordered the carbonara and I was thinking about the veal Parmesan but decided against it. Mrs. Murtaugh had put an image in my head of frisky young calves, locked into narrow stalls for their short, miserable lives, so I had the fettuccine alfredo and a side of baked clams—I wasn't in the mood for dead animal flesh but needed *some* protein.

I caught Flynn up on the case, including some of the things in Jen's diary—like her desire to come see Frankie—then asked if he'd like to help me interview the murder suspect.

"That's not my jurisdiction. And what do you need me for? Can't you handle it yourself?"

"Yeah, but it might help to have a uniform in the room. We could play a little good cop/bad cop."

He shook his head. "I don't know much about serial killers, but I do know that they're a little too self-controlled to be thrown off by that old routine. Hey, did you hear the one about the body they found in a bathtub filled with milk, corn flakes, and sugar?"

I had, but lied and asked him to tell it to me.

"So, the cops are puzzled until an FBI profiler shows up and says, 'This is obviously the work of a cereal killer.' "

I laughed politely then said, "You don't like profilers very much, do you?"

He shook his head. "That whole thing is just a bunch of mumbo-jumbo if you ask me." He looked at me and tilted his head. "Look, I know you're an expert on the matter—"

"Hardly."

"—but I just don't get how you can get inside the mind of one of these sickos and not go a little nuts yourself."

I shrugged. "It's been known to happen. It's rare but—"

"So why would you even want to do it in the first place?"

I explained to him that knowing the pattern to a killer's crimes reveals his thought process, and that profiling, when done right, with careful, studied precision, without getting drawn too much into the emotional aspect of it, can sometimes lead you almost straight to the killer's door.

He scowled. "And it doesn't make you nuts in the bargain?"

"Not if you remain detached and dispassionate about it. So, you want to help me or not?"

"You mean with this frickin' interview? It'll give me the creeps." He twitched his salt-and-pepper mustache. "And I must be a little slow. Why do you want *me* there?"

"I'm going to get him to confess—I hope—and it'll look good in the press if you're there too and get the credit."

He shook his head sadly. "So it's a pity thing."

"No"—I laughed—"I'm just returning a favor." I reminded him of some of the things he'd done for me over the past year, even though our relationship had gotten off to a rocky start.

"I don't need your frickin' favors," he grumped, going for another breadstick.

I changed the subject. "Remember Randall Corliss?" He snorted and said he did. I told him something smelled fishy about his relationship with Jennifer's family and his current interest in finding her.

"Sounds about right. What are you going to do about it?"

"I'm not sure. From the looks of things, I'd say this bastard they've got in custody killed the girl's aunt. But it does make Corliss's being on the case seem like more than just a casual coincidence."

"Un-huh. How's he connected to the girl's family again?"

"Good question. I'd ask Kristin again, but I doubt if she'd give me a straight answer."

He thought a bit. "Well, there's Corliss's ex-wife. The bastard's divorced, you know."

I smiled. "I forgot that. She might know something."

He snorted again. "Yeah, and if she does, from what we know about his character, she'd probably be pissed off enough at him to tell you anything you want to know. As long as it doesn't slow down her alimony and child support."

I laughed. "Which might make bringing up where he gets some of his money a little dicey."

He shrugged. "Not if you handle it right."

I thought it over. "You mean make her feel that he might have some hidden income he's not telling her about?"

"That would do it." He smiled.

"That's good thinking, Sheriff." I paused, took a sip of wine. "This is why I'd like you in the room with me tonight."

He snapped a breadstick in half. "I told you, I don't need your frickin' favors."

"Take a reality check, Flynn. I'm a dog trainer. I don't have a political career to protect. You do."

He waved one half of the breadstick at me in protest.

"Besides"—I stopped him—"if you're involved with the interrogation, you may pick up some insights about how to help me find Jen Vreeland. How's that for a good reason?"

He munched on the breadstick and thought it over. "You really think she might come by the kennel some night to see your frickin' dog?"

"I know she wants to. Whether she will or not—"

"And your kennel is in Rockland County, right?"

"That's right," I smiled. "Which is your jurisdiction."

He nodded and said, "I still think it's a pity thing. But if she shows up at the kennel . . ."

"And you'll help me out with the interview?"

He nodded halfheartedly. "Yeah, but won't the police and the feds have a problem with me being there?"

"The state cops I can handle. The FBI isn't in on it yet. Though they will be soon, knowing them."

"What happens when they show up?"

"You'll still get credit for the confession, if not the capture, of a dangerous criminal with over ten years of savage murders on his sheet. That's got to impress the electorate."

He shook his head. "Aren't you the one always raggin' me about bein' too concerned with what the voters think?"

"That was before I knew you, before we were friends. And I'm sorry, but I think the voters in this county need to—"

"You know what," he almost shouted, "at this point I could care less what the frickin' voters in this county think of me!"

Everyone in the restaurant stopped eating and chatting. They frankly stared at us. A few even had their mouths open.

"A little louder," I said, leaning forward. "I don't think everyone on the kitchen staff heard you."

"Fine." He actually got up, went to the kitchen and shouted through the double door, "I don't care what any of *you* thinks of me either. You got that?" Then he walked slowly back to the table, staring everyone into quiet submission.

The waiter hurried over with our plates. Left them on the table, in the wrong places, and quickly disappeared.

"That was real good, Sheriff," I said, "but you forgot your bullhorn."

He shrugged and smiled. "You know, it *felt* pretty good. And come to think of it, I guess I wouldn't mind doing a little good cop/bad cop with you tonight. Seems like I'm kinda already in the mood to play one of the parts."

"You sure are," I said, as we switched plates and got down to the business of eating dinner.

21

"The thing you need to understand about dogs," I told the Zimmermans, as Clarence jumped around in my lap and licked my face, "is that they're not genetically engineered to be house pets. They evolved as social hunters and still retain the same basic instincts as their ancestors who lived tens of thousands of years ago. When those drives and instincts aren't being satisfied, or don't have some kind of safe, positive outlet, they get restless and bored."

"So, that's why he's roaming?" asked Julie, with a look to her parents, Oscar and Iris, who were seated together on a faded green sofa. I was sitting in an armchair from the same catalogue. Julie sat cross-legged on a hooked rug. The family television was turned to the news, with the sound off.

"He's very affectionate," said Iris, hopefully.

"This isn't affection," I said, trying to keep Clarence from biting my beard.

"But look at him!" chimed Julie. "He loves you. He can tell you're a good dog trainer." She was trying to convince her mom and dad that I was the right guy for their dog.

"No, sorry. He sees me as a stranger, with lots of doggie

pheromones on my clothes. Mostly from two other unneutered males, I might add. What he really wants to do is bite me, but he feels inhibited, so he's licking me instead."

"But he's exactly like this with us, too," said Iris. She was a slender, pleasant-looking woman, a little older than I, with parchment skin and dark, deep-set eyes.

"Even when he's just come home from a long ramble?"

"No," Julie admitted. "Then he usually does nothing but sleep. He's very contented and relaxed."

"You can't wake him up when he gets like that," said Oscar, taking his eyes away from the television for a moment.

What he said about Clarence's sleep patterns put me in mind of the way Vreeland had passed out in my chair earlier. I gave a short, bitter laugh at the thought, then looked closely at Oscar Zimmerman. He had a full, thick face, and his stocky body suggested that manual labor was his lot in life, but his blue eyes held a sweet gentleness. I liked him.

Julie said, "Dad, can you turn off the TV, please?"

"Oh," he looked at me, "is this bothering you?"

"It's a little distracting," I said. "Wait a second, I want to see this." A story about the capture of the murder suspect came on; they showed photos of him and Jennifer.

"You want me to turn the sound up?" Oscar said, reaching for the remote.

"No, Julie's right. You should probably turn it off."

Julie turned her eyes from the TV and said, "Is there really a connection between Jen and this serial killer?"

"Maybe. I'm actually scheduled to interview him in about an hour."

"Really?" Julie said, her face beaming. "Could I come?"

"Julie!" said her mother.

"No," I said, "you can't come. Why would you—?"

Her mother interrupted. "Why would you even think about it?"

"I don't know. I think they're a fascinating social aberration. I'd just like to find out what makes someone like that tick, you know?"

"I'll explain it to you sometime, but we should concentrate on Clarence right now. Unless you want to pay me to sit here and watch TV and talk about serial killers."

"With what you charge?" Oscar said, clicking the TV off.

Julie said, "I'd pay to hear about your experiences with serial killers." She turned to her parents. "I would."

"Julie," said her mom, "that's enough. Honestly!

"Anyway, Dad," Julie said, "you're only paying him so much because he's the best dog trainer in the country."

"I don't think I'm the best."

"But I've seen you on TV."

"That doesn't mean I'm good. There are some real idiots on TV, trust me." I turned to her parents. "So, where does he sleep?"

"Who?"

"Clarence."

Iris said, "He likes to sleep wherever we are."

"She lets him sleep in bed with us," Oscar groused.

Iris put a hand on his knee and said, "He loves to dig under the covers and snuggle."

"If he could, he'd sleep on top of my head," said Oscar, with a sour laugh. "And if you roll over the wrong way in the middle of the night, he growls at you. He even bit me once."

"He didn't mean to," said Iris, patting his knee.

Clarence jumped down from my lap, ran over to grab a stuffed toy, brought it to me, dropped it at my feet and began to growl, his focus alternating between me and the toy.

"Well," I said, ignoring him, "I don't usually make an issue of not letting the dog sleep on the bed—I let my own dog do it—but whenever there are behavioral problems, particularly if he bites you in his sleep, that has to stop."

"Hah! That's fine with me," said Oscar.

Clarence began to bark at me, and, when that got no response, he grabbed the toy in his teeth and shook it, breaking its neck.

"But how?" Iris said. She got up and tried to take the toy. "Clarence, give! Give me the toy!" He danced away from her, growling. She sat back down and shrugged. "He's very determined about having his own way."

Clarence took the toy over to Julie, who started a game of tug-of-war with him.

"That's got to stop too." I explained the difference between den instincts—which are geared for nurturing and resting—and outdoor instincts—which are geared for chasing and biting. "You don't want to mix the two. So no more playing games with him in the house."

Julie let go of the toy and Clarence shook it again, growling. "Sorry," Julie said, both to him and me.

Clarence brought the toy back to her and she shook her head, crossed her arms, and tucked her hands tightly against her ribs. Clarence realized he wasn't getting any more action from her, so he settled down with the toy and began to chew.

"This is good," I said. "This is what you want Clarence to do inside the house, chewing but no playing."

"So how do we keep him out of the bed?" asked Iris.

I told them to get a crate.

"We have to put him in a cage?" Iris asked.

"That's not how he'll see it. He'll get used to it pretty quickly, and even start to like it. It'll be like his own little den—his comfort zone, if you will—inside the house. Just make sure it's only big enough for him to circle around and lie down in. Nothing bigger. And you'll only need to close the door on him at night. Now let's go out in the backyard and I'll show you how to get him to play fetch with a ball. Or does he already know how?"

Julie said, "He'll chase it, but he won't bring it back."

"Well, that's easy," I said, and we all got up and went out to the backyard, which was a wide space, covered with grass. There was also a flower garden next to the house, some hedges that ran along a wooden fence, and a few tall pine trees scattered around. I spotted some holes under the fence, where Clarence had dug his way to freedom.

I explained that outside the den the dog's system is geared toward searching for things to either chase and bite. "That's why he's so intent on escaping from the yard, because there's nothing much to chase and bite here, except the cat."

"He kills a lot of rats down at the barn," said Oscar.

"If you want him to, that's fine. Just make it a group activity; go with him and praise him for doing it. The point is, if we can satisfy his instincts, close to the house, that's the first step to making him feel less like roaming."

Oscar said, "And we won't need to have him fixed?"

"Fixed?" I said, with a teasing gleam in my eye. "Why? What's wrong with him?"

"I mean, everyone's been telling us to have him castrated."

"It figures. But the roaming is not just hormonal at this point, it's also habitual. So surgery wouldn't necessarily change it now. Besides, surgery is unnatural and unhealthy."

"That's not what I heard," said Julie. "I heard the surgery lowers the risk of prostate cancer."

I shook my head. "There's no direct link between having a healthy set of testicles and developing prostate cancer. In fact castrated dogs are three times more likely to get other types of cancer than dogs who haven't been 'fixed.' "

"Really?"

"Sure," I said, "you can look it up if you like. The surgery also increases the risk of urinary tract problems, it'll shorten his life span, cause problems with his skin and coat, lots of things. If you're worried about his having unwanted puppies you can always have him vasectomized."

Oscar said, "All I care about is keeping him from running off. Would an electric fence do the trick?"

"You mean an electr*on*ic fence," I said. "Yeah, it'd work, but I'd rather have you save it as a last resort. If you end up needing one, there's a guy I know in Vermont who's very conscientious about teaching the proper way to use one." I gave him Bill Grant's number then said, "Now let's get to work."

I got to work. I hooked Clarence to a fifty-foot training lead—a light one, not like the one Jamie and I had used to climb the tree outside Dana Hall—then I showed him a tennis ball.

He didn't show much interest in it, so I teased him, dancing it around his nose, then ran away, getting him to chase me. He was still hesitant, in fact he started sniffing the ground, ignoring me. So I put the leash on him, tied him to a fence post, and asked Julie to play catch with me.

"You stand over there and I'll be back here, and we'll throw the ball right past his nose, close enough so he feels like he could grab it, but won't quite be able to. Got it?"

"I think so. What'll this do?"

"It'll drive him nuts, especially if we act excited."

So we did that. We happily tossed some low grounders, right past the dog's nose until he was crazy to bite the ball. Then I unhooked the leash and began teasing him with the ball again, running away and laughing in a high, silly voice every time he tried to grab it. Then I fell down on the grass and let him jump on top of me. I laughed and praised him, still keeping him from grabbing the ball, then I jumped up and ran away again.

He was totally focused on the ball now and made several grabs at it. Each time he did I pulled it away in the nick of time, praising him all the while. Then, when his interest was at its peak, I threw the ball right past his head. It was a short throw, relatively speaking, only about twenty feet, maybe less. He raced after it and grabbed it in his mouth in mid-stride.

I praised him enthusiastically and he came running back toward me. As he did, I ran away, keeping my body at an angle, looking over my shoulder, and praising him. When he was focused on my movements, and not the ball in his mouth, I pulled a second tennis ball out of my pocket and teased him with it until he dropped the first ball. The instant he dropped it I threw the second ball, right past his head. He spun around and went racing after it. I reached down and picked up the first ball.

I repeated this pattern several times until I had him chasing the ball, bringing it back, and dropping it at my feet.

"Amazing," Julie said. "He's never done this before."

"It's just a matter of knowing how to stimulate the right instincts and emotions," I told her. "You want to try it?"

"Sure," she said, taking the tennis ball from me.

It was then that a part of my brain went forward in time to my interview with the serial killer. I'd been a little nervous about it, but as I taught Julie how to get Clarence to play fetch I realized that getting a confession from the killer was just a matter of pushing his buttons, which is what I'd done with the dog. You tease him, move away, increase his desire to talk, then continue the process over and over until you get him to open up to you and drop the confession at your feet.

I had Oscar and Iris try it, and as they did I explained that once Clarence finds that his instincts are satisfied on a daily basis, his desire to run off would decrease dramatically.

"You're going to have to do this a lot every day, though. At least half an hour, once before he eats breakfast and once before dinner. And since the behavior is not only instinctive but habitual, we're probably going to need another session to teach him the boundaries of his play area. You *could* use an electronic fence to do that, but there's a much nicer way."

"If you and Mom will take the morning shift," Julie said, "I can come by after class every day. This is kind of fun."

"It *is* fun, isn't it?" Iris said, throwing the ball. Clarence went zooming after it and grabbed it in midstride again. "He really seems to be enjoying himself."

"He's having a blast," I said with a grin.

Then I told them to never let him out of the house alone or unsupervised, to play hide-and-seek with him from time to time to increase his social attraction to them, and to always have the fifty-foot lead on whenever they played fetch, just in case. I also suggested they play the "find" game, where you hide something around the yard, like a ball or a toy, and tell the dog to go try and find it.

"And since he's a terrier," I added, "and a Patterdale at that, it's gonna take an awful lot of play to wear him out."

"You got that part right," said Oscar, laughing.

We went back inside and sat down again. Clarence sprawled out on his side, at the foot of my easy chair, his chest heaving now, and his big mouth happily chewing on the dead tennis ball.

22

I was on my way to Augusta, feeling loose and happy after playing with the dog, when I got a call from Doyle.

I said, "Let me pull over so I can talk to you."

"Pull over?"

"Yeah, I'm on the turnpike."

She laughed. "You can't drive and talk at the same time?"

"I can," I grumped, "I just don't think it's safe." I pulled onto the shoulder, put the woody in park, got out a pad and pen, and said, "So, what'd you find out?"

"First of all, that family cabin in Massachusetts? It's located about fifty miles north of Amherst." She gave me the exact location, and I do mean *exact,* and I wrote it all down.

"Okay. What else?"

"Well, I talked to Adam and a few of the girls, but Jen never described the killer to any of them. It seems like her diary is the only person she shared her true feelings with."

"I'm sorry, *who's* the only person?"

"Her diary. You a little slow tonight?"

No, I thought, but a diary isn't exactly a person, then I realized, who am I to talk, with the way I relate to dogs.

"Okay," I said. "Is that it?"

"No," she said, a little peeved. "Jeez, you think I'm not working my ass off here, covering all the bases?"

"I'm sure you are. So what else is there?"

"Corliss. I found out what he was doing on campus that day. He was with a buddy of his from the FBI."

"He's buddies with an FBI agent?"

"Yep. Name of Steve Rice. He was at Colby giving a—"

"He knows Steve Rice?"

"Yeah, why? You heard of him?"

"I know the name, though I don't think I could pick him out of a lineup. He was at a seminar I went to in Quantico."

"Well, he and Corliss are buds, apparently. Anyway, Rice was giving a lecture on law enforcement and Corliss came along, probably hoping to find a college girl he could bang."

I laughed. "You're probably right." I thought it over. "Listen, if it was Rice or Corliss that Jen saw that day . . ."

"She might have seen them, we can't say for sure. But here's the thing, Dr. Henry could have been on campus too. We just can't prove it. And he teaches at Hampshire College."

"In Amherst?"

"That's right, Amherst, Mass. Just fifty miles south of that lake cabin where Lilly Blythe was attacked."

"Okay," I said, "good work, as always."

"Thanks. And I'm gonna show Henry's picture to everyone on campus to see if anyone remembers seeing him that day."

"Where'd you get the photo?"

She laughed. "You probably haven't heard about this new law enforcement tool we got. It's called the Internet? Long story short, I went to the Hampshire College website. They've got pictures of all the faculty members. I printed Henry's."

"You're good," I said.

"No problem, partner."

I pulled back onto the turnpike and drove to Augusta, then called Jamie on my cell phone when I got close to police headquarters. (I was stopped at a light.) She and Sinclair met me in the parking lot at a quarter to eight. Sinclair handed me a dossier on the suspect, Dr. Clay Henry, only son of George and Miriam Henry of Huntsville, Ontario. The mother died of cancer in ninety-two. The father was still living.

We went inside, to Sinclair's office, and I sat behind his desk and pored over the documents. Jamie stood behind me.

The victim had been drowned, just like all the others. Jamie said she'd been working with a forensic odontologist to get a match on the teeth marks left on the body.

"Using what, the suspect's dental records?"

She nodded. "His dentist in Amherst faxed us a copy. He teaches botany there."

"Yeah, I know. Peggy Doyle told me."

"She's been busy, huh? We haven't asked him for a dental impression yet. Greg thought we should wait to see—"

"I didn't know what you'd want to do," Sinclair said.

"That's good. We don't want to tip our hand." I looked at Sinclair. "You'll be watching through the two-way mirror?"

He said he and Jamie would both be there, and that they were expecting the dental expert at any moment.

"Okay, I'm expecting Flynn, too. If he comes."

"Why Flynn?"

I explained my reasons. Jamie said, "I think that's a wonderful idea."

"Thanks. I'll give you two a signal when it's time to spring the dentist on him. Let me look at the rest of this."

There wasn't much in the file: his academic background and credentials, which were spotless, a single misdemeanor as a juvenile (he killed a neighbor's dog), and a domestic violence complaint (he'd bit his wife during sex and her injuries required stitches). There was also a list of his alleged victims, all twenty-one of them. And sure enough, Lilly Blythe—Jennifer's aunt—was one of the names on the list.

"Oh, brother," I said. "This is going to be tough."

"How so?" said Jamie.

I explained about the need to make the suspect feel that I wanted to hear his side of things when all I really wanted to do now was break his neck.

"Why?" Jamie said. "Because he killed a dog?"

"That doesn't help. But, no." I explained what I knew about Lilly Blythe's murder and its effects on Jen.

"That's awful," Jamie said, stroking my neck.

Flynn appeared in the doorway. "Hey," he said, looking a little uncomfortable. He looked at Sinclair. "Did Jack tell you he wanted me to help with the interview?"

"Yeah, that's fine. We're just about to start." He looked at me. Seeing the look in my eyes, he said, "You don't have to do this, you know, Jack. Either one of you."

"No. I'll be all right. Just give me a minute."

Flynn said, "How do you want me to play it?"

"Just do whatever you want. I trust you. The main thing you need to know is, most serial killers don't have a normal startle response to threatening stimuli, like loud noises."

"Meaning what?" Flynn said. "If I scream in his face or bang on the table he won't react?"

"It depends. He might fake a reaction. He might just act bored. His autonomic nervous system is sluggish. That's one of the reasons he kills people."

"I don't get it," said Sinclair. "I thought these sickos all came from abusive homes."

"That's how it usually starts. But you have to remember that the child's brain is still developing. So when the abuse happens, certain parts of the brain develop in abnormal ways."

I could have gone on to explain the effects of abuse on the amygdala—which controls the instinctive fight or flight response—and which may also cause a deadening of certain areas in the prefrontal cortex, which is where impulse control, judgment, and moral behaviors originate.

"It's a two-way street," I said. "The abuse starts the ball rolling and warps the neurochemistry of the killer's brain, not just his mind. Gacy had a severe brain injury as a child. Bundy was diagnosed with a manic-depressive psychosis.

"Anyway . . ." I went on, then took a few deep breaths, stood up, and said, "Let's do it."

Sinclair said, "Aren't you going to take the file?"

"Nah, I've got what I need memorized."

"That's my boy," Jamie said, proudly.

23

It was the usual interrogation room: a sturdy metal table with four sturdy metal chairs, four walls, one with a large panel of one-way glass, and some overhead fluorescents.

Sinclair introduced us to Dr. Clay Henry; a slim, casually dressed men with a thatch of light brown hair, round eyeglasses, not very thick, limpid green eyes and a tight-lipped smile. He sat straight-backed, with his hands folded on the table in front of him. He wasn't nervous or upset.

He was smaller than I'd expected him to be, but then Jen was only twelve when she saw the attack. He must have seemed huge to her at the time.

"Mr. Henry," Sinclair said, pulling out one of the chairs for me, "this is Dr. Field and Sheriff Flynn."

I took a seat and nodded at Henry, but made no move to shake his hand.

Flynn pulled out a chair and took it to a corner of the room and sat down. Nice move, I thought.

"It's *Dr*. Henry," he said. "And what's *he* doing here? I told you I won't speak to anyone from the police."

Sinclair said, "Anyone feel like coffee?"

I said, "Not for me, thanks."

Henry waved his hand but said, "I'd like a little water. And will someone tell me what the sheriff is doing here?"

Sinclair said, "It's just a security precaution."

He laughed. "You think I'm going to try to kill someone?"

Sinclair said, "Like I said, it's just a precaution," and left, closing the door behind him.

There was a brief, uncomfortable silence, which I did nothing to dispel. I didn't examine my fingernails, stare at the suspect, or look away. I just sat there.

Finally, he said, "You, um, you had some questions for me?"

"I thought you were the one who wanted to talk to me."

"I hadn't counted on an audience."

I ignored him. "Before we start, I'm not a cop, but I think I should ask you if you want to speak to a lawyer."

"Why? I haven't done anything wrong." He gave me a superior look. "Only someone who's guilty needs a lawyer."

"Fine. So how do you want to do this?"

"You ask me questions, I answer them. Once we do that, you'll see you've got the wrong man." He smirked.

"So I guess you know why you're here."

He shook his head sadly. "Some fantasy the police have cocked up about me being a serial killer. Totally ridiculous."

I nodded and smiled. "And why do you think I agreed to come talk to you?"

He thought it over, or seemed to. "You're an ex-cop, with a PhD in criminal psychology. You probably think I'm guilty like they do, and you want to get me to confess." He laughed.

"You goddamn sonovabitch," Flynn roared, jumping out of his chair. "You think slaughtering women is funny!" He came over, using his full height and girth to intimidate Henry.

Without turning, I said quietly, "Sheriff, sit down."

"I want a piece of him!" He banged the table hard, with both hands. Henry just blinked a few times, nothing more.

I turned to look at Flynn. "That's enough, okay? He wants to explain things, so let's let him do that."

Flynn reluctantly went back to his chair and sat down.

Quite calmly, Henry said, "I'd like for him to go now."

"That's out of my hands. If he goes, I have to go too."

"Why? I just want to explain that I'm innocent."

"Fine. And I'll be happy to listen to anything you have to say. But I'm not allowed to be in here alone with you. That's standard procedure when dealing with an alleged serial killer."

"Then just keep him from annoying me, do you mind?"

I looked at Flynn. "Could you just let us talk?"

"Do whatever you frickin' want," he grumbled. "Treatin' this sick bastard like he's a real human being."

"Well, he is," I said and turned to Dr. Henry. "What were we saying before he interrupted us?" (This is a good tactic, using the first person plural: we or us.) "Oh, I remember. You said you think I'm a criminal psychologist, and I was about to tell you that I don't actually have a PhD, but you're right in a way. I'm an ex-cop and I have a background in criminology. So, it looks like we both know how this is going to go."

"What do you mean?"

"Well, I'm going to try and outsmart you by asking certain questions that will draw you into a trap, and you're going to try and outsmart me by maintaining your innocence and turning my arguments against me."

He chuckled. "Sounds a bit like chess."

"Goddamn waste of time," said Flynn.

"That's it, Sheriff," I said. "One more word out of—"

"Fine. Have it your way, genius."

I turned to Henry. "That's right, it *is* like chess. Of course, we could go straight to the evidence the police have."

"What evidence?"

"I could tell you, but that would end our little game before it even got started, wouldn't it?"

He smiled. "All right, then. I think I'd enjoy a little game of chess."

"Fine, but chess has rules and so does our game."

"Fair enough." He smiled easily. "What are they?"

"We both have to tell the truth about everything."

He pulled his head back and grinned. "Ah-hah. And how do either of us know when the other one's lying?"

I shrugged. "We'll be on the honor system. Now, since you're a suspect in a murder case, I won't expect you to answer any questions that might incriminate you. How's that?"

"I don't know what you hope to accomplish, but fine."

"Good," I said, then just sat there, letting him know he had the first move.

He licked his lips. "Okay. The first thing you'll want to know, I suppose, is what I was doing out at the lake?"

"Not really. I already know that. You were watching the police recover the body of one of your victims."

He smiled again. "Okay, here we go. You know, I have a perfectly reasonable explanation for that: I was there studying the gradations in kettle bog vegetation. It's what I do."

I gave him a facial shrug. "Kettle bogs?"

"They're the remnants of ancient glacial activity. The whole area around Potter's Pond is called the Belgrade Esker and Kettle Complex. I was there studying—"

"Esker? That's what, something to do with glaciers . . . ?"

"Very good. It's when a mass of ice moves through an area, scoops out the underlying rock, and leaves behind a trail of gravel and, quite often, what's called a kettle hole. Some of these holes fill up with water, creating a bog, with its own unique forms of plant life. It's fascinating how the vegetation differs from that in a normal lake."

"So, that's what you're going to stick with? That story?"

"It's not a story, it's the truth."

"Okay," I said, then asked how he first got interested in botany. He told me he'd grown up in Canada, where there were kettle hole lakes nearby. I nodded appreciatively and drew him out on how his fascination developed. He was happy to tell me. Most people like telling stories about themselves, particularly lonely people, which is what Clay Henry was.

This is also a standard interrogation technique. You get the suspect talking about himself, get a rhythm going. Make him feel that you're genuinely interested in hearing about his life, what makes him tick. Make him want to open up to you.

"This interest in plants is a lifelong passion of yours?"

"Absolutely," he said proudly. "In fact, I was quite an outcast at school. Everyone else was interested in hockey. They couldn't wait for the lakes to freeze over every year. I was on the opposite cycle, you might say; waiting to see what little things would be the first to sprout every spring."

"I see," I said, "the thrill of new life burgeoning . . ."

"Exactly. Yes. I once spent four days waiting for a *Coptis groenlandica* bud to open. Can you imagine what the others thought? Down in their boots over the loss of a hockey rink while this beautiful white flower was bursting out of its winter hiding place . . . showing us all the meaning of life."

"The meaning of life. That must have been something."

"Yes. The bog is life manifesting in its purest form. These plants, they need nothing for sustenance but water, soil, and sunlight. Some don't even need soil. The best ones."

I nodded. "You must have given up a lot of things as a kid to have spent all that time—"

"I didn't look at it that way. It was my passion. And I know what you're trying to infer."

"Imply, you mean."

"Fine. You're implying that I'm a serial killer, since those psychopaths have the same kind of intensity and dedication to their sick, violent activities as I did to my love of botany. But it's not the same thing. Einstein was obsessed with knowing the nature of the universe. And Burbank with plants."

"Still, that kind of dedication, that purity of purpose. Very admirable. Your parents must have been proud of you."

"Of course they were."

"Now come on, Clay. Remember our rules? Honesty."

"Very well, then." His face grew dark for a moment, then he smiled. "This is where you try to get me to talk about my parents and I'm supposed to refuse or make things up. Only I won't. I don't mind giving you ammunition for your little profile of me. It won't do you any good. I'm innocent.

"The fact is, my father was a horrible, violent man who had no paternal impulses for me and my interests. In fact, he worked for a gravel company that nearly ruined the entire esker, and most of the wetlands as well, until my mentor, Dr. Reedy, launched his campaign to stop them."

"Dr. Willis Reedy, yes. I read that in the bio they gave me on you. You married his daughter Nancy, yes?"

He sighed. "Yes, well, that turned out to be a mistake. I sadly mistook what I saw of his greatness in her."

"I guess that's why you were abusive to her, then?"

"Abusive? Me? Never." He regained his composure then smiled a tired smile. "Good one, Dr. Field. Almost got me."

"Then how do you explain the domestic violence complaints?"

He took a breath. "There was *one* incident. *One*. And I didn't beat her or abuse her in any way." He went on to explain that the complaint was just a ploy on her part to win points in the divorce proceedings. "You can't make anything out of that."

"That's interesting, because I also read the hospital report. Those bites you left on her required stitches."

"I thought you might bring that up, but the truth is . . . You want honesty? Complete, and utter truth?"

"That's the deal."

"Good." He smiled. "I normally don't discuss bedroom matters with strangers, but in this case, as it's part of the game, I will. The fact is she liked that sort of thing—rough sex. That could've happened to anyone who, who, who, got . . . I don't know, caught up in the moment. Personally, I would have never done anything like that if she hadn't asked for it."

"Asked for it?"

He sighed. "I mean, if she hadn't asked me to do it."

"But you can see why the police . . ."

"Yes, yes." He was a little frustrated; but just a little, then he smiled. "But I'm telling you, it's nothing."

"Yeah, you're probably right. The cops tend to read things into incidents like that." I stopped, shook my head. "The thing is, the detectives who spoke to her got quite a different story. She said it was like you were possessed, and then when you realized what you'd done, you became a sniveling infant."

His face turned red, then he composed himself again. "Okay, that's it. This interview is over." He looked over at the mirror. "And when can I get my water?"

"If that's the way you want it." I stood up. "I told you what my agenda was going to be. I've played by the rules we agreed on, but if you think you can't stick to them—"

"No! Sit down!" He ran one hand through his hair.

Flynn stood up and took a step toward us.

Henry ignored him and said, "Please sit back down."

"Sorry, Clay. You stated that the interview was over. I have to go by your statement. I'll see about your water."

"Look, seriously, I want to talk to you. I need you to understand that I didn't do this. That I couldn't have."

I ignored him, nodded to Flynn, and we went to the door and left the botanist alone with his thoughts.

Jamie and Sinclair met me just outside the door. We closed it and Jamie said, "Jack, are you all right?"

"Don't worry, honey," I said, "I'm fine."

Sinclair said, "So, that's it? You're just walking out?"

"Walking out? Hardly. This is where it starts to get good." I turned to Flynn. "You did great."

"Thanks. Do I gotta go back in there again with him?"

"No, it'll be better for the second part of the interview if you're not there."

Sinclair said, "So, what happens now?"

"I get him to talk about himself more. He's a serial killer. There's no question about it. He barely blinked when Flynn threatened him. The other thing is, he wants to confess."

"He does?" Jamie said.

"Oh, yeah. Look, guys like him spend a lot of time thinking things through in their heads, knowing what they're doing is wrong, but being unable to stop themselves. So they have to make up stories, give themselves rationalizations for what they do. So they're dying to explain themselves to someone, but they can't try out their stories on anyone else for fear of being caught. A part of them even wants to be caught so they can stop finally doing what they're doing. That's the part of them that despises themselves for the killings. The other part, the sick part, can't tolerate the idea of being locked up and never being able to kill again. It's the only thing that makes them feel alive. They're like drunks or drug addicts. Every victim is going to be the last one, they tell themselves, then they'll stop, they'll never do it again. This guy has been ripping himself to pieces for years, and it's all dying to come out now."

24

I waited a good interval, then came back with the water bottles and placed them on the desk. I didn't take a seat, nor did I make as if to leave. I just stood there.

"Please sit down, Dr. Field? I mean, I'm sorry. You're right. Since I have nothing to hide, I'll be happy to clear up anything you think might be of—"

"Well, I don't know. I'm going to have to ask you some pretty tough questions, you understand? If you're going to cry because I've taken your queen or avoided one of your gambits . . ." I looked at the water bottles. "I thought you were thirsty."

He nodded, looked at a bottle, picked it up and opened it "Yes, yes, I am. Now please sit back down so we can talk."

"Fine." I sat down.

"Isn't the other one coming back in? The sheriff?"

"No, I don't need him anymore."

"Because you're not afraid of me now?"

"No. He was just playing the bad cop to try and rattle your nerves."

He laughed. "I'm not surprised." He gulped down some H_2O and wiped his lips. "This has been very stressful," he said calmly. "You can appreciate that. You were arrested for a murder you didn't commit once, weren't you?"

I'd forgotten about it but I had, in fact, spent more than a few hours in jail on a murder charge. "That's true. I *do* know how it feels. But, look, Clay, all I'm trying to do is get at the truth. Get your story. I was up front with you from the beginning, wasn't I? I told you I thought you were guilty and that I was going to try to get you to confess. A police officer would never have done that, would they?"

He shrugged. "Probably not. I guess I should thank you for being honest." He thought of something. "You even told me about the good cop/bad cop routine, though telling me was probably just another gambit, wasn't it?"

I shrugged. "Okay, so tell me how it happened. This biting incident with your wife. Give me your side." I smiled, reassuringly. "And don't worry that I'm going to look down on you or make assumptions. I've known a lot of people who've gotten into trouble with the law, and I've learned that you can't judge people."

He blinked slowly. "Is that so?"

"Sure, everyone has reasons for the things they do. So tell me your reasons for . . . I don't know how else to put it, for—"

"Biting her?" he said disgustedly. I nodded and he explained that he was always careful about sex, always the gentleman, never losing control in any situation. "The thing is, at some point Nancy got bored with me. She wanted something a little rougher, a little more exciting, She *wanted* it."

I nodded. "And you weren't experienced enough with that kind of sexual adventuring to know how much was too much?"

"Exactly. Exactly. If I had known I was hurting her, don't you think I would've stopped myself, in an instant?"

"But you didn't know. That's understandable. After all, you'd never done anything like that before."

"Never."

"And afterward, when she said you were like a sniveling infant—that's what she told the police, remember—that was simply her perceptions of you apologizing, asking her to forgive you."

He smiled. "See? I knew you'd get it if you just gave me a chance to explain how it really happened."

"Okay, I'm glad we cleared that up."

"Good. And you'll tell the police my side of it?"

"Of course. But this serial killer we're looking for, we're pretty sure he bit his victims in the same way, so—"

"I wouldn't know anything about that."

"So the cops aren't going to be easy to convince."

He slammed the table and it was my turn to control the startle response. "I have never hurt a woman in my life!"

"Except Nancy."

"That was an accident. That wasn't my fault."

"Right. But what you *should* have said just now is that you've never *intentionally* hurt a woman."

"Okay, then. I never wanted to, I never meant to, no."

"I believe you, Clay." He didn't say he hadn't *done* it, just that he'd never wanted to or meant to do it. That part, at least, was true. He'd probably acted out his violence against his victims almost as if doing so against his own will. The truth was starting to come to the surface.

I just sat there a moment. "Now I'm going to ask you an unsavory question. It's kind of personal."

He snorted. "Like the thing with Nancy *wasn't* personal?"

"Yes, but it's a matter of public record. What I have to ask you now isn't. It's very private. So do you mind?"

He shrugged.

"Did your father ever abuse you?" I asked.

"What kind of question is that?"

"A personal one, like I said. So?"

He shook his head, calmly. "No. God, no. Where on earth did you get that idea?"

I got the idea from the ugly facts about serial killers and the sexual abuse they were subjected to as children, but I didn't tell him that. Nor did I tell him that in studying his MO, I'd deduced that he had a very sick, twisted oral compulsion that could only have been created at a certain stage of development. And that it had probably gone on for some time after that. But I wasn't ready for that part yet.

He took a moment. "Well, since we're being honest with each other, I wouldn't put it past him, doing something like that. He had no ability to control his impulses. None."

"And you do."

"Absolutely. I am nothing like my father. Nothing."

"That's good to know, Clay. That's important."

He smiled and smoothed his jacket front. "There you go, buttering me up again. You know, if the police had a real case against me, they wouldn't need you to try your little head games on me, now would they?" He laughed. "Remember the rules—you have to be totally honest with me too."

I grudgingly agreed that so far there was some initial evidence, but it didn't add up to much of a case against him,

"What evidence?" he asked with genuine interest. (They always want to find out what the evidence is.)

I told him we weren't there to talk about the evidence, which was slight at best, then got him back on the subject of botany. His face warmed again as he talked about wildflowers and fens and ferns. After enough of this I said, "Didn't you . . . um . . . didn't you once have your own flower garden?"

"Yes. Can you imagine the kind of taunts I got over that from my schoolmates? These people, they just don't understand nature. Sad, really."

"Yeah, it is sad. I work with dogs, you know."

"Dogs?" He made it sound faintly repulsive.

"Yes, they're a part of nature. But you'd be surprised how few people realize or honor that aspect of a dog's character."

"Well." He shook his head in disdain. "I would hardly compare a dog with a wildflower, I'm sorry."

"Oh, that's right, you killed a dog once, didn't you?"

He smiled and shook his head. "That was an accident. He got into my flowers and I was just trying to scare him off."

"By cracking his skull open? Now, come on, Clay. Let's not insult each other's intelligence, shall we?"

"Fine. I know what you're getting at. All serial killers start by torturing or killing small animals." He shook his head and smiled a faintly reassuring smile. "I never tortured any animals. I tried to scare the neighbor's mangy dog because he was digging my flowers, then he lunged at me and I lost my . . . I was frightened, so I tried to stop him."

"Come on, you were frightened?" I said skeptically.

"Very well, to be totally honest, I was frightened, yes, but at some point I lost my temper and I killed that dirty creature quite gladly. But it was done in the passion of the moment. And I was fourteen. Hardly the kind of thing you'd expect from someone who carefully plans his crimes."

I nodded and we went around and around on things for a while, me gently dislodging bits of the man's psyche, then teasing them up to the surface, and Henry doing his best to come off as sincere, intelligent, and wrongfully accused. His words came in slow, detached segments whenever discussing the case, but there was an almost raptured flow when he discussed the beauty of nature, as he called it. Still, it was clear that he hated his parents; his father was violent and abusive, and his mother was overprotective when the father wasn't around, and strangely cold and distant when he was.

There was one other thing that came out during this time,

but I didn't realize its importance until later: he felt that glaciers were nature's "cleansing agents."

"Think of it," he said, his eyes glowing with fervor, "they scoured the earth clean of all impurities, leaving behind only what's truly essential to life."

"Like a baptism by ice," I suggested.

"Oh, no. Baptism is hardly an analog for what a glacier does. There's no religious hocus-pocus involved. It's real, powerful, and relentless. Nothing left but the purity of existence."

I nodded. "Plus, there's no trace evidence."

He smiled. "You said you weren't going to ask questions that might incriminate me, remember?"

"Good point," I said. "So, these kettle bogs of yours, they each have their own individual character?"

"Yes," he smiled. "It's truly remarkable."

"And I guess if you're trying to map out these differences, the best way to go about it is to keep your distance, not get up close and personal with the individual botanical specimens."

"Now, where on earth did you get that idea? That is so wrong. No, the thing to do is get as close as you can. You can't tell anything from a distance."

Good. Get the suspect to make a small lie, then confront him with the truth. "So, if that's what you were doing at the lake, then why did you need the telescope?"

He took a sharp breath. "Well, that is to say, you need to get an overview first, and *then* get up close, obviously."

"So that's what you were doing, getting the broad strokes, not getting up close and personal."

"Exactly."

I scrunched my face. "Except Potter's Pond is not a kettle lake, Clay. In fact, the Belgrade Esker is actually quite a distance to the north and west. So there'd be no reason for you to be analyzing any specimens in that area."

"Well, you obviously don't know as much about botany as

I do. As I said, the outlying region is quite important as well."

I shook my head. "Look, Clay, let's leave that aside for now. We can talk to Dr. Carla Petersen. She heads the—"

"I know who she is."

"And we had quite a conversation, she and I. She told me about interlobate moraines, tills, kames, kettle hole lakes, the whole deal. She also told me there's no reason for you to be at Potter's Pond to study kettle bog vegetation. None."

"Just a difference of opinion. Her approach and mine may be different. That's quite common in the scientific community."

"Yeah, I guess I can see that." I took a moment. "All right, let's get back to your father."

He sighed tiredly. "Do we have to?"

"No, we don't have to. But if I'm going to understand your reasons for doing what you've done—"

"I told you," he said, laughing, "I haven't done anything."

"Fine. Let's look at it from a hypothetical point of view, then. It seems to me that our serial killer, the one we're looking for, may have had a father a lot like yours. We can look for parallels and differences between the two."

"I don't know what you think you can learn from me. None of that ever happened to me, as far as I know."

"It never happened to you?"

"No. At least, not that I remember."

Good. He wasn't making a flat denial that it happened. He just denied remembering it.

"Okay, but let's say it did happen to someone like you. A bright, sensitive boy who loves nature." Then I went on to tell him the story of his early life. How the father's sick needs turned into a kind of sexual ritual that never seemed to end.

"That's disgusting."

"It *is* disgusting. But it gets worse. Because the child keeps growing, keeps getting older, but the game doesn't stop. How can it? Like you said, the father can't control himself."

Then one day, I told him, the father becomes so full of self-loathing for what he's been doing that he begins beating the mother and the young boy, beats them into silence.

He was sweating now, which is rare in a serial killer. Like I'd told Flynn, their systems don't process stress the way a normal person's do. He was even licking his lips.

"Are you thirsty? Would like some more water?" I opened a bottle for him. He took it and drank it dry, then wiped his lips. "Like you said, Clay, the man had no self-control."

"None," he agreed. "But I don't remember anything like that happening to me. I'm sorry, I just don't."

"Well, we're not talking about you, necessarily, Clay. And even if we *were,* you're completely innocent."

"That's true. I am innocent."

"You never asked for this to happen to you. But you can see now why our killer does what he does. He doesn't want to do what he does."

"No, he doesn't."

"It makes him sick to do it. But he can't stop himself."

"But he should be able to. He should be able to stop."

"He doesn't want to be like his father."

"No."

"He's determined to control himself."

"Yes, yes."

"But he can't."

"But why? Why can't he stop doing it?"

"Because those feelings are too strong, Clay. He can't stop himself any more than you could when you hurt your wife."

"I didn't mean to hurt her." He was actually on the verge of tears. "She meant the world to me."

"I know she did. It was your chance to make things right. To put all that behind you. But you couldn't, could you?"

"But I never killed anybody. I'd never hurt a fly."

"But you killed that dog, Clay." He nodded. "And I think you killed a lot of women, as well."

He took a deep breath. "But I didn't."

"Yes, but if you did, well, who could blame you? After all the terrible things that happened to you when you were young."

"But they didn't happen to me. I don't remember them."

"So you're not to blame."

"No. I never killed anyone." He stopped. "Except that horrible little dog."

"Because normally, you can control your impulses. You're not like your father."

"No. I told you, I'm nothing like him."

"That's right. Now, about the telescope."

"What?" He took a moment to process the change in topic. "How did we get back to that. I explained—"

"I know, I know. It just occurred to me that once we go to the press and tell them we've got the wrong man, we're going to have to explain that you had a legitimate reason for being at the lake. That you were studying kettle bog vegetation."

"Right. That's good."

I shook my head. "But you see, Clay, from what I understand you have quite a reputation in the field of botany. And there'll be a lot of botanists who hear that, and you know as well as I do what their reaction is going to be. 'Kettle bog vegetation at Potter's Pond?' When that story gets out, your reputation and credibility as a botanist will be gone. You realize that?"

He took a long, deep breath and looked away. "Okay, you're right. That's not what I was doing at the lake."

"You were watching the police recover one of your victims."

"No," he said patiently, "I was merely interested in what the police were doing there. You may have guessed that I've developed a certain interest in serial killers."

"You do seem to know a bit about the subject."

"Well, I've studied it. That's all. And I have a police scanner in my car—I'm sure the State Police will tell you that—and when I heard some chatter about a body being found in a lake, I drove out there to watch. Is that a crime?"

"So you lied initially about what you were doing there?"

"Wouldn't you?"

"No. Not unless I had something to hide. Look, I admit you controlled nearly everything that happened with most of your victims. But the thing is, you didn't think you'd be caught out at the lake. But you were, and now the police have evidence linking you to the crime. So it's time to finally get it all off your chest and tell your side of things."

He shook his head and tightened his lips in a smile. "There's no way I can be linked to any killing. None."

"Yes there is, Clay."

"But you said it. You said the police have no case."

"No, I said they didn't have much of one. But they'll have the evidence they need soon enough. You planned it out very carefully, I must admit. Always leaving the body in a lake or a pond, where the decay and the water would remove all trace evidence. You really thought it through. But not this time. This time you didn't have time to ditch your cell phone. The police are tracing your calls on it now."

He laughed easily and shook his head. "That phone is a prepaid cell. You can't trace any calls on that."

"That's why you bought it."

"Yes. I mean, no, but it's not possible. You're lying."

"I haven't lied to you, Clay. It's being done as we speak. They'll find the home phone number of that high school kid you called and told—"

He shook his head. "I may have dialed a wrong number—"

"That's okay. I don't expect you to tell me the truth about that. That would incriminate you. And I promised I wouldn't do that, remember?" He nodded casually. "And it is possible, I guess, that it's just one more little coincidence in a long string of them, but it's all adding up to life in prison. And once the other evidence is solid against you, you won't have a chance to explain yourself. You'll just be caught."

"What other evidence? You said there *wasn't* any."

"No, I said the evidence was slight, at best. Remember? But they're working on some things, like the calls on the cell phone and the adipocere. Do you know what that is?"

He said he didn't so I explained. Then I told him how he'd left his teeth marks on MerryAnne Moore's body when he'd bit her. When I said it, just casual and matter of fact, he sighed and shook his head, but I also saw a flush of pleasure light up his eyes for a split second. What a sick bastard.

"Adipocere also protects and retains trace evidence, if you know what I mean."

He looked sick. "I'm afraid I don't."

"I think you do." Then I gave a look to the mirror as I explained that the adipocere retained a perfect set of his teeth marks. "And those teeth marks are just as conclusive as fingerprints."

He grimaced. "That's not true. It can't be."

Sinclair came inside and said, "It's true, all right."

Flynn followed and said, "We gotcha now, you sick bastard."

Jamie and her forensic odontologist friend came into the room right behind him. The dentist was carrying a dental tray and some impression compound.

I said, "Check and mate, Clay. We're about to prove you guilty of killing MerryAnne Moore, the lady in the lake, and all twenty-one of your victims. And you'll never have a chance to explain why you did it."

"Twenty-*one*?" he said, with a shocked look.

"That's right. Twenty-one innocent women. Women with families, women with the rest of their lives ahead of them. And all your intellectual pursuits aside, and your grand ideas about glaciers and baptism by ice, you killed every one."

The dentist began troweling the compound into the tray.

Jamie said, "Dr. Henry, we're going to need you to open your mouth for us, as wide as you can."

Clay looked at her, then at me. "No, I want a lawyer."

I said, "I thought innocent men didn't need attorneys."

"I have nothing more to say. Except that you've got the number of my victims wrong. If I *were* the killer, that is."

"Sounds like a confession to me," said Sinclair.

"Too late," said Henry. "I just asked for my lawyer so you can't use anything I say after that. It's inadmissible."

Reassuringly I said, "Don't you want to explain why it happened, Clay? Why you killed them? How you didn't want to do it, but you had to? You couldn't stop yourself?"

"I couldn't stop. I tried to, but I couldn't stop. But I didn't kill twenty-one women. You have to believe me."

"I won't lie to you, Clay," I said. "I think you're a sick, twisted bastard. But I believe you."

The trouble was, I really *did* believe him. Either he'd killed a lot more than twenty-one women or else one or more of the killings we had on the books had been done by someone else—someone who'd copied his pattern and signature exactly.

"But it's not my fault. You said so. My father—"

"Yes, but your father had a chance to stop himself at first, didn't he? So did you. You didn't want to kill your first victim. When the idea came to you, you probably spent hours, maybe days or weeks, trying to talk yourself out of it. But Nancy had left you. Her father had broken all contact. You felt your life was meaningless, so you told yourself you would just kill this one woman, just to see how it felt."

"God, how do you know all this?"

"I just know, Clay. I know that the first time you had that thought, it scared you, but you brushed it aside. It was just a thought. You weren't really going to do it. But it kept coming back, that thought, and pretty soon, instead of trying to put it out of your mind, you started having other thoughts. Brutal, deadly thoughts. And instead of pushing *them* aside, you started to entertain them. You began to play with them in your mind. And before you knew what you were doing, you were planning to kill her, then to kill yourself after she was dead. At last, you thought, you'd be free. But you didn't have the courage to go through with it after she was dead, did you?"

"No. I tried. I tried to kill myself. I wish I had. I couldn't live with what I'd done. Please believe me."

"I do believe you. But the feeling of killing her was too pleasurable, wasn't it? You'd discovered an awful secret that you couldn't give up: it felt good when you killed her."

"Yes, it felt good. But it was awful too."

"That's important. That's in your favor. So tell me now, who did you kill? You have to give me their names."

"No, I didn't kill anyone. I'm not saying anything else until I speak to an attorney. I know my rights."

I tried to press him on it, but he kept his mouth shut and wouldn't say anything else. Not without his lawyer present.

The forensic dentist picked up the tray and impression compound, then we all left him there to stew in his misery and wait for his attorney to show up.

Sinclair stopped me in the hall and said, "Where'd you get all that stuff about his father? It wasn't in the file."

"I know, but it was in his head. I can't explain how I knew about it. It's kind of a Zen thing, I guess."

"God," Jamie said, "what a nightmare."

"Well, it's not over yet."

"What do you mean?" she said. "He confessed."

"Yeah. But only after he asked for a lawyer. That confession won't reach a jury. In fact, he's going to claim I confused him or tricked him into it and he's probably going to have his lawyer file a motion to dismiss the charges."

Flynn shook his head. "You're a real party poop."

"Sorry," I laughed. "But that's the way it is. On the bright side," I turned to Sinclair, "you've got enough now for a warrant to search his house. As I recall, each of the victims had a piece of jewelry missing. A watch, a bracelet, one woman was missing a diamond belly-button ring. Serial killers usually keep souvenirs of their victims." I thought of something. "They'll be well hidden, but my feeling is that you'll find them mixed in with some botanical specimens."

Sinclair nodded and said, "I'll call the State's Attorney and have them contact a judge in Massachusetts right away."

Jamie hugged me. "Good work, Jack."

"Yeah, thanks. But now that it's over I desperately need a glass of scotch and couple of dogs to play with."

"Can you wait for me?" she said, with a nod to the dentist. "Since he won't cooperate, we need to wait for a warrant. As soon as I finish, I may desperately need to join you."

"Yeah," I smiled, "I can wait."

25

The perp's lawyer showed up half an hour later, along with two FBI agents. It was just a coincidence, of course—they came in separate cars—but it *did* pique my interest.

The lawyer I knew slightly. He was Jamie's old friend, Barry Porter, a local defense attorney, a bit slimy, in my opinion. The other two, the feds, I knew as well. I'd met them during a seminar at the FBI's Behavioral Science Unit.

The older man was Wick Tanner. You might have seen him on *Oprah* during the Unabomber case. Or a jillion other places, for that matter. He was tall, spry, clear-eyed, and had stringy white hair, combed over a bald spot in back. He was wearing jeans, Reeboks, a light blue Polo shirt and a navy cotton windbreaker. Even so, he looked more dangerous than Dr. Henry did on his worst day. He taught the seminar I'd attended.

The other man I recognized as a fellow student, but couldn't think of his name. He was a few years younger than I and had on chinos, penny loafers, a plaid shirt, and a dark green sports jacket. But for the plaid shirt, and the fact that he had lighter skin and hair, he reminded me of Regis. For some reason I thought maybe he was his pal Steve Rice.

They came into Sinclair's office, where Sinclair, Jamie, and I were waiting for the warrant for the dental impression. Flynn was long gone.

"Hey, Wick," I said to Tanner. "I thought you'd have retired by now."

"Don't I wish," he sighed. He tilted his chin at the Regis clone, and said, "You remember Steve Rice."

"Hey, Steve," I said, as I got up and shook hands. I'd been right. He was the feeb who'd been with Regis on campus.

Meanwhile, I ignored Porter and he did likewise with me.

To Sinclair, Porter said, "I'd like to see my client." Then he smiled and said hello to Jamie.

She smiled and nodded, though her heart wasn't in it.

"Sure thing," said Sinclair, then called out to a trooper: "Hey, Grasso, that sicko's attorney is here."

Porter got on his high horse. "Now see here, I object to that characterization."

"I'm sorry," said Sinclair, acting sincere. "What would you rather be called, a scum-sucking attorney?"

Jamie did her best not to laugh. Me? I gave in to the impulse and chuckled.

He huffed. "I meant your calling my client a sicko."

Grasso came to the door, curled himself around the frame, and said to Porter, "Follow me."

Porter made to leave, the feds made to follow. He stopped them. "I'd like to speak to my client in private."

With that, he left, while Tanner and Rice stuck around.

"So," said Wick, "is this our guy, Jack?"

"Absolutely," said Sinclair.

"Sort of," said I.

They all looked to me for an explanation, Jamie included. So, I explained. "He's our serial killer, all right. I'm just not sure we've got the number of victims right."

"Oh, bullshit," said Rice.

"Now, now," said Tanner, "let's hear what he has to say." He turned to me. "Jack? You think there's a copycat?"

"That's one possibility, but since you're apparently taking over the case . . ." I looked at Sinclair. He gave me a sad head-shrug. "You might want to reexamine the pattern on all of the victims. There might be a slight variation in the killer's signature on one or more of them. There also might be several more bodies out there that we haven't found yet."

"What the hell makes you think that?" Rice asked.

"Steve," said Tanner with a warning tone.

"Well, I'm sorry, Wick, but we've finally got the bastard in custody and now he's gonna walk—hell, dance out of here—on one of the victims? Un-uh, sorry. I don't think so."

Sinclair said, "Well, the guy virtually confessed. But he did kind of imply—"

"What, Jack?" Tanner said to me. "He implied what?"

"It's not that he implied anything. It's just that when I told him we were going to convict him for twenty-one murders he told me we got the number wrong."

Rice huffed. "He's a serial killer." He turned to me. "He's just playing his sicko games with your head."

"It's possible," I said. "I just don't think so. I think he's right. I think we've got the numbers wrong."

Tanner said to Sinclair, "What do *you* think?"

Sinclair looked at me, then at Wick and said, "If Jack says something's off, I'd listen. That's my opinion." He shrugged. "But it's your case now."

"That's right," said Rice.

"Oh, shut up, Steve. We're done for tonight anyway. Let's get a hotel room." Wick went to the door, stopped and looked at Sinclair. "Did you make a tape of the interview?"

"Of course. I'll send a copy to the bureau first thing in the morning."

"Do it now, and have it sent to our hotel." He told Sinclair where he and Rice would be staying and started to go.

I said, "Hey, Steve, I heard you were at Colby College a few weeks back."

Tanner turned and said, "We both were. Why?"

"Oh, no reason." I paused. "You know Randall Corliss?"

"Not really." Tanner looked at the younger man. "He's an old college friend of Steve's, I think."

"Well," I said, leaning back in my chair, using my body language to let him know that it was no big deal, "since you're trying to lock up a serial killer and rapist, you might want to explain to your partner that it's not a good idea to be hanging around with crooked ex-cops who are also known rapists, of the statutory kind."

"Randy was never convicted of anything," said Rice. Tanner shot him a look. "It was consensual," he explained. "The girl was of legal age."

"No, she wasn't," I said. "Then there's his shady relationship with another rapist by the name of Eddie Cole."

"Okay, what's this about, Steve?" asked Tanner.

He gave him a hard look. "It's nothing. Trust me."

I said, "It's called guilt by association. The press would love to get their hands on this kind of stuff. Eddie Cole is a convicted pimp and drug dealer. And your pal Corliss was on his payroll."

"No he wasn't," said Rice. "That was a totally unfounded accusation."

"Only because Cole escaped from custody before he went to trial. The charges against him included kidnapping a woman who's now the state's chief medical examiner. Jamie and I could both testify to that. He also raped and nearly beat to death another woman, a math and computer science professor at Bates College." I didn't mention Tulips by name.

Rice said, "Which has nothing to do with Corliss."

"Still," I said, "it makes you wonder. How did Eddie Cole

escape from police custody? Did he have inside help?"

"Okay, Jack," said Tanner, "that's enough." He turned to Rice. "Steve, you're off this case as of now."

"Wick, you're not in a position to make that kind of decision, and you know it."

"No, he's right. It's guilt by association. If there's nothing to it, you'll be brought back in. But for now—"

"You really screwed this up, Field," Rice spat.

Tanner said, "That's it, Steve. You're going back to Boston tonight." He turned to Sinclair. "I still want that tape delivered to my hotel."

Sinclair said, "Sure, whatever you say."

Tanner and Rice left, still arguing about the younger man's relationship with Regis.

When they were gone, Sinclair turned to me. "You want to explain all that?"

"Not really."

"Okay. Does it have anything to do with this case?"

"Probably not. I just don't like Corliss very much. Besides, it's not our case anymore, remember?"

Sinclair laughed. "When did that ever stop us?"

The warrant came and Jamie and her dentist friend, whose name was Dr. Kaplan, got the impression made. When that was done we went out to the parking lot and Jamie loaded some boxes from her Jaguar into the backseat of the woody and we headed home.

"Do you really think he only killed twenty victims?" she asked, after we'd got out of town and onto Route 17.

"I think it's a good possibility."

"I didn't mean 'only' like that," she added sadly. "I mean, even one is one too many, but—"

"I don't know. We'll just have to see what develops."

We drove for a while.

She said, "He could have been playing a game, you know. Doesn't this car have a heater?"

"Sorry." I turned up the heater. "And I don't think he was cheating. It seemed to me that he was determined to play by the rules to try and beat me. If that's true, then we really do have the number of victims wrong. And it's possible that at least one of them *was* murdered by someone else. Someone who copied Henry's signature well enough to fool the experts at the FBI." Then I explained about the man Jen had seen on campus the day before she disappeared.

"Ah-hah," she said. "I thought it was odd that you brought up Regis earlier. Because I know you. You may hate him but you're not petty and vindictive."

"Anyway," I said, "Peggy Doyle's going around campus, showing Clay Henry's picture to find out if anyone else saw him that day. So he may still have been the one Jen saw. Besides, just because Regis and company were on campus doesn't mean she saw them. It could have been someone else."

"But it might have been Corliss? Or even one of the FBI agents?" She thought it over and sighed. "Well, that's just awful. It's worse, in a way, than if Henry had killed her."

"I know."

"I mean, he did his killings out of a sick compulsion. He almost couldn't help himself."

"That's right. Almost."

"But if it was Regis or one of the feds, they did it in cold blood. Oh, did you talk to Gretchen?"

"Yep. And I confirmed the reservations at the Samoset."

"That's good. It gives me less to worry about."

"You're welcome."

She huffed. "I shouldn't have to thank you, Jack. But thanks anyway." She settled in her seat. "Now I guess it's up to us to find out who this other killer is."

I laughed. "What?"

"I'm serious. We need to find that other killer."

"Honey, if there is another killer, Wick Tanner will know about it soon enough."

"What if Doyle can't find anyone who saw Clay Henry on campus that day? That would make Tanner a possible suspect, himself. After all, he knew the MO better than anyone. Maybe he knew the victim. Maybe he had a motive."

"To quote Peggy Doyle, 'That's a lot of maybes.' "

"Okay. I'll give you another one: maybe you're the only one who could solve this crime."

"Honey," I laughed, "there are a lot better detectives out there than me, and Wicklow Tanner is at the top of the list. Is it possible Wick could be a killer? Anything's possible, but it's too ridiculous. Besides, the other victim could have been killed in Ohio or Michigan, or even up in Canada. Besides, the numbers could go the other way. Henry could have killed more than twenty-one women, not less."

"His name is Wicklow?"

I nodded. "He was named after a county in Ireland."

"What makes him so great?"

"I don't know. I just know that he's got the magic touch."

"And you don't?"

"Please. He once came to a crime scene, looked around and concluded—don't ask me how—that the killer had a stutter."

"And *did* he?"

"Who?"

"The killer. Did he have a stutter?"

I nodded. "As it turns out, he did. And even Tanner himself doesn't know how he knew that. And he's the last guy in the world *anyone* would suspect of committing murder."

"Which would give him the perfect cover." She settled

back in her seat. "Still," she said, yawning, "I'd feel a lot better about it if you were working on the case too."

"I've got other things to worry about."

She took my hand. "You mean like finding Jen."

"That's right, my tired girl. Let the FBI handle this."

"If you say so." She closed her eyes to go to sleep, then opened them again. "Oh, I get it! That's why you didn't mention anything to them about the man Jennifer saw on campus that day! A part of you thinks that one of them may be . . ."

I shrugged. "It doesn't pay to show your hole card. But I still think Henry was the one who killed her aunt."

"Why? Because she was killed so close to Amherst?"

"That's right. And the MO is exactly the same. If it had been a copycat there would have to have been some sort of subtle difference in the way it was done."

"Yes, Jack, but both Tanner and Rice knew the killer's MO." She thought a bit. "But Corliss didn't. Or did he? Maybe, since he's friends with Steve Rice, he found out how Henry killed all his victims." She thought some more. "But how could someone else use Clay Henry's MO? Wouldn't they be worried he'd have an alibi?"

"No. Think about it. A copycat, if there is one, could only have known that all the bodies were found under a dock and that there was no way to trace the timeline back to any degree of accuracy. The exact time, even the day of death is uncertain, so an alibi—"

"I see where you're going. But that's not true in this case. We've got her stomach contents. Sinclair is trying to find out what her last meal was before she disappeared. If he can track that information, we'll have an accurate timeline, down to a few hours of when she died."

"That's great, honey."

"Are you sure you don't want to solve this case too?"

"Yep. I'm just a dog trainer now, remember?"

"Mm-hmm," she sighed. "Just tell that to the family."

"Whose family?"

"The one woman that Clay Henry didn't kill, remember?" She sighed. "I hope it really *wasn't* Jen's aunt."

I let out a breath. "Okay, I tell you what: as soon as I can, I'll take another look at the victim information from ViCAP, and see if there are any clues as to which one of them might have been killed by the copycat and not by Henry."

"That's good. Oh, did you get the marriage license?"

"Yes. At least I applied for it." I took the copy of the application out of my jacket pocket and gave it to her. "They'll send us the license in three days."

She opened the envelope and unfolded the piece of paper. "Good," she said, smiling. She set it down then reached into the backseat. "And look what I brought." It was a hat box. Or, more accurately, a veil box. "Want to see it?"

"Not now, honey. Surprise me later."

She started to open the box. "Why not now?"

"Anticipation," I said. "It enhances the experience."

"You're a strange man." She put the box back. "I'm glad though, that you're not like most other men. You don't care for sexy lingerie, for one thing. You think I'm sexy just wearing nothing but one of your old T-shirts."

"That's true. I don't know what it is, but you're incredibly sexy when you wear those."

"That's good." She sighed, and cuddled up next to me. "That Victoria's Secret stuff is very uncomfortable."

"You've worn it before?"

She shook her head. "Not really. Eve Arden talked me into trying some on with them once."

I laughed. "I can't imagine what that was like."

"You'd better *not* imagine it. Anyway, I'm glad you like things to be real and natural with us."

"Well, the natural part I agree with. But I'm not so sure about us being real."

"What? What's that supposed to mean?"

"I don't know. Maybe my head's in a weird place right now after doing that interview."

"I wouldn't be surprised." She shuddered.

"I know, but sometimes—not just tonight—I get the strangest feeling that we're not real people, you and I."

"What?" She laughed at the absurdity of what I'd said. "Then what are we?"

"I don't know. Sometimes I think we're just two characters in a series of mystery novels."

She laughed. "You are the oddest man." She cuddled up next to me again. "Still, I kind of like the idea of us being characters in a story. That way nothing really bad will ever happen to us."

"Yeah, well, I wouldn't be so sure about that."

"Why not?"

I shrugged. "Writers can be pretty sneaky."

26

When we got back to the house, neither one of us was in the mood to fool around, so the veil stayed safely in its box. The interview with Clay Henry had kind of sucked all the fun out of life, so we just climbed into bed and held each other for a long time and fell asleep like that. We didn't wake up until the dogs went nuts around three A.M., howling, barking, and shredding the quiet night air with their plaintive cries.

I'd been having a frenetic, frustrating dream about racing through some woods somewhere near a lake, trying to find Jen before the killer did, with Frankie and Hooch barking and howling and leading the way, stopping at every turn in the trail to look back at me and urge me on. It took me a while to realize that their barking wasn't part of the dream.

I woke up and saw Frankie standing in our bedroom, facing the window, barking at the sounds coming from the kennel.

I reached across Jamie and switched on the lamp.

"Jack?" She got up on one elbow. "What's going on?" Her eyes were puffy and she had a pillow crease down her cheek, and she looked adorable, even though she wore a terrible frown.

"I don't know. Frankie, quiet!" He kept barking so I reached for a pillow and threw it at him. (This is not a training practice I'd normally use or endorse—it was just a knee-jerk reaction, and it was just a pillow.)

He stopped, turned around, and wagged his tail at me, but the dogs in the kennel kept going.

I got out of bed and Jamie said, "What's going on?"

My first thought was Jen. Maybe she'd come by to see Frankie and the dogs were barking at her. "I don't know. Maybe Jen's here." While I threw some clothes on I said, "You stay here. I'm going to see what the noise is all about."

Jamie swung her legs over the side of the bed and began looking around for her clothes. "Is this kind of thing going to keep happening, even after we're married?" she said grumpily.

"I don't know, sweetheart. I doubt if the dogs will be aware of our marital status and change their behaviors accordingly. You left your clothes in the bathroom."

"I did?"

"Yes. In a pile on the floor."

"Don't yell at me." She brushed the hair out of her eyes.

"I'm not yelling," I laughed. "I'm just saying—"

"I'm sorry. I can't always remember to hang everything up like you want me to." She got up, still a little wobbly with sleep, and tottered into the bathroom.

I got some jeans and a T-shirt on, which was tough to do with Frankie circling around me. When I was dressed enough I went to the door and said to Jamie, "Go back to sleep. I'll take care of it." Then I raced down the stairs with Frankie leading the way.

We ran through the living room to the kitchen and out the side door. As I crossed the side yard I looked over at the carriage house to see if Leon had woken up from the noise, but there was no light on. He's a deep sleeper.

I got to the kennel and turned on the overhead lights, which increased the barking exponentially. There were only five dogs in the kennel—Vreeland's three Dalmatians, Hooch, and a Lakeland terrier named Roxy I was training for her owner. By the time I got the dogs quiet—all except Frankie, who continued to bark, and Hooch and Daisy, who weren't barking but were whining and spinning around in crazy circles—Jamie appeared in the front door of the kennel and said, "Jack, what was it? What's going on?"

"I don't know." I looked around. "No one is missing, and the doors are all locked."

She came over and put her arms around my waist. "Can we go back to bed now?"

"I guess," I said, and started to turn out the light.

Suddenly, Frankie stopped barking and I could just barely hear a car horn, somewhere in the distance. The horn wasn't honking, over and over, like you'd hear from a frustrated driver stuck in traffic. It was a steady sound as if someone had fallen forward in the driver's seat of their car, with the weight of their head resting against the steering wheel.

"Do you hear that?" I said.

"What?"

"That car horn? It's coming from the county road."

"Is that what they're barking at?"

I looked at Frankie, then at Daisy. They both had an unusually strong attachment for Jennifer, and it occurred to me that maybe Jen was in that car, hurt or something worse.

"Jack, what are you doing? Don't let the dogs out!"

But I did let them out—Daisy and Hooch, that is. Daisy and Hooch immediately ran to the back door of the kennel, which was very unusual. We never take the dogs out that way. Frankie and I followed them to the door and I opened it. All three dogs shot through the door and began running up the hill behind the kennel building, the straightest way up to the county road.

"Jack!"

"Stay here, honey."

I followed the dogs up the hill, doing my best to keep up, but it was no use. Daisy was racing, almost like a greyhound, though Frankie kept turning around to see where I was before running after her. Hooch was actually heeling—running right next to me, looking up at me the whole way.

I clambered through the thicket of alder saplings that runs along the gravel road, and by the time I got there Frankie and Daisy had disappeared around a bend in the gravel road. Oh, great, I thought, I've lost one of Vreeland's valuable show dogs. Hooch raced ahead to the curve then turned and waited for me to catch up.

"Jack! Wait for me!" Jamie was just coming up the hill.

I went back over there. "Didn't I tell you to—"

"Shut up and help me!"

I did a side-step traverse down the grade a few feet, took hold of an alder sapling with one hand, and reached down to Jamie with the other, then helped her up the rest of the hill.

We stood there a moment, panting. "Now what?"

I said, "Now we follow Hooch, I guess."

"Great," she said, looking down at our bare feet. "We're about to go running down a gravel road at three in the morning with no shoes on."

I was about to say I'd told her to stay put, but she took off after Hooch, with an, "Are you coming?" over her shoulder.

As we ran, Hooch would run ahead of us, disappearing at times around each bend in the road, then he'd come running back just close enough to make sure we were still following him. Frankie and Daisy were just gone.

We got closer and closer to the horn sound and we could

hear the sound of Daisy's whine, and Frankie's calling bark, mixed in with it. Hooch was waiting, panting, at another bend in the road, but as we approached him, he didn't turn around and head off again, like he'd been doing. He just stood patiently waiting for us, kind of smiling with his big Hooch face. The car now sounded to be just around the bend.

We came around it and saw Jennifer's rust red 1965 International Harvester Scout. The vehicle comes with a detachable roof, which wasn't in place, making it essentially a convertible. She'd driven it into a ditch and crashed the front end against a pine tree. The engine was still running and Frankie and Daisy were on the front seat next to Jennifer, taking turns licking her face. Hooch, secure in knowing we were there, ran ahead to join the other dogs.

He put his paws up on the driver's side and barked. When he did this, I saw Jennifer's hand wave weakly at the other dogs to get them to stop licking her, though her head was still resting firmly against the steering wheel.

"She's alive, thank god," said Jamie. She stopped running and bent over, breathing heavily, with her hands on her knees.

I stopped and put a hand on her back. "How are your feet?"

"Never mind that now," she said, standing straight. "I need to check her injuries."

We ran to the car and I told the dogs to get in back, which after some argument, they did. Jamie opened the door and gently palpated Jennifer's neck and back, which caused the girl to bat her hand weakly at Jamie.

Jamie said, "Take it easy, honey. It's Dr. Cutter. I'm here to help you."

"Jamie?" Jennifer said weakly. "Is Jack here too?"

"Yes, Jack's here too."

After Jamie had found no major damage to Jen's neck, she gingerly pulled the girl's head back from its resting place on the car horn and the world was still and silent again. Even Frankie and Daisy sat calmly panting in the backseat.

I got in back with them, stood behind the driver's seat—it was the bench type—and helped Jamie scooch the barely conscious girl to the other side of the car. Jamie sat in the middle, with an arm around her and her head resting on Jamie's shoulder. I held the back door open for Hooch to hop in, then got in front and took the wheel.

"Jennifer?" Jamie said. "Can you hear me?"

"I came to see Frankie," she said with her eyes closed.

"Frankie is here, honey," I said. "So is Daisy. They helped us find you."

Her eyes fluttered open. "Daisy? Daisy girl?"

"Where's your cell phone?" Jamie asked. "We need to get you to a hospital and have them check you out."

"No." I thought she meant she didn't have her cell phone, but then she said, "No hospital."

"But you need to be looked at by a doctor."

"No," she said, whining, trying to open her eyes again. "He'll find me. I have to hide."

"It's okay," I said. "You're safe with us now."

"Have you taken anything? Have you been drinking?"

"Just tired," she said, closing her eyes. "Can't sleep."

Jamie looked at me. "She needs to be seen by a doctor."

"You're a doctor," I suggested.

"No. She needs an emergency medicine specialist."

"Okay," I said, stepping on the clutch and putting the gearshift into reverse. "Let's get her and the dogs back to the house and then decide what to do."

Jamie nodded and cradled Jen in her arms. But before I could drive ten yards, two official vehicles pulled up from opposite directions and boxed us in. One was a sheriff's Jeep. The other was a Colby College Campus Security car.

27

Sheriff Flynn and Doyle got out of their vehicles and we had a brief chat, I introduced them to one another, and I got their stories.

They'd both had the same idea: to park along the county road and wait, in case Jen came back to the kennel to see Frankie. Flynn had parked on one side of my property, closer to Perseverance, and Doyle had positioned herself on the other end, closer to Hope. They'd both waited conscientiously for several hours but had finally succumbed to drowsiness. Oddly enough they'd both slept through the sounds of the car horn and the barking, and it wasn't until the noise stopped that they both woke up and decided to see what was going on.

"Okay," I said, getting back in Jen's Scout, "Jamie and I are taking her back to the house. Why don't you follow us?"

They agreed and we made a convoy back down the road through the dark autumn night.

We got Jen back to the house and I carried her inside to the guest bedroom on the first floor. We were followed closely by Frankie and Daisy. Hooch settled by the fireplace.

Flynn and Doyle went into the kitchen to make coffee. After Jamie and I put Jen onto the bed, Jamie checked her pulse and breathing.

"I think she'll be fine here," she said, which I was glad to hear. "She just needs to sleep, more than anything. If we took her to the hospital it would probably only increase her anxiety and they'd have to sedate her."

"I think you're right. Can you get her to bed? I've got to call her parents."

While she was getting Jennifer undressed and under the covers, I went into the living room to use the phone.

Doyle appeared in the kitchen doorway. "Oh, I forgot to tell you."

"What?" I asked, phone in hand.

She smiled and said, "I got a hit on Henry's picture from some of the students today."

"He was on campus the day Jennifer disappeared?"

"That's what they told me."

"Good. Good work," I said and made my calls. The call to Kristin's cell phone went directly to her voice mail—meaning it was turned off or she was out of area. The Samoset wouldn't put me through to Sonny's room. It was after 3:30.

"This is a police emergency," I said. "His daughter's been missing and has just been found. He'll want to know."

"How do I know that? Are you with the police?"

"No, I'm an ex-detective, hired by Mr. Vreeland to find the girl. Look, he'll want to know that she's safe."

"Jack!" I heard Jamie call out, "can you get these dogs away from me?"

"Hang on," I said to the operator, "let me give you to the sheriff. Flynn!" I called out. "Can you take this call?"

Jamie cried out, "Jack!"

"Just a second, honey."

Flynn came in from the kitchen and said, "Who is it?"

I told him then said, "But whatever you do, don't let this idiot switchboard operator know where Jen is."

The phone squawked. "I heard that."

He nodded and took the phone. "This is Sheriff Flynn. What?" There was a pause. "Oh, don't take it personal. He's like that with everybody."

I went to the bedroom, where Frankie and Daisy were threatening Jamie. Daisy had her lips pulled back and was growling at her. Frankie stood between Jamie and the bed, where Jennifer was lying asleep, still clothed except for her boots. Jamie stood next to the window, out of harm's way.

"They won't let me go near her."

"Frankie," I said, pointing behind me to the living room, "go lie down." The goof just stared at me and didn't move an inch. "Frankie!" He hung his head but still didn't budge.

It looked like I was going to have to change his emotional state before he'd listen. I went over to the bed and sat on the edge of it, next to Jennifer. "Come here." He obediently trotted over to me. "Now, listen, Doodle," I said, petting him, "Jennifer is fine and Jamie's just trying to help her. Okay?" He wagged his tail and lifted his head for an ear scratch. I obliged. "Now, go outside and take Daisy with you."

He looked at me, then at Jamie, then turned around and came toward Daisy, kind of dancing in her direction, trying to charm her. She got a little wiggly herself, then he danced her out of the room, where they immediately turned around and stood in the doorway to stand guard. While they stood in position, Daisy gently nudged Frankie with the side of her head.

"Good doggies. Now, Frankie, go lie down with Hooch." He just stood there. "Frankie, go lie down!"

He lay down in the doorway and Daisy followed suit.

I turned to Jamie. "Sorry, honey," I said. "That's the best I can do."

"Can I get this poor girl undressed and put to bed now?"

"Yes. I'll keep my back turned."

I started toward the door and heard Jennifer say, weakly, "Jack?"

I turned back. "Yeah?"

"I'm sorry I kissed you that day."

Jamie shot me a surprised look.

"That's okay. Just relax and get some sleep now."

"But you forgive me?"

"Yes," I said. "It never happened, remember?"

She seemed confused. "It never happened?"

"No, it did. But we were going to pretend like it didn't. Remember what I told you?"

She nodded weakly. "And you forgive me?"

"Yes. And you're safe now, so don't worry. The police have the man you're afraid of. Just relax and get some sleep."

"They caught him?"

"Yes, he's in jail right now. Now get some sleep."

"I'm so tired." She closed her eyes. "Thank you."

Jamie went toward the bed and the dogs growled at her.

I turned and gave them a look. "What did I just say?"

They wagged their tails.

Jamie said, "Jack, maybe you should just go outside and close the door. Keep them out of here."

I agreed and went out the door, preventing the dogs from coming back in by placing my body between them and the door. Then I closed it, went to the mudroom and got a leash, came back, put it on Daisy, and led her and Frankie over to one end of the sofa. Flynn was still on the phone at the other end. The dogs lay down, their eyes focused on the bedroom.

Flynn had been having pretty much the same success with the Samoset that I had. They put him through but Sonny

Vreeland wasn't answering his phone. He was now talking with the Waterville PD.

As I sat down he cupped the phone and said, "Zeke Evans says hi and congratulations."

"Tell him thanks." While Flynn did that, I called out to the kitchen. "You need any help with that?"

"It's almost ready," Doyle called back. The smell of fresh coffee was overflowing into the living room.

Jamie came out of the bedroom and the dogs stood up. Daisy began growling at her.

"Jack?" She stood halfway between the door and the sofa.

"It's okay, honey. Just let her sniff your hand." She didn't seem convinced. "It's okay. Really." Then I said in a happy tone, "Daisy, good girl, say hello."

She stopped growling and wagged her tail. Jamie came over, holding her hand out for Daisy to sniff. The dog calmed down. I told Jamie, "Now scratch under her chin."

She did and said, "Her fur is so soft."

"I know." I stroked Daisy's topline. "It's like velvet, isn't it? How's Jennifer?"

"She'll be okay, I think." She sat down next to me.

I released Daisy from the leash. She and Frankie went right over to Jennifer's door and took positions in front.

Flynn got off the phone. "You got the address for the mother's house in Waterville?"

"Yeah, let me write it down for you."

I wrote down the address, he took it and started to get up. "It's better if she gets the news in person anyway."

Doyle came in with a tray and four cups of joe, with saucers and spoons. There was a sugar bowl and small pitcher of cream on the tray as well. She set it on the coffee table.

"I didn't know how everybody took theirs," she said.

Flynn sat back down and we all took a cup and saucer and made it to our liking, then just sat sipping for a bit.

Doyle said, "I can camp out down here and keep an eye on her if you two want to get some sleep."

"That won't be necessary," I said.

"The hell," said Doyle. "Anyways," she added with a sour laugh, "I had a pretty good nap up on the road."

Flynn got up. "I'd better go. I'll send a fax to the press office at the statehouse after I notify the parents."

"Yeah, just don't let anyone know where she is," I said. "And leave me and Jamie out of it entirely; this was all you and Doyle."

He picked up his hat and said, "I told you before, I don't need your—"

"Look, Sheriff, I want to be left out of it. Jen'll be safer that way. And you ought to try the Samoset first," I told him. "Kristin might be there with Sonny. And he might be a little hard to wake up. He takes GHB to relax."

Flynn shook his head. "What a family."

After he left I got some pillows and a quilt for Doyle. She insisted on staying on the sofa the rest of the night. She kicked off her shoes and tested the sofa for springiness.

Jamie and I said good night and were halfway to the stairs when I said, "Have you got the photo with you?"

"What photo?" Doyle said.

"The one of Clay Henry that you showed around on campus earlier."

She nodded. "It's in the car. Why?"

"Since we now know he was on campus, I want to show it to Jen after she's had some sleep."

"I'll go get it."

"It can wait till tomorrow morning."

Then, while Doyle was getting comfy, Jamie and I went upstairs to bed, leaving Hooch by the fireplace.

"What was all that about her kissing you?" she said as we got under the covers.

"It was nothing," I said.

Jamie put her head on my shoulder and got nestled next to me. "It didn't sound like nothing."

I pulled a strand of her hair out of my mouth. "She's a mixed-up girl," I said, then told her what happened that day.

"And you didn't tell me about it?"

"Nothing to tell, really. It's not like she was serious. Besides, she made me promise not to."

"Un-huh. So are you planning to go on kissing other girls after we're married?"

I laughed. "Just the nutcases."

She chuckled, then sighed. "She's not a—"

"I know. But her *mother* is."

"Wait. Don't tell me you kissed Kristin too?"

"I mean, her stepmother. And no, I didn't kiss her. She kissed me." I finally told her about that day in the kennel.

"Looks like I'm going to have to keep an eye on you."

"Don't worry. I'm the luckiest guy in the world and I know it. I'm not going to do anything to ruin that."

"You'd better not." She sighed and hugged me.

"In fact, I'll do my best to enhance it."

She got up on one elbow. "I'm not sure I know what that means."

"Nothing. I was just thinking about what Peggy Doyle told Zeke Evans when he came to Colby the other night, remember? He said, 'You ruined my evening,' and she said, 'I didn't ruin your evening, Zeke, I enhanced it.' "

"Oh, I remember." She chuckled. "That was cute. Well, just be careful how you enhance things, okay?"

"Okay." I yawned and said, "Maybe we could sleep in."

She sighed. "I wish. I still have a ton of work to do on the case, and you have to drive me back up to Augusta in the morning, remember?"

"Oh, right. I forgot."

She sighed. "I can get a state trooper to drive me if you want to get a little extra sleep."

"No, I was thinking of Jennifer," I said. "I guess we can let Doyle stay with her till I get back from dropping you off."

"You never told me that her father took GHB."

"I know. It didn't seem relevant. I've still got a bottle of his stuff."

She got up on one elbow. "Why?"

"I confiscated it from him while he was asleep."

"And why haven't you gotten rid of it?"

"I don't know. I was toying with the idea, if we ever found Jen, of giving her some to help recover her repressed memories. That's one of its medical uses, you know."

"And are you a psychiatrist?"

"No."

"A medical doctor?"

"No."

"Then what the hell were you thinking?"

"Honey, I didn't say I was actually going to do it, it was just an idea. I want to help her sort all this stuff out if I can, that's all."

"That's fine, but it's not your job, is it? Where's the bottle now?"

"In the medicine cabinet. Why?"

"So I can pour it down the bathroom sink in the morning."

"Don't you trust me?"

"What do you think?" She snuggled up next to me again. After a while she said, "I'm really glad Peggy Doyle's here."

"Yep. With Doyle and the dogs, I'd say that girl's got some pretty good protection."

She nodded, then yawned and closed her eyes. "But who's going to protect her from herself?"

28

Jen was still asleep when I got up the next morning. For that matter, so were Doyle and Jamie, but I had to get up early so I could get the dogs exercised and fed before taking Jamie to the capital. I also had to drop Leon off in Perseverance so he could catch the school bus to take him to his day in detention.

The first order of business was to take Frankie and Daisy out for bathroom duty, along with Hooch, but the two canine bodyguards weren't interested in leaving Jen's door. In fact, Daisy growled at me when I first came down the stairs. Frankie gave her a nudge with his nose and she calmed down.

So I had to do the trick with the leash again to get Daisy to move. She unwillingly came with me and Hoochie outside, where there was a cool, light mist hanging over the property.

I tried to get her down the front steps, but she quickly spraddled her legs on the porch, left a huge puddle there, and then began pulling as hard as she could to go back inside, her toenails scratching for purchase on the wooden surface. I took her back inside and left Hooch outside, on solo urine duty.

"Okay, Doodle," I said, unhooking Daisy from the leash.

"Your turn." He wouldn't get up. "Frankie." He just stared at me as Daisy settled next to him. "Okay, then you get the same treatment." I leaned down and hooked the leash to his collar. He didn't get up. I gave a tug. He just grunted and stayed put. Dogs don't know anything about the laws of physics, but some of them (bulldogs, beagles, and pugs are the best examples) sure know how to use their centers of gravity against you when they don't want to move.

I dragged him past Doyle then through the mudroom and out the front door, closed it and the screen door, unhooked the leash and said, "Okay, now go pee!"

He got to his feet, shook himself, then turned around and scratched at the screen to be let back inside. This was very uncharacteristic. He normally has a very passionate approach to urination. In fact, at times it seems as if his only mission in life is to pee as much and as often as possible.

"Fine," I said, draping the leash around my neck, "but I'm not going to be responsible for what happens to your bladder." I let him inside and he bounded back to Jen's door.

I got one of the dog towels from the mudroom and soaked up Daisy's urine, then looked around for Hooch and saw him down by the play yard, patrolling the perimeter and marking every other fence post. I called, "Heyo!" and he turned and came lumbering back to me. We went to the carriage house to rouse Leon and Magee. Then I took Hooch and the terrier to the kennel, freed Roxy and the two male Dalmatians, Rorschach and Seurat, and we all went out to play in the morning mist.

After I was done taking care of the dogs, I started making breakfast: Denver omelets, juice, coffee, and toast. After I'd chopped the peppers and onions, I started sweating them in a little garlic butter (I hate when the veggies in an omelet are raw), I went out to the living room, where Doyle was still asleep on the sofa.

"Hey, partner," I said, "time to get up."

"Mmmm?" she said, still groggy.

"Come on. Wake up. Shift's over."

She opened her eyes, looked at me, then looked around to orient herself. "Oh, yeah," she said. "Anything happen?"

"Nope. She's still safe and sound."

"Good." She sat up and stretched. "Oh," she groaned, "what time is it? Where's the—?"

I pointed toward the downstairs bathroom. "It's a little after nine. You want some coffee? Something to eat?"

"Yeah, just let me pee first."

"Okay. When you're done I'm going to need you to get me that picture of Clay Henry from your car."

"Okay." She got up and padded off to the bathroom.

I went to the kitchen to stir the peppers and onions, with Hooch at my heels. After a bit Doyle came in with the black-and-white fax photo of our killer. It looked just like him—the round glasses and the thatched hair.

"Thanks, this should ease her mind. Can you take over for me while I look in on Jen?" I nodded to the brick of pepper jack on the cutting board. "Just grate the cheese for me. I'll be right back."

"You got it, boss," she said, putting on an apron.

I poured a glass of orange juice and grabbed a banana and one of Mrs. Murtaugh's blueberry muffins, then went to the bedroom to check on Jen. Frankie and Daisy saw me, got up, and followed me inside. Jen was bunched up under the covers in the fetal position, her pink and green hair tumbled across her face and pillow.

I set the glass of juice, the banana, and the muffin for her on the nightstand, and put Clay Henry's picture next to them. I found a pen next to the lamp and wrote a note on the back of the photo: "We got him. He's in jail." I figured that since some of the students that Doyle canvassed had seen Dr.

Henry on campus the day before Jen disappeared, that she'd seen him too, and that he was her aunt's killer. I hoped that when she woke up and saw the note, then turned the picture over, she'd feel relieved that he was now in custody.

As I closed the door, leaving the dogs inside to protect her, I looked back and saw them curl up next to her bed.

I finished making the omelets and Jamie and Leon joined us for breakfast. I asked Doyle if she wouldn't mind sticking around until I got back from doing my morning chauffeur duties.

"Sure," she said. "Unless you'd like *me* to drive them?"

I looked at Jamie and Leon. They had no problem with that.

"Okay, then. I'll stay here on Jen duty."

They left after breakfast. Hooch and I settled on the sofa to keep an eye on the news, if there was any, with the sound turned down low so I could also keep an ear on Jennie's bedroom.

Farrell Woods showed up at nine and I gave him the keys to the Suburban so he could do the morning pickups. Around ten, I heard the crunch of tires on gravel again. It was too soon for Woods to be back, so I went outside to see Kristin and Sonny, arriving together, in separate cars.

I met them at the bottom of the steps and we went inside.

"She's still asleep," I said quietly as we came into the living room. "Would you like something to drink?" I asked.

"No thanks," said Sonny. "Can't I talk to her?"

"Well," I said, looking over at the door. "I think it'd be better to wait until she wakes up. But it's your call."

He looked at Kristin. She said, "Don't look at me. She's *your* daughter."

He looked down at his suede desert boots, then gave me an apologetic facial shrug. "I'll just go have a look-see."

"Fine with me," I said. "But be prepared. Frankie and Daisy have decided it's their job to protect her."

He nodded. "Daisy's always been like that. I'll just take a quick peek, though."

Before he got to the door, we heard the sound of an engine starting up in the driveway. A dog began barking outside. They looked at me for an explanation. I had none—Farrell Woods was still out doing the morning rounds and Mrs. Murtaugh lives just across the road and doesn't keep her car at the kennel. Then it hit me—it had to be Jennifer.

I cursed and ran to the door just in time to see her brake lights go on as she took the turn from the driveway onto the county road. Frankie was chasing after her and barking. I called him. Several times, in fact. Finally on the fourth or fifth try, he came running back.

I ran to the woody and got in but it wouldn't start. I tried turning it over several times but all I got was the starter motor. The engine wouldn't catch. I looked over at Woods's empty pickup, but realized he had his keys with him.

Kristin and Sonny had followed me outside. They just stood there, helpless. "My car won't start," I shouted. "Let's take the Land Rover." I got out and we ran over to it and piled in, but it was the same story. The starter engaged but that was it.

I got out to look at the engine and noticed that the hood had been opened but hadn't been closed all the way. As I pulled the hood high I told Kristin, "Try your car." She ran to the Mercedes while I looked at the Land Rover's engine. Its distributor cap was gone. Meanwhile, Kristin couldn't start her car either.

I ran over and checked under *her* hood and found the same thing. No distributor cap.

I said, "I'd better call the sheriff and have him start looking for Jen."

I ran back inside to call Flynn, with Frankie at my heels and Hooch joining in on the excitement. Flynn said he'd put the word out to his staff and that he'd put a call in to the State Police as well as all other local authorities.

I hung up and explained to Kristin and Sonny what was going on at Flynn's end, and answered their questions as best I could. Then I said, "I want to check out her room. You two should look around for those missing distributor caps."

They left to do that and I went into the bedroom. The window was wide open. Daisy was gone. So were the banana and the muffin. The juice glass was empty. The photo of Clay Henry was on the bed. I picked it up. Scrawled across the top were the words, "IT'S NOT *HIM*!!!! WRONG MAN!!!"

I sat on the bed, feeling like I'd been punched in the gut. I cursed myself for being an idiot, then took a few deep breaths and went outside to show Sonny and Kristin the photo and help them find the missing distributor caps.

After looking everywhere we could think of, we gave up. She'd apparently taken all three with her.

We went back inside and I went to the phone to call a parts store. While I was dialing I said, "I'll say one thing for you two—you raised a pretty smart girl. She's a lot of trouble, but she's smart."

Kristin said, "Sounds like you, Jack." Then to Sonny, she said, "Where are you going?"

He shrugged apologetically. "I need to use the bathroom."

She shook her head. "Let me check your pockets first."

He smiled good-naturedly and opened his arms wide so she could frisk his safari jacket and pants pockets. When she didn't find anything he said, "See? I can obey orders."

"Yeah, fine," she said, then plopped onto the couch.

I got through to the parts department and ordered three distributor caps. They said they only had models for the

Land Rover and the Mercedes, not the woody, and that they'd be delivered by six o'clock. It was half past ten.

"Great," I said, and hung up. I sat next to Kristin and told her the good news/bad news.

"That's all right," she said. "I'll call a rental agency. We're not hanging around here till six." She looked around the room. "You've done some remodeling."

"Yeah, it's been a lot of work." I thought it over. "Wait, I don't remember you being here before."

"Sure, I was here last Christmas, remember? I brought Jen by to play with Frankie?"

"Right. And to get recommendations for Daisy's trainer."

"Anyway," she said, "I really like what you've done with the place. Especially your sconces."

"Oh," I almost blushed, "that was Jamie's idea." I handed her the phone. Just then the toilet flushed and Sonny came out of the bathroom, looking loopier than usual.

He stumbled his way over to the easy chair and laughed. "You forgot to check my shorts," he said to Kristin, then dropped into the chair and promptly fell asleep.

Kristin looked at me and shook her head as she dialed the operator. "I told you he couldn't handle all this stress."

29

While we waited for Sonny to wake up, and for the rental car to arrive, I grilled Kristin on her, or the Blythe family's, relationship with Randall Corliss, but got nowhere. I decided to switch tactics.

"What can you tell me about Sonny's will?"

"His will? Why?"

"Because I want to know about it. It might be relevant. Do you inherit anything if he dies, or if Jennifer does?"

"You think *I* want her dead?"

"No. Just answer the question."

She looked over at her sleeping husband. "It's—it's a complicated situation."

"How so?"

"Sonny inherited the company from his parents. His money is controlled by the provisions of his own inheritance. He can't change that with a will of his own."

"So, his parents didn't want their money going to Sonny's wives, just to his children?"

"Something like that. It's more complicated, but yes."

I thought about it. "And that's why you got pregnant?"

She glared at me. "I ought to slap you, you know that?"

"So I'm right." Before she could say anything I added, "I mean that you don't inherit if Sonny dies."

She nodded. "I'd get a little, but not much."

"But Jen and your baby, when it's born, do?"

"It *all* goes to them eventually, yes."

"And you'd be in control of how that money is spent until the child reaches maturity."

"Where is this headed? I don't want anything to happen to Jen *or* Sonny. I love them both dearly. And when it comes to money, I have plenty of my own, you know."

"Sure, but how much is Sonny worth?"

She looked down at her Timberlands. "A hundred million."

"Wow. That's a lot of vitamins." I shook my head. "And *you'd* have to design a helluva lot of sets and costumes to make that kind of dough."

"Jack, I don't care about the money. You should know that better than anyone. Why are you asking me all this?"

I ignored her question. "So, according to his parents' will, when is the money turned over to Sonny's children?"

She told me it was supposed to go into a trust, with limited access given to Sonny and his wife, until the child turns twenty-one, and that the trust starts at age six.

I thought this over. "That's about how old Jennifer was when her mother died."

"Yeah. So?"

"So, it seems an odd coincidence, don't you think? She dies just when the money goes out of his control?"

"No," she shook her head. "No way. Sonny . . ." She looked over at him. "He wouldn't . . ." She looked back at me, fear in her eyes. "There's another provision."

I waited to hear what it was.

She stared at her lap again. "Once the child is six, a

substantial portion of the money is to be handled by the child's mother. It's out of Sonny's hands then." She looked back at me. "His parents didn't trust him, apparently."

I looked at the man, who was now drooling all over his safari jacket. "Can you blame them? And if the mother decides to file for a divorce or if she dies?"

"Sonny takes control. But he wouldn't have killed Rose."

"Someone did. Unless it really was a suicide, but I'm starting to have my doubts about that. And we know for sure that someone killed her sister Lilly."

"That's another thing." She sighed. "From what I know, Lilly Blythe was in a bitter custody battle with Sonny at the time of her death. She wanted control of Jen's future."

"And inheritance?"

She nodded. "She claimed that Sonny was an unfit parent and that Rose had asked her to look after Jen if anything happened to her. It was even written in Rose's suicide note."

I nodded. "How long had this battle been going on?"

"Just a year or so."

I shook my head. "Well, Jen was five or six when her mother died, and twelve or so when her aunt was murdered. That would mean that Lilly Blythe waited six or seven years to act on her sister's wishes."

She shrugged. "The story I got is that Lilly had some drug problems for a few years. And a gambling habit, and a string of loser boyfriends. She finally got it together, I guess, and—"

"What was their relationship like?"

"Who, the twins? How should I know? Jack, what does this have to do with—"

"You must have overheard someone talking about them at some family gathering. Sonny may have brought the subject up."

"You really think all this matters?"

"I don't know. It might."

She shook her head and sighed. "Well, from what I know, they weren't lovey-dovey, the way you usually think of twins. They spent years not speaking to one another." She thought of something. "Although it's odd. Rose had put together some money—she had quite a living allowance and had put some aside, close to a million dollars, I think—and she left all that to Lilly when she died."

"Interesting. What kind of background did they come from?"

She told me that Rose and Lilly Blythe had been born into a modest lifestyle in Denville, New Jersey.

"But they have a lake cabin in Massachusetts?"

She shrugged. "It's the only valuable property they owned. It belonged to Rose and Lilly's grandmother, on their mother's side. It was just a shack, really, until Sonny stepped in and revamped the place. The mother and father divorced. He stayed in New Jersey. She moved back in with her mother in Amherst."

She went on to tell me that Rose and Sonny met while she was working as a waitress at the Short Hills Country Club. "Meanwhile, Lilly was in Manhattan, struggling to become a model or an actress or something. They were both quite lovely to look at, very striking."

I thought it over. "Did you ever hear any stories about them switching identities?"

"No, I don't recall any. Why, is that something—?"

I shrugged. "Some twins like to play head games with their sister's boyfriends. It's just a thought."

She cocked her head. "You think that Rose's suicide was mistaken identity? And that her sister Lilly was actually—?"

"Anything's possible. I read the police report. They didn't do a full autopsy. The identification was made by Sonny himself. There was no mention of dental records or—"

"But, Jack, that's insane."

"It's a possibility. Look, the two deaths may be totally unrelated. That's one possibility. But let's say that Sonny wanted Rose dead so he could control Jen's money. So he calls someone he knows to have it done, but Rose somehow overhears their conversation. So she invites Lilly to the cabin, lets her borrow some of her fancy, vitamin-money-bought clothes, then sends her into the arms of this hired killer. When the sister dies, she's now free from Sonny and has a million dollars to boot. Time passes, she has expensive tastes, the money runs out, and she wants her daughter back, not to mention control of the girl's inheritance.

"Look," I went on, "Jen seems convinced that her mother was murdered. Maybe she really *was,* seven years after her apparent suicide. Maybe Sonny found out about the switch—"

"But Sonny couldn't have done it, Jack. It's just not in his nature."

"Maybe not, but I'm starting to think that Jen isn't so screwy after all." We sat for a moment or two. "Look, all I'm suggesting is that it *could've* happened that way."

"That's just awful. But even if Sonny wanted her dead, who could he have possibly hired to—oh, my god! I just realized, when Randy was in college, he and a friend of his had summer jobs at the lake. They were caretakers for some of the cabins."

"When was this?"

"I don't know. Like I said, he was in college at the time. He's in his mid-thirties. *You* do the math."

I did, and it fit roughly with the time of Rose Vreeland's suicide. "Who was the friend?"

"What friend?"

"This friend of Regis, from college."

"I don't know."

I shook my head. "I wish you had told me this before."

She sighed. "Me too. But you were acting so territorial about him that I—"

"Jesus, Kristin, the man is a rapist. At the very least he's guilty of statutory rape. And he may be a killer. He's now on a short list of sus—"

"Oh, god. Poor Jen."

"Yeah, and poor Rose and Lilly. Don't forget them. And maybe poor you, after the baby is born."

"Oh, crap. I hadn't even thought about that."

Just then we heard Farrell Woods come back with the Suburban. We got up and I went over to Sonny and tilted his head back so he wouldn't dribble all over my leather chair.

"What'd you do that for?"

"Sorry. I get enough drool from Frankie and Hooch."

"You're such a jerk."

As we went outside I asked, "How long has Sonny been addicted to GHB?"

"I don't know that he *is* addicted. And I don't know when it started. I think probably after his first wife died."

"Have you ever used it?"

She nodded sadly. "A few times. It does wonders for depression when my drugs don't work right." She explained that the dosage on her prescriptions can be tricky, and there were occasions when she felt herself plunging into a depression and the GHB immediately brought her out of it. "I've learned how to manage the drugs so that hasn't happened in years."

"That's good, but I think Sonny should see a neurologist." She seemed puzzled so I said, "Some of the symptoms he described could be signs of a tumor, and the GHB could be masking them. Plus, I just think he should be in a mental hospital."

"Hah! That's not going to happen."

"Why? If he refuses to check himself in voluntarily, you could easily have him committed."

She shook her head. "No way. I spent a few months in one of those places, and I'm not doing it to him."

This was news to me and I said nothing about it. I just felt bad that she'd had to go through that experience.

We got to the kennel, where Woods had already taken the dogs inside. "Yo, Farrell," I called over the barking.

He turned and smiled. "Hey, Jackie boy, what's up?"

When I explained about the distributor caps he expressed his concern and asked if there was anything he could do.

I told him no, but I needed to use the Suburban.

"It's your car," he said, putting Oscar, a chocolate lab puppy, into one of the pens—the one with the pine tree motif. The little guy settled down immediately, looked up at Woods and wagged his tail. "Good boy, Oscar," Woods said, closing the gate. He turned back to me and said, "By the way, the Blue D'Artes already have a gig on the day of your funeral."

"You mean wedding."

"Call it whatever you want. But I mentioned it to Tulips and she says she can get a trio together. And she's got the perfect song for your first dance: 'Love Is Here to Stay.' "

"God bless her," I said. It hadn't occurred to me to ask for the Gershwin tune, and I suddenly felt myself actually looking forward to the reception for the first time.

"But she doesn't know that Peter, Paul, and Mary tune."

"You mean, 'There Is Love'? That's okay."

"She said she could learn it, if you want."

"What the hell." It would make Jamie's mother happy. In fact, it would probably make her cry. "Sure, why not?"

He came over to us and handed me the keys to the Suburban. "Oh, and she said she's got a rough computer graphic done for you to look at. Whatever that means."

"Thanks," I said.

We went back to the house where Kristin used the phone to cancel the rental car. Then I cancelled the parts delivery. When I was done she said, "How long will it take you to get the distributor caps?"

"I have to go to Rockland. At least an hour."

She looked at Sonny's unconscious body. "Okay. I'd better stay with sleeping beauty. And it's not a Peter, Paul, and Mary song, by the way."

"What?"

" 'There Is Love.' Technically, it's a Paul Stookey song. Or Noel Stookey, as he likes to be called. He sang it himself at *our* wedding." She gave a nod to Sonny.

"Wow."

She shrugged. "Sonny gives a lot of money to certain political causes, Central American refugee funds among them. I guess Noel was grateful."

"You'd think he'd get tired of singing it."

"I thought so, too. But he says he doesn't."

"Okay. I'll be back as soon as I can. Do you know where Regis lives?"

"He has a condo in Lewiston. Why?"

"I'll need the address. And listen, can you do something for me while I'm gone?"

"What?"

"Call him. Tell him you think you know where Jen is. Pick the last place on earth she'd actually go."

"That's easy. Las Vegas."

"Really? She doesn't like Vegas?"

"Hates it. Sonny took her to a vitamin convention there once. She still talks about how superficial it is."

"Okay, good. Tell him you think she's in Vegas, that you want him to go there, and that you have more money for him. Can you *get* enough cash together to interest him?"

"Of course. Where do I meet him?"

"I don't know. It'll be an undercover thing. I'll have an ex-lady cop I know rig a wire so she can listen in on your conversation with him. Pick some bar or restaurant where he'd be likely to meet you. But not in Lewiston. I want him away from his condo for a while."

She took a deep breath. "So I'm going to be a detective?"

"Sort of. Set up the meeting for around seven."

"Okay." She gave me a plaintive look. "Is he really a suspect?"

"I don't know, that's what I want to find out. But don't get too fancy and try to get him to confess or anything."

"I won't."

On the drive down to Rockland I called Jamie and told her what was up. She'd done all she could on the autopsy of the lady in the lake and was stuck at the office, going over budgets and things of that nature. I asked her if she could requisition copies of the police report on Rose Vreeland's suicide and the autopsy on Lilly Blythe's murder.

"I suppose so. Why?"

"I just want you to double check everything to make sure no mistakes were made." There was no point going into all the possible scenarios. Then I asked her to pull any background info she could on Regis and Steve Rice. "But it has to be done without alerting the FBI about what we're up to."

"Okay. I can get Greg Sinclair to help, if I need to. Barry Porter has filed a motion to exclude the confession."

"That figures. When is the judge hearing it?"

"Tomorrow morning. Jack, without that confession, we may not have enough evidence to hold him. Not to mention the fact that Gretchen screwed up the photos of the bite marks and we have to get someone else to do them all over again."

"How'd she screw them up?"

She sighed. "She didn't make the proper notes on each

photo. We can tell by looking at them which pictures were taken with the UV filter, but without those notes . . ."

"See? I told you she wasn't reliable."

"No, you said she was lazy. We've got to get someone else to retake everything now."

"So, she's out as our wedding photographer. Okay, I've got to call Kristin and Doyle now to set up the meeting." I remembered something I wanted to tell her. "Oh, I forgot. Kristin said she loves your sconces in our living room."

"She did?" She sounded happy. "That's nice to hear."

"Yep, she was very complimentary about them." I thought of something else and laughed.

"Now what?" Jamie asked.

"Adam," I said, still chuckling. "He's a pretty good photographer. Maybe *he* could do our wedding."

"Okay, call him. Seriously, I'm not having one of your ex-girlfriends take our wedding pictures, no matter how—"

"Don't worry. I wasn't even thinking about Giselle."

"Her name is Giselle?"

"Bye, honey. I've got to call Doyle about tonight."

I called Doyle and told her what I was planning to do. She immediately hopped on board, though she said, "How did you know I can rig a wire?"

"After the way you took Jen's computer apart, I thought you might know your way around an electronic wire."

"I think I can come up with something," she said. "The only thing is, I'm on duty tonight, starting at six."

I thought it over. There was no point in trying to get her to call in sick. She wouldn't shirk her daily responsibilities. "Okay, we'll set the meeting for four."

I called Kristin and asked if she'd called Corliss yet.

"Jack, I'm going to do it. I just have to get my courage—"

"It's not that. I just need you to change the time of your meeting to four o'clock."

"Okay. I'll call him right now."

I called Jamie back and told her about the rescheduling.

She said that was fine, then said, "Giselle, huh? Wasn't she a supermodel before she became a photographer?"

"I don't know," I lied. "It's a common name."

"Really? Since when?"

"It's fairly common in the fashion world. There's another Giselle who's a big star right now, I think."

"You think? Jesus, Jack, you really *don't* like Victoria's Secret underwear, do you? And didn't your Giselle get married recently to some rock and roll—"

"How should I know who she's married to? I haven't spoken to her in—"

"Well, I'm Googling her right now."

"Google away, honey."

"I am."

"Good. You're still stuck with a dog trainer for a future husband, not a rock star. Though I actually know a couple of musicians I could introduce you to. They're both a little rough around the edges, though."

"Hah! Like you're *not*? Ah-hah! I knew it!"

"What? You Googled her already?"

"Of course. I have DSL. Oh, now *this* is interesting . . ."

"Gotta get off now, sweetheart. I'm driving."

"I'm Googling you *next,* Jack."

"Bye!"

30

Kristin chose the Jameson Tavern in Freeport, insisting that she needed to do a little shopping at the outlet stores to calm her nerves before her undercover meeting.

I wasn't familiar with it but Doyle was. So was Jamie, for that matter, but it was Peggy who'd be manning the wire while James and I were far away in Lewiston, sitting on Corliss's condo and waiting for him to leave.

It was about three, with a low, dark sky, threatening rain, when Corliss came dancing out of the left front door of the building, a four-unit modern, made of concrete and big wooden beams with lots of plate glass windows at odd, though pleasant angles, overlooking the river. He got in his Corvette, which was parked out front, and roared off.

I turned to Jamie. "Ready?"

"Boy, am I. How do we get in?"

I showed her my lock-picking tools.

"Okay. I'm ready if *you* are. What if someone's home in one of the other units?"

"Well, we'll just have to be very quiet."

Rain started to splatter on the windshield as we got out and went up the three concrete steps to the twin wooden doors, painted pine green, and took a position in front of the one on the left. By the time we were in position it had really started to pour. We stood safely dry under the overhang and I said, "Stand behind me. That way, if anyone sees us from the street, it'll just look like I'm having trouble with my keys."

She did and I inserted two of the tools into the hole and maneuvered them around for a while until I heard a click. I opened the door and we went into the entryway, where I saw a flashing red light next to a security panel and keyboard.

"Oh, shit."

"What is it?"

I pointed. "I should have checked for an alarm system."

She clutched my arm. "Then let's get out of here."

"Just a minute." I stood there thinking.

"Jack!"

"Honey, relax. We've got at least thirty seconds for me to try to guess his security code."

"Okay," she said, "and what if you don't guess right?"

"Then we'll split, obviously." I thought it over and said, "Okay, here goes nothing." I pressed the buttons to spell out 69VETTE and the red light went off and the green one came on.

Jamie breathed a sigh of relief. "That was lucky."

"Yeah," I agreed, "but he *is* a bit of a dumbass. The damn security code is written on his license plate for anyone to see. He really must love that car. Okay, let's look around."

"What are we looking for, exactly?"

"I wish I knew. Don't turn the light on!" I quickly switched it off.

In the interim we had a brief, bright glimpse of the décor in the living room—all black leather furniture, with chrome lamps, a chrome and glass coffee table, and mirrors everywhere. The only other color observable was red. The rough concrete walls were papered with a red, velourlike material, with silver and black deco-like stripes. It didn't fit the architectural style of the building at all, though it fit Corliss to a tee.

Jamie said, "Nice color scheme. And why freak out about the lights?"

I pointed to the picture window, which was being pelted with rain. It looked out over the Androscoggin River. There were several houses and condos across the water. "I'm just being cautious. Let's find the bedroom and start there."

Jamie hesitated. "Do I have to go in there?"

"What's the matter?"

"Well, the living room is creepy enough."

"Honey, we're not here to redecorate, we're here to find evidence." I opened the bedroom door. The drapes were closed and it was pitch black inside. I took a Maglite from my jacket and switched it on.

"Which brings me back to my first question . . ."

"I don't know what evidence, exactly." I shone the flash around the room. "I have several theories to go on, and—"

"Now, tell me this is normal." She looked the room over, disapprovingly. "And are those black leather bedcovers?"

I went over to the king-size bed and felt them. "No, they're some kind of synthetic fabric. Do they still make pleather?" I looked overhead, then flashed the beam up to the ceiling. "Check this out!" The entire ceiling was one big smoked-glass mirror, not just the part over the bed.

Jamie shuddered, or pretended to. The rain was beating hard against the bedroom window, though the sound it made was somewhat muffled by the heavy black drapes. Even so, we both heard the unmistakable sound of a lock turning in the front door and immediately stared at each other and froze.

"Jack, quick!" she finally breathed. "Under the bed!"

A light went on in the other room. We scrambled for cover

under the bed and made it just in time. We'd barely scooted behind the faux-leather covers—me on my back, Jamie on her tummy—when the light in the bedroom went on and we heard soggy footsteps on the maroon carpet. I felt a knoblike something sticking into the small of my back.

I put my mouth next to Jamie's ear. "Turn off your cell phone."

I felt her nod her head, then felt her snake one arm down to her slacks. She pulled out the tiny phone and did something with her hand. There were several soft clicking sounds which, fortunately, were covered by the ring of Regis's telephone.

Corliss came over to the bed, sprawled across it, which caused the bedsprings to jam into my nose, and we heard him pick up the receiver.

"Yeah?" he said. "No, I'm on my way. Have you got the money with you?" He listened. "Good. I'll be there on time. Don't get your panties—wait, there's my other line. I'll see you at four." He pressed a button on the handset and said, "Yeah?" There was a pause. "Where the hell have you been?" Another pause. "That's ridiculous. That lake is the last place that girl would go." A pause. "Don't worry. I'll take care of it." Another pause. "I don't think that's such a good idea." Pause. "Because I'm not driving down there." Pause. "Will you relax? I'm meeting her stepmother in an hour. She says Jen might have gone to Vegas." Pause. "Relax, I said. I'll call you if I find out something. Until then, stay cool." Pause. "Good. Oh, one other thing. This is gonna cost you." Pause. "Well, that's just too bad. You shoulda thoughta that before the whole thing started."

He hung up the phone and said, "Moron." Then, to no one in particular he said, "Now, where's that goddamn raincoat?"

We heard the closet doors open and the sound of hangers being pushed back and forth. Then he found what he was looking for, and turned the light out as he left the room.

We waited a good minute after the front door closed before we decided it was safe to come out from under the bed. Once we were vertical, Jamie fiddled with her cell phone while I went straight to the phone by the bed, got out a pen and a scrap of paper from the pocket of my jacket, and pressed *69 on the phone.

"The number of your last incoming call," the operator said, "was . . ." then gave me the number. I wrote it down, but declined to press "one" when prompted to do so in order for the phone company to reconnect me.

"What are you doing?" Jamie asked.

"I star-six-nined the last caller." I waved the scrap of paper at her.

"Brilliant! But not as brilliant as me!"

She clicked a couple of numbers on her cell phone, listened for a moment, pressed another couple of numbers, then held it up to my ear.

"What is it?"

"The answering machine at my office. I recorded everything Corliss said. At least, I hope I did."

She was right. His half of both conversations was playing back in my ear. "Quick thinking, James. Now we may have enough probable cause to get a warrant for his safe."

"What safe?"

I told her about the knob that was sticking into my back while we were hiding. "It's under the bed. I'll bet you anything, if there's any incriminating evidence hidden in this condo, that's where we're going to find it."

I pulled the bed back and showed her the dial on a floor safe. She said, "You mean you can't crack it, Sherlock?"

"I'm a dog trainer, honey, not a safecracker."

"Before you two get too happy with yourselves," a voice said quietly, from behind us, "you might want to put your hands up in the air. And don't turn around. I've got a gun."

I stood up. Jamie looked at me, eyes wide. We put our hands up.

"Who are you?" I said to the voice behind us.

"Never mind who I am," he whispered.

"How'd you get in?"

"What is this, twenty questions? There's a window in the bathroom."

"Yeah? And what are you doing here?"

"No more questions," he whispered.

I tried to place the man's voice, if it *was* a man. It sounded familiar, but it was impossible to tell because of the way he was whispering, which may have been why he (or she) was doing it. It's a handy way to disguise your voice.

I said, "How do we know you've got a gun?"

He answered with a soft thumping sound. The gun had a silencer. He blew a hole in the mirrored ceiling and shards of glass fell around our heads and shoulders.

I said, "Okay, okay!"

"Like I said, no more questions."

I had something else I wanted to ask him, something important. I don't know if I ever did. The next thing I remember is waking up alone in a bed of glass.

Jamie was gone. So was our whispering friend.

31

I got to my knees and looked over at the nightstand to check the red digital read-out on the alarm clock. It was only 3:15. It seemed like a lifetime had passed. I stumbled on rubber legs around the room, but Jamie was gone. The safe had been opened. It was empty. I went to the living room and saw that the front door had been left slightly ajar.

I made my way back to the bedroom, my gut doing flip-flops, my head spinning, and sat next to the phone.

I called Flynn.

"I'm busy," he grumbled. "This better be important."

I told him the situation.

"Oh, no. Oh, Jesus. What's the address?"

I told him where Corliss lived. "My brain's a little fuzzy," I said. "Should I call the locals?"

"You haven't called them yet?"

"No. I guess I should though. I don't know. My head is—"

"Don't call anyone. I'll be there in half an hour."

"I'm calling Doyle." I explained where she was and why.

"That's a good idea. But stay put till I get there."

"Don't worry. I can barely sit up straight, let alone drive. And even if I *could*, I wouldn't know where to—"

"I know, I know. Just sit tight."

I hung up and sat there, my brain racing with questions, but there were no answers. No good ones, anyway.

Finally, I called Doyle and told her what was going on.

"Okay, I'll abort and be there as soon as I can."

"No, Flynn's on his way. This guy, whoever he is, I think he and Corliss are in on this together somehow. Not the kidnapping, but the killing. I think it may be Rice, I'm not sure. I think Corliss may be blackmailing him."

"You sound a little loopy, Jack. Are you all right?"

"No!" I heard the exasperation in my voice and tried a calmer tone. "I'm trying to tell you, we need Corliss to lead us to wherever this guy's got Jamie."

"Have you tried her cell phone?"

"What?" It hadn't occurred to me.

"Well, try it."

"Okay. I'll call you right back." I dialed Jamie's cell phone. It rang, but she didn't answer. Then I thought I heard her familiar Mozart prelude ringing somewhere nearby. I left the phone off the hook and tried to trace the sound. It seemed to be coming from the living room. Maybe she'd dropped the phone there on her way out. Or her kidnapper had.

No, it was coming from just outside the front door. I opened it all the way and found Jamie lying facedown at the bottom of the steps, drenched with rain, her left arm flung out over her head with the cell phone still playing Mozart. I stumbled down to her and lifted her head up out of the puddles and turned her shoulders so she was face up. I sat there, cradling her, with her head in my lap. The raindrops hit her face and her eyes fluttered. (So did my heart, a little.)

"Honey, honey? Talk to me. Are you okay?"

"Jack?" She opened her eyes. "Are you all right?"

"I'm fine, sweetheart. And you?"

"I tried to follow him, but I got woozy." She tried to sit up. I held her in place. "Let go of me. I can sit up. I'm fine." I let go of her with my right arm and supported her back with my left.

She sat up and then fainted back in my arms.

I held her like that and brushed the rain away with my right hand. "Ssshh. It's okay, honey. Just relax."

"Oh," she said, "you're all wet."

"I know. It's okay."

She looked up at me. "I tried to follow him so I could identify him, but I fell down."

"It's okay."

"No, but I wanted to see him. I should have stayed with you. To make sure you were all right."

"You did the right thing."

"You were unconscious, but breathing. Your breathing was steady. I wanted to look at him before I came back—"

"It's a good thing you didn't. He might've killed you."

She nodded. "He could have killed us both."

"I know. So? Did you get a look at him?"

She shook her head. "Just from the back. I couldn't tell you anything. I know he opened the safe, though."

"Yeah, I saw it."

"Oh, and I got his license plate. I *think* I did."

"That's good, honey. How did you—?" She tried to sit up again. "Just lie down for a minute."

"I'm fine, now. Really." She sat up and showed me her cell phone. Corliss's home number was displayed. "It's gone now. Someone must have called me while I was unconscious."

"That's okay. We'll figure it somehow." I stood up and held a hand out to her. "Can you make it to the car?"

"Yes, but shouldn't we go back inside?"

I shook my head. "Not right now." I walked her to the car and explained about Flynn and Doyle.

"You should call them back." She handed me her cell phone.

"It would erase the license plate number, if it's still stored somewhere in your outgoing numbers. That's another reason we're going to the car. My cell phone is inside."

"Oh, right. It may be stored in my outgoing calls." She pressed some buttons, located the license plate number, then clicked some more numbers. "Now it's stored permanently in my phone's memory." She pressed a few digits, we got in the car and she said, "Uncle Horace, it's Jamie." There was a pause. "No, I'm all right. I'm with Jack. He wants to talk to you."

I took the phone and caught him up on the situation.

"Okay," he said, "just stay put. I'm almost there." I could hear his siren in the background of the call. He said, "Did you get a make on the car?"

"I don't know." To Jamie I said, "Do you remember what kind of car it was?"

"I don't remember. I was looking at the license plate."

I told Flynn this and we hung up. Then I said to Jamie, "Okay, just because your focus was on one detail doesn't mean your mind hasn't stored other sensory data. So let's do an exercise I learned in acting class."

"You've got to be kidding."

"It may help you remember some details about the killer."

"Fine. What's the exercise?"

"It's called sense memory. You focus on one specific sensory detail."

She closed her eyes. "Okay."

"Now concentrate on how the rain felt." She did and started to breathe hard. She clutched my hand. "It's okay. You're just experiencing the emotions you had when you went after the guy. That's why they use it in acting class. Sensory information is on the same neurological pathway as emotions. I'm telling you, this guy Stanislavsky was a genius—"

"Jack! It was a blue car. Four doors. It was a . . . wait a minute. I can almost see it." She opened her eyes. "It was a Ford Taurus. Dark blue, and I can see the whole license number now: M10D3R." She clicked her phone open and looked up the number. "Look! 610337! It's exactly right!"

"That's great, honey."

"This is amazing, but a little overpowering. Did you do this with all your witnesses when you were with the NYPD?"

"Sort of. It's standard police procedure, at least part of it is. You always ask a witness to remember any little detail they can. When they remember sensory details, they almost always remember things they weren't even aware of at the time. And they tend to get emotional about it, too."

I called Flynn back and gave him the make and model and license plate number of our attacker's car, and he put it on the radio. Then I called Doyle to let her know what was up, then asked her to let me speak to Kristin.

There was a pause, during which I thought I heard a faint siren in the background. "I—she's not here. We're meeting in the parking lot at a quarter to."

"You don't know where she is?"

"In one of the stores, I suppose. I'm not even in Freeport yet. I'm on my way."

"You're talking on your cell phone and driving?" I said jokingly. "Don't you know how dangerous that is?"

She laughed. "So is breaking into people's condos."

"True, that," I said, then told her to give Kristin further instructions. "We want Corliss out of town for a while, and we don't want him coming back to his apartment before he goes."

"So, she should get him on the next flight to Vegas?"

"Exactly. Have her throw in an added bonus and a clothing allowance. That ought to do it."

She laughed. "True, that."

Once I finished the call Jamie insisted that we had to go to the hospital. "Head injuries can be very serious. And we've both been knocked out twice in one week."

I said, "No, they're going to ask too many questions."

There was no discussion as far as she was concerned. "If you're worried about questions, we'll go to Rockland Memorial. I'm still on staff there. But we're going."

"Whatever you say, sweetheart. Let's wait for Flynn, though. He can escort us. I'm not a hundred percent sure if either one of us should be driving just yet."

"See what I mean?"

"I just said I'd go, didn't I?"

"One of us could have a subdural hematoma. Or both of us. We wouldn't even show any symptoms till hours from now."

"Okay, okay."

She put her head on my shoulder and said, "Some detectives we turned out to be."

"Are you kidding me? We were very good detectives today. Plus we were very lucky."

"Lucky to be alive."

"No, think of the information we have now. We know Corliss is somehow involved in Lilly Blythe's murder, or at least he probably knows who the killer is. We also know that he's not just looking for Jen because Kristin is paying him to find her. He has another motive. And you, my sweet, were wonderful. It was very brave of you to go after him and get the license plate number—"

"Which I only remembered thanks to you and Stanislavsky."

"That reminds me, there's just one other thing . . ."

"What?"

I hated to think what I was thinking, but I had to know for sure. "Was it a man or a woman you saw?"

"What do you mean? He was a man, obviously."

"Are you a hundred percent sure?"

"Yes. At least I *think* so."

"Well, make sure. Do the exercise again."

"No, Jack. I'm not Meryl Streep."

"Just do it, please?"

She closed her eyes and repictured the person she'd followed out of the condo. She shook her head and opened her eyes. "Sorry. I can't say for sure. I think it was a man, but I suppose it *could* have been a woman."

"Well, thanks for trying."

"Do you think he wants to kill Jen?"

"Who, our attacker? I don't know. My thought is, if he, or she, were a real killer we'd both be dead right now. Are you tired? You want to close your eyes till Flynn—?"

"No, the last thing we should do now is go to sleep." She looked up at me. "We might go into a coma."

I chuckled. "I think you're worrying too much, but fine." So I put in *The Best of the Who* and we waited for Flynn to arrive.

32

We got checked out at the hospital, including a CAT scan, and everything was all right with our sub-durae. Doyle met us there and informed us that Regis was on his way to Vegas. She also played the tape she'd gotten of his conversation with Kristin. There was nothing of any particular value on it, but that was okay. We'd gotten more than we'd bargained for by breaking in to his condo.

The next day (Friday) the judge agreed with Barry Porter that Henry's taped confession wasn't admissible, or at least that it wasn't enough to hold him on. The prosecutor argued that the bite mark evidence would be in soon and that it would be reckless and irresponsible to release a serial killer. The judge grudgingly gave them until Monday afternoon to come up with more evidence and set a hearing for two P.M.

The rest of the day came and went with no real news about Jen's whereabouts or the identity of the man (or woman) at the condo. The car Jamie saw was registered to Steve Rice, but he and the car were both missing. Jen's I.H. Scout was found at the Portland airport, but there was no record of her booking a flight or renting another car.

"There's one thing, though," Sinclair told me. "The only activity on her credit cards was at an electronics store in Amherst. She bought a giant plasma-screen television."

"Doesn't her grandmother live in Amherst?"

"I don't know. I'll check into it."

This is one of the frustrating things about detective work. You put all the effort you can into a case and then suddenly nothing happens. You just have to wait for a break.

Jamie, meanwhile, was working almost twenty-four hours a day at the ME's office, trying to find some scrap of evidence to present to the judge. I didn't see much of her.

The next development in the case came after I had just finished my Saturday-morning segment on the TV station in Portland. Frankie and I were in the makeup room. (Lily Chow, my producer, insists I always bring him with me.) Annette, the makeup artist, was taking off my pancake and powder, when Wick Tanner appeared in the doorway.

"So, you're a celebrity now," he grinned.

"Hey, Wick. And you're not?" Frankie growled at him. "Knock it off," I told him. "Hey," I said to Wick, "maybe you could introduce me to Oprah. She's a big dog lover, I hear."

He chuckled. "I'll make a note. Is there someplace private we could talk?"

"Sure. Where would you—?"

He looked around at the hair and makeup people. "Let's do it in my car. I'll be waiting in the parking lot."

"Okay. See you in a few."

I found him leaning casually against his government-issue Town Car. Despite his casual manner, his eyes were serious.

Frankie's throat started to rattle with a low growl. "Okay," I told him. "That's enough." To Wick I said, "I don't know what's wrong with him today. So, what did you want to talk about?"

He waved a file folder. It wasn't thick yet seemed to weigh him down. "About what's in here, for one thing. I also wanted to let you know that Steve Rice has disappeared."

This was no surprise. "No kidding. Any idea why?"

He tilted his head toward the car's interior, got in and clicked the passenger-side doors open. I let Frankie into the backseat with a quick "Behave yourself," then I got in too. Frankie had stopped growling but was panting.

Wick set the file folder on the dash. It was starting to loom in my imagination, like some wildly secret set of documents that might burn my eyes if I were to read them.

I said nothing; I just waited.

He said, "Despite what's going on with the hearing on Monday, we've just about got Henry ready to confess to all twenty-one killings," he said, "but I still think you were right about one of them not being his handiwork."

I waited some more. Frankie continued panting nervously. I couldn't pay attention to him, though. This might be big.

He sighed. "The thing is, I knew one of the victims."

(I told you it would be big.) "You knew her *personally*?"

" 'Fraid so. Very personally. We were having an affair."

"Okay," I said, trying to get my bearings. "You need to tell me which of the victims you knew and how you knew her."

"I know. That's why I'm here. You see, we offered Henry a deal if he copped to all the killings."

I asked what kind of deal they could offer a serial killer, and he told me that if Henry behaves himself in prison the deal is, he can have his own garden. Then he told me that Henry wanted to be sent to one of three prisons: Oxford, Wisconsin, McKean, Pennsylvania, or Elkton, Ohio.

"Did he give any indication why he chose those prisons?"

"No, and we haven't been able to come up with a reason for it, but if he confesses to all the killings, he gets what he wants." His face grew dark again. "Anyway, some of the head boys, Thom Harris and Don Case—I don't know if you know them—have a different take on this whole thing than I do."

I told him I knew the names of the two men, but hadn't met them personally, and knew nothing about their style.

"Don is a bit of a stickler for procedure, and Thom Harris, I don't know, I guess you'd say he has a more nuanced approach. Anyway, this woman—the thirteenth victim—Case and Harris were the only ones who knew about our relationship."

The thirteenth victim: meaning Lilly Blythe (as if I didn't know that already). "You said you were having an affair. As in, past tense?"

He nodded. "I ended it a few months before she died, but she wasn't happy about it. She wanted me to divorce my wife, you know the routine. Then, after a few months of dramatic phone calls and whatnot, I didn't hear from her for a while."

"Then her body turned up in a lake somewhere?"

"Yeah, we even had a witness. The only eyewitness in all of the murders."

That would be Jen, I thought to myself. Frankie, I noticed, was still stressed out, still panting.

He went on, "She turned out to be unreliable, though. It's in the file." He sighed, looked down at his lap. "I told Case and Harris about the affair right away. Even told them to take me off the case and look at *me* for the killing."

I chuckled and said, "That's so like you, Wick. Always aboveboard and upfront about everything."

He shook his head. "Not everything. Just ask my wife."

"She didn't know about the affair?"

"If she did, it's not because I told her about it. So when this woman turned up as a victim, I had some meetings with

Case and Harris, and we hashed it over and they came up with an alternate scenario, which was borne out around the next week or so."

I waited to hear what that alternate scenario was.

"They decided that Henry—of course, we didn't know his name or anything about him at the time, that was *your* contribution—"

"Yeah, yeah. So what did the three of you decide?"

"That Henry—or whoever the killer would turn out to be—knew I was on the case, and somehow got wind of my affair, and did it as a revenge thing. Killed her. Or maybe it was a warning. And sure enough, a few weeks later, I got a letter telling me that my wife would be next if I didn't back off."

I thought it over. "And they checked out the letter?"

"Oh, absolutely. I mean, like I said, Case was a stickler. He wouldn't let something like that go."

"They had handwriting experts look it over?"

"Yes, and a forensic linguist."

"And?"

"It wasn't my handwriting or my grammatical style. That took me off the hook and they put me back on the case. Harris, meanwhile—and I knew him better, on a more personal level than Case—didn't have any doubts about it not being me. The bureau put a watch on my wife and nothing else changed. We chalked it up as one more victim for the guy."

"Was the killer's pattern the same?"

"To a tee."

"Well," I said, "that's a bit of a problem, then isn't it? It has to be a copy cat, done by somebody who knew all the details of Henry's MO, but not by Henry himself."

"I know. Serial killers kill out of a sick, frustrated urge. So if he killed her for revenge or as a warning—"

"—then the M.O. would show that. The same kind of sick, sexual intensity wouldn't be there."

"You don't have to tell me, Jack. But Case and Harris pointed out that with the bodies found in water, several months after the victims were killed—"

"—there wasn't enough trace evidence left to prove exactly how these women died. That's a good point." I thought of something. "Your wife's name is Doris?"

"Dolores."

"Did she have access to your files?"

He looked at me. "You think *she* might have done it?"

"Anything's possible. You must have considered it."

He shrugged. "I had a passing thought about it, certainly. And it's possible she could have gone through my things. I *have* taken files home with me on occasion. Then there's my laptop, though it has a security code. I doubt if she would have killed her, though. It's not her style. Killing me? Yeah, maybe."

"Still, I don't know," he went on, "I worry sometimes that maybe my marriage colored my acceptance of the official stance, you know? It was more convenient for me to not look into it any further. The only thing is . . ." He let it hang.

"What?"

"Well, hadn't it occurred to you that I'm no longer working out of the main office in Washington, but out of a boondock, regional office?"

"Well, Boston is hardly the boondocks, but yeah. I guess I wondered about that."

"It was this *case*. It put me in the doghouse but good."

"Then how did you get back on it?"

He shrugged. "I have you to thank for that. You found the guy here in Maine. That makes it my beat." He took a moment then said, "So, what do you think?"

"About what?"

"About Henry not doing one of the murders."

I said, "I think it's probably true."

"Maybe this will help." He handed me the folder.

I didn't open it. I just held it in my hand, trying not to let my hand tremble or give me away. "What's in it?"

"Everything that should've been put into the official file but wasn't."

"And why are you giving it to me?"

"I know," he said glumly. "The case is officially closed. And I'm not in a position to open it up again but—"

"You want *me* to do it?"

He put the key in but didn't start the car. "Just read the file. You always had a handle on this case, even when it was just a hypothetical class assignment. You were the only one who knew it was a real case."

"That's 'cause I was not just a cop, but a dog trainer as well." He was puzzled. "Look, we all knew that open cases weren't discussed in a classroom situation, but when I thought about it, I knew that the killer had to have an oral fixation, meaning he probably bit his victims."

"Which nobody knew about for sure until this body, and the adipocere, proved you right."

"I know. And this is where it gets back to dog training. You see, Freud says that—"

"What does Sigmund Freud have to do with dog training?"

"A lot more than you'd expect. Freud says that when an impulse is screwed around with—I'm paraphrasing, of course—especially during a developmental phase, you get neurotic or compulsive behavior later on in life. The thing is, before I attended that seminar I'd been working with a dog who obsessively licked doorknobs whenever someone entered or left her owners' apartment and I realized that her compulsive behavior came from having her oral impulses stifled when she was a puppy. It's Ockham's razor. The simplest explanation is always the best.

"Then," I went on, "when everyone at the seminar was

coming up with all these Byzantine explanations for why the bodies were always found in a lake or a pond, I thought, there's got to be a simpler scenario. And it hit me—the killer wasn't necessarily obsessed with water, he was just being practical, placing the bodies where they wouldn't be found; or if they *were* found, the trace evidence would have all been washed away. And my first thought was that he'd probably left bite marks on his victims. *That* was the trace evidence he didn't want discovered."

Tanner got a faraway look in his eyes. "I remember."

"Yeah, and *I* remember your reaction to hearing my theory of the case. Like a lightbulb went off in your head."

"So?"

"So, it was a *live* lightbulb, not a dead one. To me it seemed obvious why you reacted that way—it was an open case."

We sat in silence for a while. The sun was up and the air was bright. Life went on at the TV station; people came and went in the parking lot. A few news vans backed out of their spaces, going out on assignments somewhere.

I looked back at Frankie. He'd stopped panting but his eyes were glued to the back of Wick Tanner's head. I looked over at Tanner again. He seemed tired and bent, like his shoes were lined with kryptonite.

I said, "This woman you were having the affair with, was she killed before or after we broke it down at that seminar?"

"After."

"And I don't suppose you included the class list in that little folder of yours?"

"Oh, I'm sure Case and Harris checked out everyone at that seminar, including you, Jack."

"And Steve Rice?"

He nodded. "That's another story. It turns out that Steve Rice is actually Stefano Rizzoli, of the Boston mafia."

I let out a surprised laugh. "He infiltrated the FBI?"

"He sure did." He shook his head.

"And that's why he's in the wind now? Or did he have something to do with Lilly Blythe's murder?"

"I wish I knew. It may be another reason the Bureau is willing to let Henry cop to all twenty-one killings."

I nodded and said, "Because if the story about Rice comes out, it'll be bad publicity."

"It'll be worse than a public scandal, it'll mean . . ."

He didn't finish, and I knew why. Finding one Mafia mole in the Bureau would mean there might be others. Maybe dozens of them. And the Bureau had to stop any leaks about Rice so they could go quietly about the business of cleaning house.

I said, "So, the Bureau is okay with Henry copping to a murder he didn't do?"

He shrugged. "It's a matter of which is more important; finding one possible killer or saving the Bureau itself."

I shook my head. "This kinda stinks, you *know* that."

"Not just kinda, Jack. It reeks."

I looked at the file. "And the FBI isn't going to come down on me for trying to find Lilly Blythe's real killer?"

He stared at me. "You already knew about my affair?"

I shook my head. "After Henry said we got the number wrong, I went over the list. All of his victims were killed either in the spring or fall, with the bodies being found six months later. But Lilly Blythe was killed in July. I didn't know anything about her until now."

He took this in, smiled, and said, "I'm glad I brought you the file then. You're already a step ahead of me."

"So," I asked him again, "are Case and Harris going to come down on me for looking into this on my own?"

"I don't think so. That is, as long as they have no idea of what you're up to, I think you're in the clear."

I gave a sour laugh. "Thanks a lot."

"Sorry. I'm just trying to do the right thing."

"Hah." I shook my head and opened my door. "You realize that if you *did* kill her, I'll find out about it."

"I'm not worried." He smiled a sad smile. "Not about that, anyway."

"What are you worried about?"

"Just read the file." He started the car. "If you need me I'll be in Amherst, finishing the search on Henry's home."

I had to wonder, if only briefly, whether he'd be looking for Jen Vreeland while he was there, too. Then I put the thought out of my mind, got Frankie out of the back, and we went to my car. Frankie kept looking back over his shoulder at Wick's car.

I took the file home and looked it over, then rechecked the files from ViCAP and ViCLAS. When I had what I needed to know, I called Dr. Carla Petersen at home. I gave her the locations of the three prisons that Henry was negotiating to be sent to, and the locations where all the bodies were found, including Lilly Blythe's.

"Well," she said, "I can tell you that all three prisons are located near an esker bog complex. Same with the locations for all but one of the killings."

"You mean the one near Amherst, Mass?"

"That's right. How did you—?"

"Been doing my homework, teach. Thanks."

33

On Sunday morning, Adam brought the photos he'd taken of Jen. He also brought along Jen's friend, Darcelle. We all sat on the white wooden front steps of my house and looked through the photos. There were only five that had what I needed—shots of Steve Rice, Randy Corliss, and Wick Tanner. And only one of them showed enough detail to be of any use. There were no shots of Clay Henry, but I didn't expect any. The students who'd "remembered" seeing Henry on campus probably only did so because they'd seen him on the news. Either that or Peggy Doyle had lied about it.

I said, "I think I'll keep this one, if you don't mind."

"Fine with me. You paid for it."

Darcelle said, "Mr. Field?"

"Call me Jack."

"Okay. Remember you said if we thought of anything that might help, we should tell you about it?"

I said I did.

"Well, I remember something Jen said. She said the man who attacked her mother reminded her of her father, sort of."

I sat a minute absorbing that information. "You don't suppose it actually *was* her father she saw, do you?"

She shrugged a smile. "I think she'd remember *that*."

Yeah, I thought, or she might try to block it from her memory but wouldn't be able to erase it entirely, and she'd be left with a hazy feeling that the man had only *looked* like her father, even though it actually *was* him. Then there was another possibility: that she'd actually seen Sonny kill her mother six years earlier, and that the attack on her aunt jolted her memory circuits enough to make the connection to the second murder. This was getting way too complicated.

"Mr. Field?"

"What?"

"You . . . I'm sorry, you seemed sort of out of it."

"Sorry, I was thinking. And call me Jack. Why didn't you tell me about this before?"

"Well," she hesitated, "Sabrina was sort of . . ."

Adam said, "Sabrina was trying to get them all to say that *I'd* done something to hurt Jennifer. Like I would ev—"

"It wasn't like that, exactly." Darcelle shrugged. "Sabrina just thought that you should kind of investigate Adam, and the more we talked about it with her the less I remembered what Jennifer actually said to me."

"Well, it's a good thing you told me now. Thanks."

"I mean, after all," she made a facial shrug, "how could *he* have done anything?" She put a hand on Adam's neck and his face brightened. "I mean, he's totally harmless."

Adam's face fell. Being thought of as "harmless" was not going to help him get girls.

I said to Adam. "What are you doing this coming Saturday afternoon?"

He looked at Darcelle as if he thought I were about to invite them both, as a couple, to some event. She rolled her eyes at him and he said, "Nothing, I don't think. Why?"

"Jamie and I are getting married. We need someone to take our wedding pictures."

He smiled. "Really? You want *me* to do it?"

"You're a good photographer. We'll pay you, of course."

"Hey, I'd do it just for the experience."

"Well, the going price is five hundred bucks. Maybe you could use the money to upgrade your wardrobe a little."

Darcelle nodded emphatically and Adam hung his head.

"Sorry," I said, "it was just a thought. But don't get too creative with the pictures. They're just wedding photos."

He smiled and nodded. "I gotcha."

After he left I tried to reach Kelso again, but there was no answer. Then I called Kristin to find out the address of Jen's grandmother—that is, her mom's mother—in Amherst.

She gave me the info and said, "I can't talk long, I'm on another call with London. I really need to get over there. But I need to know, do you still suspect Sonny of murder?"

"Sweetheart, I've got a whole laundry list of possible suspects at this point."

"You didn't answer the question. Is Sonny on the list?"

"I'll know more when I talk to some people."

"You still didn't—oh, you're impossible. I've got to go."

Then I called Victor "Slick-Vic" DeMarco, an "alleged" mob boss I knew in Buffalo. I'd helped convict his son's killer during the Allison DeMarco case and hoped he'd remember that when he got my call so early on Sunday morning.

"Victor, it's Jack Field. Remember me?"

"The dog-training detective?"

I laughed. "That's right. How's your little Shih tzu?"

"Fine," he laughed. "She's in my lap right now." He spoke to the dog, "Aren't you, my little cuddle-bug?" He spoke to me again. "So, why the phone call?"

"I need a favor."

"Hey, whatever it is, you got it."

"Thanks," I said, then told him what I needed.

There was a long pause. Finally he said, "I'm gonna need to know what this is about."

"I can't tell you much, sorry. I just want some background on a guy who might be connected in Boston."

"Who?"

I told him about Steve Rice, AKA Stefan Rizzoli.

"Nope, never hearda him. But that don't mean nothin'. He sighed. "I'll make a coupla calls and call you right back."

"Thanks." I gave him my number.

While I was waiting, I called Jamie to tell her about Adam being our new wedding photographer and about my planned excursion to Beantown and various environs.

She said, "Be careful, honey."

"I will."

"I'd come with you, but I've got court tomorrow and—"

"I know."

"Maybe you should take Flynn along. Or Peggy Doyle."

"No, I'll be all right."

"Then take Frankie."

"Frankie?"

"You're going to try and find Jen aren't you?"

"Among other things."

"Well then, take the dog with you."

"I don't want to drive all the way down there, and the airlines won't—"

She huffed. "Then call the Belfast airport. Hire a private plane. Do I have to do all your thinking for you?"

"Not *all* of it," I laughed. "Thanks. I think I *will* take Frankie along." After all, I thought, I was in dogged pursuit of a killer. What could be more appropriate than to bring a dog with me?

"That has nothing to do with it," said Jamie. "Don't you get it? That dog—and I mean he loves Jennifer—is trying to tell you who the killer is."

"You mean that's why he's been growling at—"

"What do you think? Aren't you the one who's always saying you should listen to what the dog is trying to tell you? And how hard are you listening to Frankie right now?"

"Well, anyway," I said, "that's why I'm going to Boston. I mean, after all," I said, before she could interrupt, "who's gonna take my dog's word for the killer's identity?"

"Who? Who's going to take Frankie's word for it? The answer's simple—you, you dope!"

"Well," I said, still hedging, "we'll see."

34

The flight was quick and Frankie and I grabbed a cab at the airport. I put the luggage in the trunk and gave the driver, a gnarly-faced Irishman named McMurtry, the address.

"Beautiful dog," he said, as he pulled into traffic. "So you're paying a visit to the alleged head of the Scarpelli crime family. Funny thing, you don't look like a wise guy."

"What are you, an ex-cop?"

"Could be."

"Yeah, I thought so. Me too."

"No kidding." His smile lit up the rear-view.

"Fifteen years," I told him, "NYPD."

"So that's what this is about? You workin' a case?"

"In a way."

He shook his head, leaned on his horn, took an impossible opening in a traffic circle, and said, "You need any backup?"

"I hope not. Were you a detective?"

"Hah!" he said, and made another improbable and foolhardy turn at full speed. "Would I need to drive cab with that kind of pension dough? No, I was a beat cop my whole career."

"Yeah?" I said, gripping the handle over the door, "so was my old man. In San Diego."

"Now there's a nice place to retayuh."

We zoomed through Boston traffic and talked about "the job" until the subject of my investigation resurfaced.

"Sorry. I can't really talk about it."

"Figures," he said and clammed up. He also slowed down.

I knew what was going through his head. He thought I wasn't letting him in on things because of the typical disdain most detectives have for unis. "It isn't that," I said, "it's just that there's a lot of secrecy involved here. If I let you know what's going on, it might put you in danger."

"Sure, sure," he said. "Like I never put my ass on the line before?"

I laughed. "I'm sure you did, plenty of times. But I'm not about to put you in a situation—"

"Ah, screw you." He drove a bit then said, disdainfully, " 'New York's finest' my ass. I'll put the Boston PD against your guys any day of the week, except maybe that one Tuesday."

I knew the Tuesday he was referring to—September 11, 2001. "I gotta hand it to 'em. They did just fine that day."

"They did what they could. And I *will* say one thing, I doubt if any of our guys could drive these streets like you. Where the hell are we?"

"You think I don't know where I'm goin'?"

"I'm sure *you* do." He took two left turns and I could have sworn we were headed back to the airport. "But I have no idea where I am. Aren't we supposed to be going north?"

"This *is* north."

"But you just took two left—"

He laughed sourly. "This is Boston, pal. Just shut up and let me drive."

I did and it wasn't long before we got to the address that Vic DeMarco had given me. McMurtry pulled to a stop in front of an ivy-covered mansion, surrounded by a high stone wall with a wrought-iron gate. He turned off the meter.

I got out some money but he said, "Keep it. I'll wait."

"Okay, we should only be gone about ten, fifteen minutes."

"You taking the dog with you?"

"Yeah. He's my ice-breaker."

"Hah! What happens if you're gone longer than that? You want me to break the door down and save your sorry ass? Or is he an attack dog, this one?"

"Well, he is pretty fierce. When it comes to chew toys." We both chuckled as I got out. "If I'm gone too long, call your pals at the local precinct." I pointed to the St. Christopher medal hanging from his rear-view mirror. "Meanwhile, put in a few good words for us with the man upstairs."

"Will do."

About twenty minutes later Frankie and I were escorted off the property by two well-muscled gentlemen. I opened the cab door and the dog jumped in. I got in, sat beside him, and straightened my clothes a little.

McMurtry looked at me through the mirror. "Nice lip. I guess it didn't go so well, huh?"

"Could have gone a little easier."

He started the engine. "I guess the dog let you down, huh? Where to now?" I gave him an address and he said, "You got it."

He drove for a while, with the occasional lingering glance at my bruised and bloody kisser, which Frankie was occasionally licking.

"You want to file an assault charge?"

"No."

"Un-huh. So, did you get what you wanted? Besides the split lip, I mean."

"Sort of. At least now I know someone's been lying to me. I just don't know who yet, the mob or the feds."

"Un-huh." He nodded. "No chatter—just like a dick."

"Look, I'd tell you what happened in there, but we came to sort of a tacit agreement about me not divulging the partic—"

"Like I said, typical detective bullshit."

We drove in silence for a long time and got to an upper-middle class neighborhood with pretty trees and wide lawns, some of which were being mowed leisurely; a nice pastime for the man of the house on a quiet Sunday afternoon. Where I was going, the man of the house wouldn't be home. He was in Amherst, going through Clay Henry's personal belongings, trying to find enough evidence to keep the killer in custody for committing twenty-one murders, one of which he didn't actually commit.

We came to a nice two-story with a Victorian air, though it was probably built in the fifties. McMurtry pulled the cab to a stop. "Same deal here, or is your face gonna survive this one?"

I laughed. "I should be okay. Frankie, let's go. Can you pop the trunk?"

He did and said, "You staying or you want me to wait?"

"I just need my briefcase. I'll be back in a bit. If you want to wait that's up to you, though I'll probably be a little longer this time."

"What do I care? I got the meter running."

Frankie and I went up the curving front walk, past some rose bushes, then up three stone steps to a wooden porch, and I rang the bell. Dolores Tanner opened the door. She was wearing khaki slacks, Reeboks, and a simple blouse under a lilac cardigan sweater. She gave me a part-friendly, though also partially blank look.

"Yes?"

"Hi. My name is Jack Field. This is Frankie."

She said, "Hi, Frankie."

He wagged his tail and she leaned down to pet his ears, then turned her head back to me with a questioning look. She also gave my split lip the once-over.

I said, "I don't know if you remember me, but we met once about seven years ago at a party in Washington. I was a student in one of your husband's seminars."

"Oh, I'm sorry. I'm not sure I *do* remember. Wick had so many students. And, I'm sorry, he isn't here right now."

"I know. I need to talk to you about a case."

She seemed mildly puzzled but let us in.

"Would you like something to drink?" she said, leading us into the gleaming, white kitchen. "Some water for your dog?"

"Yeah, that would be nice. He's probably thirsty."

She led me to an antique dinner table with matching chairs. I sat down and put the briefcase on the table while she went to the sink and filled a glass mixing bowl with water.

She came back and placed the bowl in front of the dog, who immediately began lapping it up. She smiled and took a chair across from me, looked at Frankie, and said, "He *is* thirsty. And you? Would you like something for that split lip?"

"No, I'm fine. It's just one of the things you have to deal with when asking certain people certain types of questions. So," I changed the subject, "Wick didn't mention me or the case I'm working on?"

"No. I haven't spoken to him in a few days. He's been pretty busy—"

"—working on a case. I know." I sighed. "I hate to have to ask you this, but my investigation involves a woman he was having an affair with several years ago."

She sat back in her chair and smoothed the creases in her

khaki slacks. Her blue eyes stared at me. "I'm sorry. You must be mistaken. My husband has never been unfaith—"

"Yeah, I *could* be wrong. But the thing is, he confessed the affair to me himself, yesterday."

She just stared for a moment. "Now, why on earth would he do that? And who are you again?"

I told her.

"You're a *dog* trainer?"

"And a former detective with the NYPD."

She stood up. "Well, I'm glad to have met you and Frankie, now I'll have to ask the two of you—"

"Sit down, Mrs. Tanner," I said quietly.

She cocked her head. "This is my house, and I will not—"

"I'm sorry." I opened the briefcase. "Sit down, please. I want you to look at the file Wick gave me."

"What file?" she said, still standing.

"It's an official FBI file about the murder of Lilly Blythe, the woman your husband was involved with. At the time of her murder, he was looked at as a possible suspect."

"I don't believe you." She sat down and pushed the file toward her. She opened the folder and began reading. Frankie came over and put his head in her lap. She gently stroked his fur as she scanned the pages. After going over two or three of them, she glanced back at me. "So it's true."

"I'm sorry."

She sat back and smoothed her dress a little. "And why are you investigating this now?"

I explained briefly about Jen and her aunt, and the fact that Clay Henry was a suspect but hadn't done the crime.

"And you think Wick did? But the file says—"

"I can't say what I think, one way or another, except that Clay Henry didn't do this murder and the FBI is pressuring him to confess to it."

She stared past me out the window. Frankie lay down on

the tile floor and began licking himself. I turned my head slightly and saw a lovely maple tree in the backyard, with leaves starting to turn a deep red. It was a suburban dream, this house, this yard, and I was the blue-meanie intent on wrecking that dream.

I said, "Do you have any recollection of the case?"

"I'm sorry?" she said, coming back to the moment. "Oh. Yes, now that I've read the file, I'm afraid I do. Wick mentioned it, which I thought was a little odd at the time. He rarely talked about his work. Of course"—she looked down at the table—"he never said anything about his . . . affair with the dead woman, why would he? But it *was* odd."

"He kept his work and his private life separate?"

"Very much so. He likes to say that this," she said, waving her hand, referring to their lovely home, "is our haven from the terrible things that go on out there in the world, and that he doesn't want to bring that world, the world he lives and works in, into our private lives." She looked up at me. "I guess this is one time he failed to live up to his high ideals. Not to mention his wedding vows."

"I'm sorry."

"Yeah, me too." She didn't seem upset about what she'd learned, though she could've been hiding it. She looked down at Frankie. His head was resting on his front paws and he had his eyes closed. "What must it be like to be a dog," she said, wistfully.

I nodded, then said, "What else do you remember?"

She looked at me. "Nothing. It was seven years ago. The only thing I *do* remember is his mentioning the case. And that it disrupted our Thanksgiving that year. Which wasn't unusual."

"And nothing odd happened earlier that summer? In July?"

She gave me a puzzled look. "July? Not that I . . . now,

wait a minute. That's so strange that you mention July, because I *do* remember having a brief period that summer, wondering if he *was* having an affair."

"Really? What made you wonder about it?"

She shook her head. "There was a phone call one night. He's always getting phone calls at odd hours, but his reaction to this one was different. I don't know. He said it was about a case, but he was acting secretive. No, not secretive. Just . . . what's the word. I don't know. Normally he's so matter of fact about being woken up at one in the morning. Not this time. It was as if he were trying to act casual, but you could tell it was just an act." She remembered the scene in her mind. "He got out of bed and got dressed and left the house and I didn't hear from him until two days later when he called me from Boston. We were still living in D.C. then."

I knew it was a long shot but I said, "I don't suppose you remember the exact day this happened?"

She smiled an ah-hah kind of smile and said, "Oddly enough, I do. Or at least I can find *out* what day it was." She got up and went to a drawer. She went through some papers and old calendars and found the one she was looking for. She came back. "He was supposed to take the girls to summer camp the next day." She flipped open the day planner, found the day her daughters were to start camp and told me the date.

It was the same day that Lilly Blythe was attacked.

"Well," I said, pretending to act casual, "it probably doesn't mean anything."

She smiled a sad smile. "Now *you're* doing it."

"What's that?"

"Acting casual, but it's just an act." She thought a bit. "It was the same day this woman was killed, wasn't it?"

I smiled. "I wouldn't make too much of that."

"Are you serious? That's quite a coincidence."

"Yes, but it's circumstantial. There could be any number of possible explanations for it."

She stared out the window again. "He did it." She looked at me again. "Didn't he? He brought his world into our home."

"There's no proof of that. Look, you're forgetting that he *asked* me to look into it. Why would he do that if he's guilty?"

She laughed. "To throw you off? And you don't understand. I've been living with him for over twenty years. I know him, or thought I did. And I'm telling you, he changed after that case. He was like a different person. He began having nightmares, his behavior became erratic. That's why the Bureau transferred us."

"That might not mean what you think. The woman he'd been seeing was murdered. It would be only natural for him to—"

"He did it," she said sadly, then her face changed. "Will you catch him?" She reached out and grabbed my hand. "Will you be able to prove this one way or the other?"

"I don't know," I said, and meant it. "If he's guilty, I'm sure as hell going to try to put him behind bars." I cocked my head and tried to smile. "He may *not* be, though. It's one thing to cheat on your wife. Killing someone is another thing entirely."

"Is it really? Funny," she looked out the window again, "the way I feel right now it doesn't seem all that different."

I wondered briefly if she'd been taking GABA like Sonny Vreeland—her reactions to our meeting were strangely detached.

I thanked her for her time, put the file folder back in my briefcase, stood up, which woke up Frankie, and we went back out to the cab.

The day had grown late. Afternoon shadows were creeping across the tidy green lawns. The men with the mowers were inside, watching college football games or doing whatever it is suburban husbands do. (I'd know soon enough, with the wedding now a week away.)

One old gent was still outside, right across the street, puffing on a pipe and raking a few early autumn leaves. He saw Frankie and me, leaned on his rake a moment, and gave us a smiling, neighborly nod and wave. I waved back. Frankie trotted to the cab and pawed at the door.

McMurtry clicked the trunk open and I put the briefcase inside, then opened the door for Frankie and we got in.

"So, where to now, boss? Back to the airport?"

"No. I need to rent a car. I'm going to Amherst."

"Well, that'll be a fine fare," he said, starting the engine. "Just let me make a quick phone call to the wife."

"Look, that's not necessary."

"The hell it isn't. She loves the extra money but she hates it when I don't check in regular."

"That's not what I meant. I couldn't ask you to . . ."

"No sweat," he said, popping open a cell phone. He speed-dialed a number and said, "Honey, it's Joe. I've got an out-of-town fare." Pause. "Amherst." Pause. "I hadn't thought about it. I'll probably just grab something on the way. Don't wait up. I'll be home pretty late." Pause. "I love you too, baby."

He closed the phone. "Okay, Amherst, here we come."

He put it in gear and as we pulled into the street, the old gent across the way waved again and we both waved back.

McMurtry looked at me in the mirror and said, "That's a serious look you got on your face, bud. You want to talk about it? After all, it's a long drive . . ."

It *was* a long drive. Even so, I still kept my mouth shut about the case. I had some serious things to think about.

Finally, the silence from the front seat became unbearable so I leaned forward and said, "Look, I'll make you a deal.

We'll trade cell phone numbers and I'll call you when I'm done with the case and tell you all about it."

"Yeah?" he looked at me askance.

I nodded. "Meanwhile, we can enjoy the drive and talk about anything else you want to talk about."

"Fair enough," he said.

"And I'm getting a little hungry. Why don't you pull off somewhere and let me buy you dinner?"

He smiled. "Now I know you're a right guy. No frickin' detective ever bought me so much as a ham sandwich before."

35

The next day was overcast. I got up late, left Frankie at the motel, rented a car, filled her up and bought some dog food and a can opener at the Stop'n'Save, came back to the motel and fed the dog, which is when I noticed a strange clinking sound coming from his collar. At first I thought that his tags had got tangled up or something, but when I examined it I noticed that he was wearing a *new* tag, only it wasn't a tag at all. He now had a St. Christopher medal hanging around his neck.

Thanks, Joe, I may need it, I thought smiling and watching Frankie wolf down his chow.

When he was done I took out him for a quick pee and poop, then we took a drive, under the hanging clouds, to pay a visit to Jen's grandmother. On the way I got a call from Jamie.

"Hi, honey," she said. "Where are you?"

I told her and described yesterday's activities, including what happened at the mansion.

"Put some Polysporin on it," she said of my split lip. "*And* you're not going to believe this. Remember you asked me to recheck the autopsies on the Blythe twins, Lilly and Rose? Well get this, Jen's mother, Rose Vreeland, our supposed suicide, had never given birth."

"That *is* interesting. And you know this how?"

"Well, they didn't do a full autopsy, but they *did* take a full set of X rays. I looked them over and found no distention in the articulation between the femur and the innominate bone—"

"In English, please."

She laughed. "Never mind. She'd never given birth, her hip bones prove it. Meanwhile, our murder victim, Lilly—and this is according to her X rays and the condition of her uterine canal, which they *did* examine during the autopsy—had given birth several times and had even had a tubal ligation done."

"Hmm," I said, remembering the crazy scenario I'd dazzled Kristin with, "but there's no record of Lilly ever having any children, at least not that we know of, so that *could* have been Rose's body, not her sister's."

"I know. You already suspected that as a possibility, didn't you? That's why you asked me to look into this in the first place. You suspected something wasn't kosher."

"I had a wild hunch, yeah. So why didn't they do a complete autopsy on the first death?"

"The woman was depressed, talking about suicide, and there was lake water in her lungs. There was no poison or other suspicious toxin in her blood. They figured that was all the autopsy they needed."

I said, "That sucks."

"It happens. So what are you going to do about this new information?"

"I don't know. We have no way of knowing if there was an identity switch and if Lilly was actually murdered and Rose knew about it, or if Lilly committed suicide and Rose just took that as an opportunity to trade places with her sister."

"But why would she do that? It seems to me that she had the better life of the two women."

"I know. Maybe I'll learn more about it when I talk to their mother. I'm on my way over there right now."

"Okay. Good luck. Will you call me when you're finished?"

"Maybe. I have to find a way to trick the killer first."

"How are you going to do that?"

"I don't know, honey. I'll call you when I figure it all out."

"Okay. Clay Henry's hearing is in a couple of hours. I'm still preparing my testimony. Wish me luck! Call me!"

"I will." I pulled up to Mrs. Blythe's house. "Bye."

It was a modest, unimposing home, two stories tall, with a sagging roof over the porch and an unkempt lawn, no fence, and from what I could see, a backyard that was indistinguishable from an asphalt alley behind the property.

As I got out, and put the strap of the briefcase over my shoulder, I glanced up at one of the second-floor windows and saw a young woman's face peering through the glass. I just had a brief glimpse of her features through the cloudy reflections, before the curtains closed, but she was a strikingly pretty girl with short brown hair. There was something familiar about her, something that reminded me of that photograph of Jen's mother.

Frankie was staring at the house too. He started to whine and I realized why the young woman looked so familiar.

"So, we've found Jennifer, huh, boy?" He wagged his tail happily. "Well, she saw us *too,* fella, so what do you want to bet that she's racing out the back door right about now?"

He pulled at the leash and I had the momentary urge to let him go after Jen, but since I didn't know how far she might travel or what the local traffic was like, I kept him in a heel and we walked up to the front steps. From behind the house we heard the sound of a car starting up and driving off, though it could have been a coincidence. Maybe Jen was about to burst through the front door, welcoming us with open arms.

I knocked on the door. A few moments passed and an old woman, probably in her seventies, opened it a crack.

"Yes?" she said, but didn't undo the chain. I could hear the sound of a game show, blaring loudly from the living room.

"Hi, Mrs. Blythe. Can Jen come out to play?"

"What?"

"Sorry. I'm Jack Field. This is Frankie, one of Jen's favorite dogs. Could we have a word with her?"

"She's not here." She started to close the door.

"Fine," I said, "but could I ask you a few questions about your daughter Lilly's murder?"

The door stopped closing, then slowly opened again. Her steely eyes squinted at me. "Who are you again?"

I told her, with the added fillip that I was Jennifer's former employer.

"Hold on a minute." She closed the door. Some time passed and I thought I heard voices coming from inside, but it was hard to tell with the TV turned up so loud.

The door opened again—just a crack, like before. Mrs. Blythe stood there smiling. "Well, why didn't you say who you were?" She undid the chain and opened the door wide. "Come in and bring that little rascal with you." Frankie wagged his tail. "Jennifer's not here, but we can talk some."

She led us into the living room, which hadn't been redecorated since Nixon was in office, and I mean when he was vice president. We sat on some old chairs with faded upholstery that may have been red once, and once she got her knees under her, she crossed her paperthin–hands across her lap.

She wore a faded floral-print housedress that had once been festooned with spring blossoms. Her smile was warm and genuine, though, and she seemed happy to have company.

"Would you like some tea or coffee?"

"None for me, thanks. And Frankie doesn't take stimulants. Is it okay if I go upstairs a minute and say hello to Jen?"

"No," she said, crossly. "I told you she's not here."

"Come on. That's what you tell *every*body."

"Well, I'm telling *you*." She picked up a remote and clicked off the television, a very large, brand-new, plasma-screen model. "What did you want to know about poor Lilly? That happened nearly seven years ago."

I looked around and wondered why, except for the TV, none of Sonny's money had ended up here. He'd spent a bundle to have the lake cabin remodeled. Why not spruce up his mother-in-law's house? I pretty much knew that Jen had bought the new television, but thought maybe that the old woman had gotten used to her old furniture and refused to let Jen buy her anything new to replace it. Some old folks are like that.

"Well?" said Mrs. Blythe.

"The thing is, some new evidence has come up and I'm hoping to track down the man who killed Lilly."

"Are you a detective?"

"I used to be, in New York. The thing is—"

"What new evidence?"

I nodded. "Well, we know now that Lilly was having an affair with a married man at the time of her—"

"I wouldn't put it past her."

"Could I ask you something about your other daughter?"

"No," she snorted. "I have no other daughter."

"I mean Rose. I know she died *too,* but—"

"She was dead to me long before that. What about Lilly?"

I sat back a little. "Why was she dead to you?"

"I never talk about her or mention her name. I know she's Jen's mother, more's the pity, but I'm not going to talk about her or allow you to keep mentioning her name in my house."

"Can you at least tell me why?"

"I can but I won't. What about Lilly? Did this married man of hers kill her?"

"I'm looking into that as one possibility, yes. Is there anything you remember from that time that didn't come out in the police investigation?"

She sighed. "That poor girl. She was such a good, sweet thing until her wretched sister died. Then she became just like her. Drinking, whoring around, no morals. I don't know what in hell got into her."

She started rambling on about Rose, even though she'd declared the subject off-limits. And in the course of her tirade it came out—and this was just her opinion—that Rose had probably killed her own sons, Jennifer's two younger brothers, the ones Doyle told me had apparently died of SIDS.

Shocked, I said, "That's quite an accusation."

She snorted. "You didn't know her." She leaned forward and whispered. "I don't like to talk about it, but I'm sure she did it because of the will."

This hinted of something about the will that Kristin hadn't mentioned to me. "What exactly about the will—?"

She snorted again. "Sonny's parents made a provision that if Sonny had a son, all the money would go to him." She let that hang. "Well, it's obvious, isn't it?" She leaned forward again and whispered. "She killed my two grandsons so she could keep her dirty hands all over her stupid husband's money. Then she went so far as to have an operation so she couldn't get pregnant again, just in case." She sat back. "I'm telling you, she was the one who'd be likely to fool around with a married man, not Lilly. Did it all the time behind Sonny's back, not that he would've noticed, the fool."

I felt the room tilt. Apparently my idea that Rose had had her sister killed was not far off. In fact, it fit what Jamie had told me over the phone perfectly. Lilly, not Rose, was the "suicide." And she'd been pregnant at the time. Maybe it was a boy and maybe Sonny was the father, and maybe Rose found out about it and had her killed. It would be a powerful motive. I hated to think, though, what knowing the truth about her mother might do to Jen's mental state. And I understood now the reason for Mrs. Blythe's whispering jags. She hadn't wanted Jen, who I'm sure was upstairs, listening in, to know some of these things.

I didn't want to tell Mrs. Blythe what I was thinking, either. The poor woman already lost two daughters, not to mention two grandsons. That was quite enough for her to bear.

I also understood now her protectiveness about Jen. Even though I was supposedly a friend, she didn't know that for sure and was not about to place the girl's life in danger by letting me know that Jen and Daisy were just upstairs, probably sitting on the top step, Jen listening intently to what she could hear of our conversation. In fact, Frankie was now staring in that direction.

"What's the matter, Mr. Field? Am I shocking you?"

"I think so, a little. Do you still have any of Lilly's things? A diary, or maybe some jewelry?"

"Why?"

"They may help me bring her killer to justice."

She thought about it, pulled herself out of her chair, said, "Wait here," and tottered off to another room. I heard a door close upstairs. After a bit, Frankie got up and put his head in my lap and I stroked his ears. I noticed some dog hair on the arms of the chair. It looked like Dalmatian hair to me.

I said to Frankie, "What do you think, boy?" I brushed a grayish clump off the arm and held it under his nose. "Is this Daisy's fur?" He wagged his tail in agreement.

Mrs. Blythe came back in, handed me a manila envelope and sat down. "That's all I've got. She didn't keep a diary. There's a few letters from when she was living in New York.

And a silver locket. She didn't go in much for fine jewelry and gew-gaws." She leaned forward and whispered, "Not like her sister Rose. All *she* ever thought about was diamonds."

"Thanks," I said and opened the briefcase. "I'll get these things back to you as soon as possible." I put the envelope inside. I got out one of Adam's photographs, took a Sharpie and circled the face of one of the men in the background and wrote underneath it, "This him?" Underneath that, in smaller letters, I wrote, "Please come to the wedding on Sat. Jamie and I really want you there."

Then I stood up, handed Mrs. Blythe the photograph and said, "If you see Jen, will you give her this for me?"

"You sure you won't stay a bit longer? I just got cable." She gave a nod to the TV. "And that nice TV."

"I'd love to," I said, "but I have some things I have to take care of. Just see that Jennifer gets that photo."

She threw it down on the end table, next to what used to be a bronze lamp, and said, "I don't know where she is or when I'll see her again."

"I understand. Don't get up. I'll let myself out. Come on, Frankie." The dog followed me to the door, I turned and said, "Thanks for your help. I'll let you know what happens," but she'd clicked the television on again and didn't hear me.

I put Frankie in the car then sat with one hip on the fender for a bit, looking up at the second-story window. I also opened the envelope and riffed through Lilly's letters a little, then put my hand through the chain of the locket and held it up for inspection. It was silver and was in the shape of a heart, with the initials L.M.B. engraved on the back.

A few minutes went by and I saw the curtains move. The pretty face I'd seen before reappeared. She didn't open the window and call out to me. She didn't do much of anything but hold up an 8" × 10" photo and slowly and solemnly nod her head, confirming what I'd suspected—that it *was* him.

36

I drove around town, looking for a jewelry store or a pawnshop. I found a little place on Main Street with three pawnbroker's balls hanging over the door. In the front window I saw some electronic equipment, a few guitars, and a saxophone. There were also two signs, one that read, NOTARY PUBLIC and another that said, CUSTOM ENGRAVING.

Just what I needed.

I parked and took Frankie inside with me and spoke to the old man behind the counter. I showed him Lilly Blythe's locket and asked if he could engrave it for me.

"A nice engraving it's already got," he said, referring to the cursive L.M.B. on the back. "What for do you want to change it? You're going to marry the girl, maybe?"

"No, she's dead. Can you add a little something for me?"

He shrugged an "of course." "What you want it should say?"

"I don't know, anything. Just put some kind of symbol on it that only you know the meaning of. It's going to be used as evidence in a murder investigation."

"Tampering with evidence, you're asking me to do?" He handed it back to me. "No, thank you."

He was Jewish—either that or he wore a yarmulke for some other reason—so I said, "How's about a word in Hebrew or something? Just don't make it too obvious. You see, I don't want the killer to know it's there."

"Ah," he smiled. "So it's to be a trap for her killer, then? This I can do." He took the locket back, looked at it through a loupe and said, "Very tiny, I could make it. Certainly. Right where the period is after the *B*, maybe." He thought of something, shrugged and smiled. "I could put the Hebrew word *oth*, which some say is the mark of Cain. It can also mean evidence, which would be fitting, yes?"

"Very fitting indeed. But it has to be as small as you can possibly—"

He waved a hand. "Trust me. Microscopic, it will be."

He went about his business, placing the locket between two halves of a small vise wrapped in black velvet, then shining a bright light on it, then peering through the loupe, then gently carving the word onto the silver. He brushed away the tiny shavings, unscrewed the vise, dropped the locket into his hand, and said, "I challenge you to find any mark."

I took it and looked it over. The period after the *B* was a little larger than before. "And that's it?"

He shrugged. "All except the twenty dollars you owe me."

I paid him, had him fill out a receipt, asked him to notarize it, then took the locket, which according to him now held the mark of the human race's first murderer.

I put it back in the envelope, sealed it, left the shop, and let Frankie walk around Main Street and sniff a little.

"What do you think, Frankie?" he looked up at me. "You think this'll work?"

He had no opinion on the matter so I put him in the car then drove south on West Street then to Clay Henry's house on Autumn Lane. It wasn't hard to find. There were a dozen FBI vehicles parked out front. It was a little after one.

"Sorry," an agent in dark glasses—though it was cloudy out—told me, his hands up, "you can't come through here."

"Yeah, okay, but you might want to tell Wick Tanner that Jack Field wants to talk to him."

"The famous Jack Field?" He grinned. "Right this way."

"Any luck?" I said to Wick, looking around at the casual destruction that the gang of men in blue jumpsuits had done to what looked like a normal professor's digs.

He shook his head. "Nope. We haven't found a thing."

Frankie growled. "Easy, boy," I said.

Tanner looked down at the dog and said, "You have to bring your dog with you everywhere you go?"

"Sorry about that. He's good company."

He gave me skeptical look. "What happened to your face?"

I touched my lip. "I was in Boston doing a little investigating and my lip ran into somebody's fist. Did you look through all his botanical specimens?"

"What specimens?" he scoffed. "There aren't any."

I thought it over for a second. "Have you got a warrant to search his office on campus?"

"Of course. But there's nothing there either."

I thought it over. "Well, I don't know. He's a botanist. Maybe the botany department has got some kind of wildflower display somewhere on the college grounds and . . ."

It hit him. "Jesus, how could we have overlooked that?" He called out to another agent. "Jenkins, we need a warrant to search the campus."

"Okay," Jenkins said, "are we done here?"

"No. Go over everything again, but I'll need a couple of bodies to come with me." He turned to me. "Good thinking, Jack."

"Thanks. By the way," I said, showing him the manila envelope, "I did a little checking into the Lilly Blythe case and I think maybe we were off-base a little."

He took the envelope. "Why is that? And by the way," he added with sneer, "thanks for talking to my wife."

"You knew I'd have to talk to her."

He nodded, grudgingly. "So, what's your take?"

I shrugged. "I think it was Henry's work after all."

"Huh. And what's in here?" he said, meaning the envelope.

"Some of Lilly's things. I got them from her mother. Your wife gives you an alibi for the time of the attack, so . . ."

"That's not what she told *me*."

"I wouldn't worry about that," I said quietly. "I think she was a little upset to learn about the affair. I think she said what she did to me mostly out of anger."

"Okay, so you think I'm in the clear, which I already knew. Could it have been someone else?"

I shrugged. "I suppose it *could* have, but honestly? My feeling—and I'm sorry to put it like this—is that it had to be either you or Clay Henry. That's where the evidence was pointing. But I'm leaning pretty heavily in his direction now."

He nodded. "You want to share your thought process?"

"Well, Henry is obsessed with the changing seasons. Each of his victims was killed either in the spring, and the body was found in the fall, or vice versa. He said in the interview that he was on a "different cycle" from other people. Spring and fall, that was his cycle. But Lilly was killed in July."

"Okay. But that means he *didn't* kill her."

"No, just the opposite. Remember we said that if there was a different pattern to that *one* killing, it would indicate one of two things: someone else did it as a copycat crime, or Henry did it himself but strayed in some way from his usual MO? And since the theory is that he did it out of revenge, the murder would have had a slightly different pattern."

He nodded. "So, he really *did* do it."

"Well, I knew that *you* didn't do it. I mean, I had to look into it, but I had no doubts about your innocence."

"Well, thanks. What am I supposed to do with this?" He held up the envelope.

"Just take a look through it, if you want. There are some letters and trinkets, I guess."

"You didn't look through it yourself?"

"No," I lied. "It didn't seem right, somehow."

He frowned. "So why should *I*?"

I shrugged. "She was your . . . that is, she was someone who was important to you once. I just thought you might like to see whatever's in there. You can keep her things for a few days, I guess, but the mother will want them back eventually."

"Of course. Are you coming with us to the campus?"

I was dying to but thought it would be better if I let him take the next step without me around, looking over his shoulder, so to speak. "No, I have to get back to Maine. Is there an airport near here?"

"Yeah, a couple. There's one in Worcester and a smaller airfield just south of here in Chicopee. That's probably the quickest route." He gave me directions.

"Thanks. Here's the thing, though: I think you should talk to someone in the botany department. My feeling is that if Henry's got a display of some sort on campus, there'll be a specific wildflower that's only found in the area where each of the bodies was located. One flower per body. That's my theory. And that Henry's trophies will be buried underneath each of those specific flowers."

"Good thinking." He smiled and nodded. "You know what, Jack? You turned out to be a pretty good student."

"Thanks," I said and smiled, though it galled me to do it. "I had a pretty good teacher. Come on, Frankie."

When we got to the car, the clouds cleared briefly and there was an intimation of sunshine in the air as if a few very scattered but very persistent solar photons had finally broken through the suspended water molecules. But the moment passed and they were quickly swallowed up again in gray.

I started the engine. "Well, Frankie, it looks like you were right about him, huh?"

37

"That was *great,*" I said as Jamie cuddled up next to me.

She pulled my right arm across her naked body and said, "I guess I missed you while you were gone."

"If that's the case," I said, "I need to take more trips."

She laughed softly.

Frankie, seeing that the coast was clear, jumped up and curled into a ball in his usual spot at the foot of our bed.

Jamie and I talked a bit about the wedding, making some future plans, and the like. It was mostly Jamie chattering about things and me occasionally saying, "Un-huh," "I know, honey," "I think so too," and the like. Then our minds slowly gravitated back to the case.

Frankie and I had taken a plane from the Westover Field in Chicopee, and when I got back to the kennel there was some good news and some bad news: The FBI had found all twenty-one of Clay Henry's souvenirs (including Lilly Blythe's silver locket, which was found personally by Wick Tanner, big surprise). Each one had been buried under a wildflower, as I'd predicted.

I'd tried to contact Tanner's department heads at the Bureau, Don Case and Thom Harris, but no matter how many phone calls I made, I couldn't get through to them. Finally, I sent a copy of the notarized receipt for the engraving I'd had done on the locket, along with a note explaining its significance. I sent it special overnight delivery, return receipt requested, and was still waiting for the post office to notify me that they'd taken delivery.

As for as the rest of Henry's trophies (the real ones), they were found a little too late in the day to keep him in custody. The judge had already released him due to lack of evidence. He paid the $25,000 bond and walked away. Of course, with new evidence came a new murder charge, but unfortunately Henry was nowhere to be found. He'd disappeared.

"They found them in his house?" Jamie asked.

"What, Henry's souvenirs? No, at the college. He has a nice house, actually. On Autumn Lane, which is appropriate."

"Why?"

"He either killed his victims or watched their bodies being pulled out of a lake each fall." I paused. "Oddly enough . . ."

"What?" She tensed up, thinking I was about to say something ominous.

"Nothing. I just used to date a girl named Autumn Lane."

She thought about that for a moment, then shoved me.

"Anyway, if he's smart," I told her, "he'll leave Maine and go someplace new like Ohio or Michigan."

"Why those places?"

"They have glacial esker bogs there." I paused a moment. "If he's *not* smart, I think *you* need to be careful."

She turned to look at me. "What do you mean?"

"Haven't you noticed that you're his type? Even Leon noticed it when I was telling him about the case."

She turned back around and squeezed herself tightly against me. "You don't really think . . . ?"

I explained how his mind works, how we'd interrupted his cycle when we arrested him, that he had to kill again, and soon, and that, except for the fact that she had a higher profile than his usual victims (being in law enforcement and occasionally in the news), she made an almost perfect target.

"That explains the way he looked at me at the hearing."

I got up on one elbow. "He did what?"

She nodded, though her back was still turned. "It was very unsettling. He just stared at me and smiled the whole time. I couldn't even look at him."

"Well, you have to be very, *very* careful, then, honey. I'm serious. He's got to kill someone soon, before all the leaves fall off and the trees become bare."

"I will, I promise. Can we talk about something else now?"

"No. Maybe I should stay with you twenty-four hours a day until they find him."

"No. You have dogs to take care of."

"Okay, then you should request a State Police bodyguard. And I mean a twenty-four watch on you."

"I'll be careful, don't worry. Besides, he's probably on his way to Ohio, like you said. Let's go to sleep."

I settled in and held her close, hoping nothing bad would happen. Frankie let out a sigh and fell asleep.

"What was she like?" Jamie said as we closed our eyes.

"Who?"

"Your ex-girlfriend."

"Which one? You mean Giselle?"

"No. You know . . . Autumn Lane."

"Never heard of her," I said and we laughed a little, then finally drifted off.

Wednesday brought fine weather, though it was a bit chill. Henry was still missing. By now no one but his defense attorney, Barry Porter, had any doubts about his guilt. Porter probably didn't have doubts either, he just acted as if his client was innocent and no wonder he'd disappeared when he'd been wrongfully accused, etc.

Thursday brought more bad news.

First Regis called me. He was back from his wild goose chase in Vegas and had found his condo broken into, his safe rifled, and his ceiling mirror shot to hell. He wanted to know if I'd had anything to do with it.

"Why would you think that?"

"Call it a gut instinct. When things didn't pan out in Vegas, I figured it for a setup, and who'd have a better reason for getting me out of town than you, you prick?"

"Why me? Haven't you been keeping tabs on your enemies list? You've got a helluva lot of them."

"Yeah, maybe, but you're the only one whose ex-girlfriend set me up on this phony search. How'd you figure out the security code on my alarm system?"

"I have no idea what you're talking about, but if it *had* been me, my first guess on the code would've been what you've got plastered all over your license plate."

"Shit! It *was* you!"

I laughed. "I never said that."

"I want the things you took."

"If *I'd* taken the stuff in your safe, Corliss, don't you think your little blackmail scheme would be all over the news by now?"

"Shit! How do you?—I mean, what blackmail scheme? I don't know what the hell you're talking about."

"I'd keep looking over my shoulder if I were you."

The second bit of bad news was worse—much worse from my standpoint. Julie Zimmerman called a little while later to tell me that Clarence had run off again. Her mother had taken him out in the backyard but had forgotten to put the long leash on him first, as I'd instructed her to do. She went back inside to get it, but was distracted by a phone call.

Clarence waited semipatiently at the back door, even barking at her for a while to come out and play with him, but by the time she'd finished her call, the little guy was gone.

"When did this happen?" I asked, squelching a desire to blame her mother, or myself.

"Yesterday afternoon. He hasn't been back home, Jack."

"Have you been out looking for him?"

"Yes. We all have. I'm really worried."

So was I, but I said, "Well, let's hope he shows up soon."

"He was doing so well. He never used to wait for us to come play with him like he was doing with my mom yesterday." She paused. "There's one other thing I should tell you."

"What's that?"

"I—I couldn't help it. I wanted to know what he was like. So I sent a letter to that serial killer."

My knees got weak. "Did you tell him about Clarence?"

"Sort of. I mentioned that I knew you and that you'd helped train my dog."

I took a deep breath. "Well, let's hope there's no connection between him and Clarence's disappearance."

"But he wouldn't have done anything to him, would he?"

"I don't know. Don't even think about it. Let's just hope that Clarence comes trotting home like usual, okay?"

"Okay," she said meekly.

That evening I got a call from Congressman Schiff, of all people. He'd gotten a report about a dead dog near Vassalboro and had driven out to find the body. There was a purple wildflower stuck in his mouth and he'd been strangled with a rope, not unlike the ones found on MerryAnn Moore's body.

"Ah, no, it's probably Clarence. Where's the body now?"

"In my cruiser. What do you want me to do with him?"

"Bring him here. Better yet, take him to the ME's office in Augusta. I'll call Jamie and meet you there."

"Why the morgue? It's just a dog."

"It's close to the forensics lab. That flower is a message from our serial killer. It may tell us where he's hiding."

"Okay, then. I'm on my way."

I called Jamie, told her what had happened, then drove to Augusta as fast as I could and went straight to the lab.

It was Clarence all right. I felt my face tighten as I saw his lifeless form stretched out on the steel examining table.

Jamie came over to me and put her hand on the small of my back, comforting me. Schiff stood there awkwardly, not saying anything, just holding his hat in one hand and rubbing the back of his neck with the other. What exactly can you say with a dead dog in the room?

After a moment Jamie led me to the table and I looked down at the little guy. Both his eyes were still bulged open. I tried to close them but they wouldn't close. I kept trying until Jamie came over and took my hand away.

"I should have trained him better," I said. "This wouldn't have happened."

"You don't know that. Henry is a psychopath. He may have been driving by and seen the dog in the yard." (She was more right than she knew.) "We don't know how it happened." She brushed the tears from my eyes. "It's not your fault, honey."

"Do you, um . . ." Congressman Schiff hemmed, "that is, I should get back out on patrol unless you need me for anything?"

"No, that's fine," I said. "Thanks for calling me. You did a good thing." I put out my hand.

He came over and shook it. "This is a rotten situation."

"Yeah," I said, trying to keep my voice from cracking. "Where . . . you didn't say before exactly where you found him."

"He was . . . his legs were stuck in a mailbox just outside the post office."

"Jesus."

"A ten-year-old girl found him like that, first thing this morning. She was mailing invitations to her birthday party."

"Ah, poor kid."

"She was pretty broken up. Well . . ." he put on his hat. "I'd better get going."

He left and Jamie took my arm and said, "I combed out his fur." She showed me a brown paper bag. "I found pollen and some soil. We can have the lab check it out. Do you want me to perform a necropsy?"

"No, no. Don't cut him up. What's the point? He was strangled, right? Where's the rope?"

She showed me another evidence bag. I didn't open it. She said, "At least now maybe he's gotten it out of his system."

I was confused. "Who?"

"Henry. You said he needed to kill again and he has."

"I wish it were that easy. No, this is just the tip of the ice-berg. He's going to kill another woman again. And very soon."

She put her arms around me and held me tight.

I had some brief, livid fantasies about what I wanted to do to Clay Henry when I found him, then said, "Can I take his body and the samples you got with me? And the flower?"

She nodded. "Where do you want to take them?"

"I guess I'll take Clarence over to the Zimmerman's. They might want to bury him in the yard or something. The other stuff I'll take up to Colby College. I want Dr. Petersen to have a look at them."

"Okay." She got the evidence bags together. "Do you want to reschedule the rehearsal dinner?"

"Do what?"

"It's tonight. You have to come to the rehearsal, of course. But the dinner is mostly so the two families can get to know each other. I know how much you hate social gath—"

"I'll be all right."

"If you're not feeling up to it . . ."

"I'll be fine. Just let me take care of Clarence first, and I'll call you later, okay?" I picked up the dog's body and put it gently over my shoulder, the way you would to burp a baby. "And be careful, honey."

"I will."

"I'm serious. This man is very clever and very dangerous. You have to promise me you'll be on the lookout for him."

"Okay, I promise. Can I help you out to your car?"

"No, I've got it."

She kissed me and handed me the evidence bags, opened the door for me and I went through it. As it swung closed, I turned and saw her sag into a chair. She put her head in her hands and her shoulders began to shake as she sobbed quietly alone.

How I wanted to stay with her and join her and hold her close and let my own tears burst out, but I had things to do and very little time to waste on pointless emotion.

Besides, I thought, as I walked purposefully down the corridor, keeping my face blank, I'll have plenty of time to do my own crying once I'm alone in the car, taking Clarence home to his final rest.

38

The Zimmermans refused to let me give them their money back. I wrote them a check and everything, but Oscar just ripped it in two. (Julie was at school, which was good.)

"You did all right," Oscar said. "Clarence was really coming along until . . ."

Iris said, "It's all my fault."

I said, "It's nobody's fault. Nobody but the bastard who killed him, that is."

"Will you find him? Will you make him pay for this?"

I nodded grimly.

I finally met Dr. Carla Petersen face-to-face, between classes. She was quite pretty, in a Lauren Hutton sort of way. She was sorry to hear about Clarence, but told me she had a full schedule and wouldn't be able to examine the samples I'd brought until after five o'clock. I told her that we didn't have much time, so she agreed to get to it as quickly as she could. "Maybe I can do some work on it between classes," she said. "I'll call you as soon I have any ideas on where the poor dog's been."

I drove to the airport in Portland, met my dad and my sister Annabelle, and her husband Barry, and three of their four kids, Julie, Garret, and Lacy (Devi, their oldest, was in college and she couldn't make the trip). After they got their luggage, I helped them rent a minivan and they followed me to the Samoset and got checked in. I gave them a map of the area and said I'd meet them at the church in New Hope at seven.

"Where are you rushing off to, son?" my dad wanted know.

"Sorry, everybody, I've got some things to take care of. I'll see you all tonight."

I called Flynn, Sinclair, and Doyle, told them what was up, and that we might have a possible location for where Clay Henry was hiding as soon as I heard back from Dr. Petersen. Flynn was coming to the rehearsal anyway, but the others said they'd be standing by when the information came through.

I tried calling Jamie several times but couldn't reach her. I kept getting her voice mail, which put me in a worried state. I prayed to God that Henry wasn't after her.

I got home, made sure Leon got dressed, took care of the dogs, got Leon dressed again, even had Frankie and Hooch try on their tuxes. I wanted to get them used to wearing the damn things. We all got to the church at ten past seven.

I looked around, hoping Jamie wouldn't be mad at me for being late, but she wasn't there. She was late herself, which caused me to worry even more.

My cell phone rang and I thought it might be her, but it was Dr. Petersen. The combination of soil samples and botanical specimens found in Clarence's fur could have only come from one place, she said. The area around Potter's Pond.

Of course. He had to have a place near there to hole up in for when his latest victim was discovered. A shack, a lean-to, maybe nothing more than hole in a rock. Jesus, we had him. I quickly called Sinclair and told him what I knew. While I was talking to him I got another call. It was Jamie.

"Honey, where *are* you?"

"Sorry. I'll be there in ten minutes."

"I've been worried sick about you."

"I know. I'm sorry. I had to . . . oh, no. Oh, that's just terrible."

"What is? What's wrong?"

"There's an old woman by the side of the road. It's just starting to pour and her car broke down. She needs a ride."

"Well don't stop! Call the police."

"But, Jack, she's just a helpless old lady with a cane. It's pouring buckets and it'll only take a second." I heard her roll down her window and say something to the old woman.

"Jamie! Do not stop your car!"

"Sorry. I already stopped. Jack, she dropped her cane!"

I took a breath. "Honey, where are you?"

"I don't know. I'm on 17, just outside the city limits."

"Well, roll up your window and keep driving. Jamie? Jamie? Jamie, are you there?"

The phone was dead.

Everyone came over to see what I was yelling about.

"Jack," Laura Cutter said, "what is it?"

"Ah, it's nothing," I said, trying to control my breathing. "She's just . . . she's a little late. She'll be here. Excuse me a minute . . ."

I went outside. Flynn followed me. So did Frankie and Hooch. I called Jamie's cell back, but it had been turned off.

"Okay," said Flynn, his hand on my shoulder, "what's wrong?"

"She's gone. She's gone. She stopped to help some old woman by the side of the road and now her phone's off!"

"Do you know where she is?"

I told him Jamie's location. He got on his cell phone and placed two calls, one to the sheriff 's office, and one to State Police HQ. When he got off he said, "They've got two cruisers in that area now. If they find anything, they'll call me right back."

"I hate this. Jesus. Why didn't she listen to me?"

"Maybe it's nothing."

I nodded but said, "I have a bad feeling." It was still dry where we were, but I could feel the storm coming our way.

My cell phone rang. It was her. "Jack?" She sounded weak and helpless. "Please help me?"

Flynn's phone rang and he clicked it open. "Flynn."

"Where are you?" I asked her. "What's going on?"

A male voice came on the line. "Say goodbye to your precious sweetheart, Dr. Field."

"Listen, Clay," I tried to keep my voice calm, "don't hurt her. Don't you dare hurt—"

"Don't worry, Dr. Field. You'll see her again. Next spring when the ice melts and the lakes begin to thaw."

He hung up.

Flynn got off his call. "They found her car abandoned near Church Hill Road."

"He's got her. He's got her. He's heading toward Potter's Pond." I raced to my car. "We've got to go after them."

"Jack! We'll take my Jeep. We can use the siren."

We ran to his Jeep and got in, the two dogs included.

"Can't you leave the damn dogs behind for once?"

"No, the mood they're in, they'll follow us. And I don't want them running behind us all night."

He shook his head then started the siren and we spit gravel out of the church parking lot. As soon as we were past the lone traffic light in New Hope, he got on his radio. "I want some choppers, all available cruisers, and as many men as possible. This is an attempted assassination of a state government official."

We roared through the towns and past farms and had been on the road about ten minutes, with my heart not able to stop pounding and my mind not able to stop racing, when a call came in on the radio. A chopper had spotted Henry's car traveling at a leisurely pace, just south of Potter's Pond Road.

We were less than three minutes away. We caught up with the rainstorm first, though, and were inundated with it.

As we passed the turnpike cutoff, we were joined by two cruisers, an unmarked State Police car, with Sinclair at the wheel, and a Colby College security vehicle, with Doyle driving. Sinclair sped ahead of us, while Doyle and the cruisers brought up the rear. We could see Henry's taillights up the road.

We followed him at full-speed as he turned up a cramped, muddy road, bordered on all sides by pine trees, and with no way to maneuver past him.

Flynn was behind Sinclair and Henry, with Peggy Doyle and the troopers still bringing up the rear.

We splashed our way around a sharp curve and there was a sudden clearing to the left. Flynn veered off, missing a couple of trees, and gunned his Jeep, first past Sinclair, and then past Henry, then pulled back onto the road and blocked the killer's path. The front brake lights on the green sedan glared bright yellow in the rain. Henry crashed into the side of Flynn's Jeep. Sinclair stopped in time but was immediately hit from behind by Doyle.

We all got out, though Henry stayed safely inside his car. Flynn, Sinclair, and the troopers all had their weapons drawn, their knees bent, looking serious as all hell.

"Get out of the car, now!" Sinclair ordered Henry.

I ran to the car shouting, "Where is she? Where's Jamie?"

Doyle tried to hold me back. "It's okay, Jack. We've got him now."

I pushed past her, putting myself between Sinclair and Flynn and their drawn pistols. I banged on the wet window.

Henry looked at me with blank eyes but wouldn't open the door. My fists smeared the window again. He just blinked at me, uncomprehendingly. He was wearing a wig, a dress, and theatrical makeup to make him look like an old woman. There was a wooden cane and a revolver on the seat next to him.

"What do you want?" he cried finally. "I haven't done anything wrong."

"Where's Jamie?"

He didn't answer.

"Let us handle it, Jack," Sinclair said, as he and Flynn stepped forward.

"Like hell I will," I said, and turned my eyes down to the side of the road, looking for a rock to bust the window with. I found one big enough to do the trick, and lifted it up over my head.

"Jack," Flynn said, "put it down."

Oops—too late!

I smacked it as hard as I could against the window and Henry was covered in green pebbles of safety glass. The wind and the rain blew into the open space. I reached through it, my hands dripping with rain, and grabbed him around the neck with trembling hands.

"Where is she?"

He just sat there, blinking.

I squeezed harder. "I said—"

"In the trunk," he croaked, then reached under the dash to release the lock. I heard it click, let go of him and ran around to the back, followed by Frankie and Hooch.

I lifted the lid and found my darling girl, still fully clothed, with her wrists and ankles bound with rope and a piece of duct tape across her mouth. Her eyes were open and they were the most beautiful eyes I'd ever seen.

I leaned forward and gently pulled the tape away.

"Oh, Jack, thank god."

"Honey, are you okay?" I could feel my heart pounding in time to the pelting of the raindrops.

"I'm fine. He didn't do anything to me. He just tied me up. He had a gun. I'm sorry. I should have been more—"

"Sshh. It's all right. You're safe now."

"You told me to be careful and I was stupid. I was really, really stup—"

"Sshh," I said, trying my best to undo her knots with my rain-slippery fingers. When I was done she tried to hug me but could only clutch my arms. Frankie and Hooch were dancing around me, trying to jump up. They still had their tuxes on.

"Wait, honey," I said, "let me get your wrists."

Flynn and Sinclair were still standing crouched next to the car, ordering Henry to get out.

Then, while I undid Jamie's ankles, Doyle went around the passenger side, broke the window with another rock, opened the door, got in, twisted around and used her legs to kick Henry out of the car and onto the wet ground.

I helped Jamie out of the trunk. She wanted to hold on to me and kiss me and such, but I had something else on my mind—mainly murdering Clay Henry.

She must have read my mind because she pulled away and said, "Where is he?"

"Come on," Flynn said, trying to pull Henry up off the ground, "on your feet."

"I didn't do anything wrong," Henry whimpered.

Flynn, Sinclair, and Doyle got Henry on his feet. Flynn

and Doyle held him upright while Sinclair cuffed him.

We heard another car approaching from behind us. Jamie went around the front of the car to confront her attacker. He looked up piteously and she immediately spit in his face.

"I'm sorry," Henry said. "I didn't want to hurt you."

"The hell you didn't."

Frankie and Hooch jumped in his car and found the gun and cane, then bounded out, proudly clutching their prizes between their teeth. Hooch had the cane in his mouth, Frankie the gun in his.

"Frankie, out!" I said as I heard a car door open behind us. Frankie dropped the gun into the mud.

Jamie spat a few choice words at Henry, then kneed him in the groin. He crumpled, whining, to the wet road.

A voice said, "Stop! You're violating my client's rights."

It was Barry Porter; he came striding forward.

I came up behind Jamie and gently held her by the arm. "Honey," I said, "that wasn't right."

She shook her head, nodded sadly, though her face was still furious, and said, "I know, but it sure *felt* good."

"It isn't that," I said, trying to lighten the tone. "It's just that you should've shifted your weight onto your left leg a little before you kneed him. It would have given you a little more oomph. And you should have grabbed him by the shoulders first and kind of held him in place while you did it."

Henry was still whining and squirming in the mud.

"This is outrageous," Porter said, coming to where we stood. "I'm filing a lawsuit against all of you."

"What the hell are you doing here?" Flynn said.

"I—I got an emergency phone call from my client. He informed me that he was being harassed by the State Police."

To Jamie I said, "Here, let me show you how it's *supposed* to be done."

I grabbed the attorney by the shoulders, planted my

weight on my left leg, and in short order, the two of them—the lawyer and his client—were moaning in the mud.

Frankie and Hooch, who rarely pass up on an opportunity to empty their bladders, saw this as a golden moment (so to speak). Frankie sprayed Henry's head, Hooch, still holding the cane in his mouth, did the same for Porter.

"Good dogs!" Jamie said, laughing.

39

It was Saturday, my wedding day, and I had just finished tying my bow tie and was about to put on my tuxedo jacket when Kelso came into my bedroom, dressed to the nines.

He was quite handsome in an easygoing way, and I thought, briefly, that he looked exactly the way Regis thought, or wished, he did.

"What are you doing here?" I asked.

"I don't know. I thought I'd be your best man."

"Sorry." I put on the jacket. "The part's been filled. Hooch is doing it."

He laughed an easy laugh. "That figures. Oh, there's a couple of FBI agents downstairs, looking for you."

I gave him a look. "They have names?"

"I'm pretty sure they do," he laughed, "but they didn't tell me what they were."

"Okay. Let's go talk to them."

We went downstairs and he said, "So, where *is* Hooch?"

"In the salon. He and Frankie are getting a bath. You look great."

"Thanks. I owe it all to clean living."

"And ten million bucks or so."

He grinned. "There's that."

Waiting for us in the living room were two men, a shortish, serious-faced type with medium brown hair, and a taller, more relaxed fellow with hair the color, I hate to say it, of yellow spring roses.

The short one stuck out his hand. "Don Case," he said with a sudden smile that brightened his face. "This is Thom Harris. Sorry to come at a bad time."

"That's okay," I said, going to my office.

They followed me. Kelso lingered in the doorway, leaning against the jamb and looking like an ad for something. He pulled out a cigarette.

Case said, "We heard that you had some information for us about the Clay Henry killings."

"True, that," I said, quoting Peggy Doyle and sitting behind my desk. I unlocked the top drawer and took out an envelope.

Case came over while Harris looked around the office.

"Nice," was all he said.

I handed Case the envelope. While he opened it I said, "Henry confessed to twenty-one killings, but he lied."

"Is that so?" Case said.

"Yep. Lilly Blythe was murdered by Wick Tanner."

Both men were shocked. Case said, "I seriously doubt—"

"Tanner and his men found Henry's mementos at his little campus garden, right?"

"Yeah?" said Case. He took a receipt out of the envelope.

I said, "Including an engraved silver locket, belonging to Lilly Blythe?" He nodded. "That notarized receipt is from a pawnshop in Amherst, Massachusetts. I had the item listed on it engraved about an hour or so before Tanner found Henry's keepsakes. If you look through a magnifying glass, you'll find a tiny Hebrew word, which means 'evidence' in English. It's engraved into the period after the letter *B* on the back. I gave that locket to Tanner immediately after I had it engraved. Both the pawnshop owner and I will testify to that. I also mailed you a copy of the affidavit."

Harris looked at Case then said to me, "We never got it."

"I sent it overnight delivery two days ago. In fact, the return receipt just arrived this morning." I took it out of the drawer and handed it to Case. "You signed for it."

He looked it over. "This isn't my signature."

I thought about it. "Has Tanner been in Washington?"

He nodded. "You're saying Agent Tanner planted the locket with the other items?"

"How else could it have gotten there?"

They looked at each other and shook their heads.

"Look, you already know about Tanner's affair with Lilly Blythe. I spoke to his wife too, by the way. She can't confirm his alibi for the day Lilly Blythe went missing."

Case sighed. "You're a little late with this."

I stood up. "Why's that?"

"Wick Tanner has disappeared."

I shrugged. "Well, *you're* a little late responding to my dozen phone calls, and the letter, though my guess is that Tanner saw to it that you never received it."

"Which would have been shortly before he disappeared."

"And you're more than a little late getting here. And if I don't get a move on, I'm going to be late for my wedding." I went to the door. Kelso unleaned himself from the doorjamb.

I stopped and turned. "One more thing, Steve Rice was not working for the Boston mafia. Tanner made that up, too. And he probably stole Rice's car." (Rice was still missing.)

"What? You think Tanner killed Agent Rice?"

I shrugged. "That's up to you to find out. I've got someplace to be right now. You can let yourselves out."

There was the usual to-do, with people acting badly out of nervous frustration and saying a lot of unnecessary and stupid things, which I did my best to ignore, until finally I was standing at the altar, with Hooch, Frankie, and Kelso, in that order, on my left, all dressed in tuxedos, waiting for the music to start, and Eve Arden in their pink gowns, on my right, when Jennifer, not Jamie, appeared at the back of the church. She was still a brunette and looked quite pretty in her tea-length dress and high heels.

She saw me looking at her, nodded, then took a seat in the back, on the left side of the church.

I saw a flash pop in her direction, looked over at Adam, caught his eye, then shook my head, and circled my finger around to the altar area, reminding him that he was there to photograph the wedding, not his make-believe girlfriend.

He shrugged an apology and got back to work.

My sister Annabelle caught my eye and smiled and nodded through her tears. "You look so handsome," she mouthed.

"Thanks," I mouthed back.

My dad was next to her, holding her hand and beaming.

The music started (finally) and Jamie and Jonas appeared in the back of the church.

She looked so beautiful as she came toward me, smiling and crying behind her veil, taking one step, then stopping, then taking another step, doing the bride's formal dance, holding the bouquet in front of her, and I felt my heart burst until I saw Wick Tanner appear in the door behind them.

He had on a dark suit, slightly rumpled, to go with the wild look in his eyes and the rough texture of his unshaven face. I couldn't tell for sure, since his body was hidden by Jamie and her father, but he seemed to have a gun at his side.

As Jonas brought Jamie up to my side, and put her hand in mine, and the preacher started in on "dearly beloved" and whatnot, I glanced back and saw Jen looking behind her, up the aisle, not at Jamie and the preacher. She saw Tanner, then sprang from her seat, moved hurriedly past the people sitting in her row, and raced toward the side exit, to the left of the pulpit and flowers.

Tanner raised his pistol and fired a shot at her.

There were a number of screams. I didn't count how many.

Tanner missed Jen and she kept running.

Flynn erupted from his seat and sprinted toward Tanner, shouting, "Drop it!"

Tanner turned quickly and shot him in the hip.

Frankie saw Jen racing toward the exit and pulled at the leash, barking his head off. He pulled so hard that the leash slipped out of Kelso's hand.

The crowd was still screaming. Then Tanner raised his arm again to take another shot, and they ducked down, out of the line of fire.

Jen went out the side exit.

A bullet hit a hinge on the door, ricocheted off, and broke a piece of the stain-glassed window behind the minister.

Tanner ran down the left side of the church, after Jennifer.

I let go of Jamie's hand to go after him.

Frankie had already followed Jen out the door.

Kelso tried to follow but tripped over Hooch and knocked over a tall, white wicker flower stand.

"Jack, wait!" Jamie grabbed my sleeve. She looked at the minister then back at me and said, "Quick, Jack! Do you?"

"I do," I said breathlessly.

"Me too," she said, then gave another quick look at the cleric.

"Good enough for me," he said. "I now pronounce you—"

Jamie threw her bouquet at him, he caught it and bobbled it in his hands. There was a ruffle of taffeta and Eve Arden lunged at him, each trying to be the first to grab it.

Jamie and I went racing after Jen and Tanner, with Jamie shouting to the guests, "See you at the reception!"

We got to the door, burst through, and ran outside. Jamie was doing her best to keep up with me and keep her train out of the way at the same time.

Adam was right behind us calling, "Jen! Run!" and snapping pictures of the debacle.

Jen was headed over the hill behind the church, scattering fallen leaves in her wake. She'd been a star forward on the basketball team and had a pretty damn good set of legs.

Tanner stopped running after her, stood still, and took careful aim, but before he could squeeze off a shot, Frankie jumped him from behind and knocked him down—then, when he was on his back, the dog went for his throat. Good boy!

"Okay, Frankie, off!" I shouted but he couldn't hear me.

"Let him kill the bastard," Jamie said, pulling at her train furiously, which now had dozens of autumn leaves attached to the fabric. "He just spoiled our wedding!"

"Yeah, but Tanner's got a gun and Frankie doesn't."

"Get him off! Get him off!" Tanner cried, writhing around in the grass and the dead leaves.

We got to them just as a muffled shot stopped Frankie in his tracks and he crumpled in a lifeless heap next to Tanner.

Tanner tried another shot, but I kicked the gun out of his hand, then kicked him hard on the jaw. He went out cold.

For good measure, Jamie kicked him again.

Three times; kick, KICK, K-I-C-K!

I fell on my knees next to Frankie's body. "Good boy!" I cried. "Don't leave me. Frankie! Frankie!"

Leon came running up. "Oh, no. Not Frankie!"

"Jack, don't move him!" Jamie said, but I couldn't help myself. I began to cradle him in my arms. She maneuvered her dress out of the way and grabbed my collar to pull me away.

I landed on my butt on the grass.

"I'm a doctor, Jack, remember?" she said, kneeling down beside Frankie. "Let me check him out."

"Please don't let him die."

Then, the same way Jamie's doctor's instincts took over, my cop instincts made me crawl over to retrieve Tanner's weapon to make sure he couldn't grab it again if he came to.

"How's he doing?" asked Leon, close to tears.

"I don't know." I turned to Jamie. "Is he okay?"

"Is he okay?" someone echoed from the back of the church.

I turned and saw the entire wedding party, in all their finery, standing in a clump around the back of the church.

Some were holding each other or just holding hands. Some, like the preacher, stood as lonely, shocked figures, praying silently. Some of the women just stood there, with their hands to their mouths, their mascara running down their cheeks. My sister Annabelle was one of them. Her husband Barry had his arm around her and the kids were gathered behind her, crying and clutching at her skirt. My old dad, looking handsome in his tux and silver hair, stood next to them, teary-eyed. Nobody wanted the dog to die. They all stared at us with plaintive eyes. All except one of Jamie's cousins, who was calmly videotaping the event.

Kelso and Hooch broke through the crowd and came running up to us. Kelso, I noticed, had blood running down his face from a gash in his forehead.

"Jesus, Jack," he said, looking at Frankie. "I'm sorry."

Still on my knees, I turned to Jamie and my precious dog. "So?" I pleaded with her.

"He's still alive, Jack," she said, her sweet eyes brimming with hope. "He's breathing. He's still alive."

"Ah, that's good. Will he make it?"

"I don't know." She brushed a tear from her cheek. "I

think he's got a punctured lung. We have to get him to a vet as soon as possible."

Flynn came limping up and joined Leon, Kelso, and Hooch.

"He's going to be okay," I said, putting my arms under the dog's body. "I have to get him to the vet."

"I'll go get the car," Kelso said.

"Let's take mine," Jamie said. "It's the green Jaguar parked out front. The keys are in it."

Kelso nodded and ran toward the parking lot, with Hooch bounding along beside him.

Jamie said to Flynn, "You've been shot."

"Ah, it's just a flesh wound." Then he told us he'd gone to his car and radioed for help.

"You need a doctor," Jamie said.

"I'll be all right. The police are on the way. You go, I'll stay here and take care of this bastard."

"Thanks, Sheriff," I said. "He's going to make it."

I got to my feet and looked down at Jamie. "Thank you, honey," I said to her. She reached up and grabbed my arm and used it for leverage. I noticed finally that her dress and veil were stained with blood, her face smeared with mascara.

A few more people came to us and gathered around.

"Some wedding, huh?" Jamie said to them, brushing the leaves and blades of grass off her gown.

Leon said, "Yo, Jack, I'm coming with you guys."

"No," I said over my shoulder as I started to run toward the car, "you stay here and keep an eye on Hooch."

"But, yo, Jack!"

"Stay here, Leon."

I raced toward the parking lot with Frankie in my arms. Kelso already had the car started and waiting for us.

Jamie was struggling to stay right behind me, still dressed in her heels.

"Are you okay, Dr. Cutter?" someone shouted.

She stopped a moment, turned to the crowd, and shouted, "It's Mrs. Field! I just got married! Call me Mrs. Field!"

Then she picked up her train, kicked off her shoes, and followed me, running as fast as she could.

With Frankie in my arms, we got in the back of the car—which had been decorated with shaving cream and had some old shoes and tin cans attached to the bumper—and Kelso took off.

The crowd hesitated, then a group of them ran after us and threw rice at the car. The old shoes and tin cans clattered behind us as we raced away.

40

Frankie was in surgery for over an hour. We called my vet, Dr. Stanhope (Jamie's cell phone was in the glove box), just as he was closing his clinic in West Rockport for the afternoon.

His vet tech had already gone home so Jamie put a surgical gown over her wedding gown and pitched in, helping with the IV and manning the anesthesia. I stayed during the first part of the process—the insertion of the IV and the X rays—talking to Frankie and stroking his fur, but couldn't handle it when the scalpel came out and Dr. Stanhope started the incision.

I found Kelso, still in the waiting room. He'd been on Jamie's cell phone the whole time, going through every number in its memory bank and telling everyone what was going on. He also got word that Flynn was okay, and had been taken to Rockland Memorial to have his gunshot wound attended to.

The FBI had Wick Tanner in custody and all local law enforcement personnel were out combing the hills, looking for Jennifer Vreeland.

"Don't worry," I told him. "Once she hears that Wick Tanner is finally locked up, I think she'll reappear."

He also said that after we'd left the church, Laura Cutter

had gathered everyone together and insisted that the food she'd made for the reception not go to waste, so the entire wedding party was at the reception, waiting for us.

"I hope they don't expect us to actually show up," I said.

When Jamie and Dr. Stanhope finally came out—both smiling—telling me Frankie was stable and was going to recover, all the tension went out of my body. I'd only been more relieved once in my life, that I could recall, and that was when I'd found Jamie still alive in the trunk of Clay Henry's car.

After Jamie and I had hugged and kissed and I'd listened and relistened to the doctor's prognosis (Frankie was stable but sedated and would need to spend a few nights at the clinic, he said, "resting comfortably"), Kelso gave his report to Jamie.

"Okay," she took my hand, "we'd better get over to my mom's house now, before everyone goes home."

"You're not serious," I said.

"Yes. I'm going to dance with my father, then I'm going to dance with you. And we're going to cut the cake."

"But look at our clothes. We're both a mess."

She huffed. "It's at my mother's house. I'm sure I can find something to wear." She sized up Kelso's shirt and jacket. "And you and Lou can switch clothes, can't you?"

I looked at Kelso. He shrugged. We took off our jackets and shirts and studs, and traded clothes.

We got to Laura Cutter's house just before sunset and there were twinkling lights strung on every possible tree branch, wound around every tree trunk, and decorating every inch of the house itself. With the fading daylight and the autumn leaves, it was like entering a fairy wonderland.

Once Jamie had changed into a clean dress—a very nice red evening gown—we answered a lot of questions, said thanks to a lot of congratulatory remarks, and did all the usual things.

"So," I finally said to Laura, as I held a glass of champagne in one hand, "where'd you get all the pretty lights?"

"Didn't you know? Your ex-girlfriend, the set designer, came by early this morning with a whole crew. They put them up. She said it would be her wedding present to you two."

"It's beautiful. And awfully nice of her, considering the fact that we didn't invite her to the wedding."

She nodded. "Which was Jamie's idea, no doubt."

"No, mine, actually. Shall we dance?"

Tulips and her combo sounded great, and when Jamie and I finally had our first dance together as a married couple, she sang "Our Love Is Here to Stay," as advertised: *"It's very clear, our love is here to stay."*

As we danced I said to Jamie, "You seem content."

"I am. Very content."

"Aren't you upset that Wick Tanner ruined our wedding?"

She shrugged. "That's what our life is like, Jack. And that's what it'll probably always be like. One adventure after another." She put her head on my shoulder and said, "Anyway, he didn't *ruin* our wedding, he en*hanced* it."

So I danced with my arms around my sweetheart and let my eyes wander around the yard, saw my sister dancing with her husband, gazing into his eyes, and my dad dancing and flirting with Jamie's mom, and a nicely dressed Peggy Doyle in the arms of one Lou Kelso, with her head resting nicely on said Kelso's shoulder, and a kid named Leon dancing with a big orange dog, who for some reason was wearing a tuxedo jacket and a bow tie.

It was a great party.

I wish you could have been there.

Epilogue

It probably goes without saying, since nearly everybody has seen the wedding video on one of the cable news outlets by now, but Jamie and I became famous as "that couple in Maine" whose nuptials were interrupted by an FBI profiler gone mad. As usual, they played it to death.

Meanwhile, Tanner was indicted on a capital murder charge under a federal statute and was facing the death penalty. He chose to confess to everything in exchange for life in prison.

He admitted that he'd killed the woman he'd been having an affair with, the one he *thought* was Lilly Blythe. He did it in a fit of rage and when it was over, Steve Rice and Randy Corliss helped him dispose of the body. Corliss had been blackmailing him ever since.

Rice had too, in a way; using what he knew about the crime to make his way up the ranks at the bureau.

Tanner also confessed to killing Steve Rice. He gave up the location of Rice's car, which he'd stolen. It was at the bottom of a lake near Auburn. Rice's body was found inside the trunk. He'd been dead since the night I interviewed Clay Henry.

Corliss was arrested for being an accomplice to murder (after the fact) and for blackmail, and when it hit the news his ratings in the polls for the recall election for county sheriff took a pretty bad hit. The odd thing was that there were *some* people still willing to *vote* for him!

Nevertheless, Sheriff Flynn kept his job and Peggy Doyle came in second, once all the votes were tallied. Flynn promptly announced his retirement and named Doyle as his replacement. The voters were puzzled but not unhappy with his decision.

No one but Jamie and I knew that Tanner's original victim was really Rose Vreeland and that she'd killed her twin sister years earlier, making it look like a suicide. And we had no reason to spill the beans. They were both dead, and revealing the truth now would only hurt the living, namely Jennifer.

I'd been right about her—Jen, that is. Once she learned that Wick Tanner was in jail, she immediately showed up at the kennel to see if Frankie was okay and if she could say hello.

I told her that he was still at the clinic, and that it wouldn't be a good idea for him to see her or play with her until after he'd fully recovered.

"Why?" she asked sadly, as if I'd made my proscription because I was mad or because something was wrong with her.

"Because he'll be so happy to see you," I explained, "that he might tear out his stitches and need more surgery."

"Oh," she laughed, relieved to know that she and Frankie were still safe territory. Then she smiled shyly and told me she was going to try to make up the work she'd missed at school and had even been accepted back on the basketball team. "When the season's over and things settle down," she said, "do you think maybe I could have that job you offered me before?"

I said I thought we could work something out, as long as she promised me to come and talk to me about anything that was ever bothering her, and that she'd see a therapist to help her deal with the things that had happened to her as a child.

"Don't worry." She rolled her eyes. "I've been on the net looking for shrinks. I may be crazy but I'm not stupid."

Leon made friends with the kids at school who'd been verbally abusive to him, especially Jason—the kid whose nose he'd broken. In fact, they quickly became best friends. It turned out that Jason was a big dog lover like Leon and even brought his own dogs, Senator and Grendel, to the kennel fairly often to run around the play yard with Magee. Leon even taught Jason some of the training techniques he'd learned from me.

Principal van Noy called to tell me there had been a new development at school, though, one he hoped would finally teach me to keep my big mouth shut. The kids were no longer using the "n" word, they'd started calling each other futtshicker instead.

About a week after the wedding I got a call from the warden at the prison. Clay Henry was being moved to a federal penitentiary in Ohio in a few days and wanted to talk to me before he left.

"No thanks," I said. "Did he say what it was about?"

"I'm just the messenger," the warden said and hung up.

Later that day, Barry Porter called with the same strange, and unwelcome, invitation. "He has an affidavit he wants you to deliver to the authorities in Canada."

"Fat chance. What's it about?"

"All I know is he wants to talk to you."

"Yeah, all right," I huffed. "When do I see him?"

"Sometime this afternoon?"

"I have some dogs to take care of. How's four o'clock?"

"I'll make the arrangements."

So at four on the dot they took me into one of those visitation rooms with the bulletproof glass and the grimy telephones you talk to the perpetrators on. I took a seat on a wooden stool, which was bolted to the cement floor, and a little while later Henry came in, dressed in prison orange.

He took his seat and picked up the handset. I picked up mine. "Thanks for coming," he said.

"Yeah, yeah, what do you want?"

"I need to ask you a favor, but I need to tell you something first. Please? Don't hang up. I'm sorry for what I did to Dr. Cutter."

"Save it," I said. "We both know it's bullshit."

"It isn't. I *am* sorry. Though you're right, in a way."

"I'm listening."

"What I mean is, I know I'd do it again if I had the chance. I'm self-aware enough for that at least. But I *am* sorry about it. You played a good game and beat me fair and—"

"Can the crap. What's the favor?"

"My attorney has an affidavit. I'd like you to—"

"I already know about that. Why should I?"

He took a breath. "After our interview I remembered some things about my father, and you were right about what he did to me. I want you to put him in jail for that. In a way he's as responsible for all these murders as I am."

"I don't really know if that's the case, Clay. I have no way of knowing that it was your father that did this to you. For all I know it could have been an uncle or a teacher."

"But it *was* my father. He did horrible things."

"Maybe so, but I can't take *your* word for it. Besides, the statute of limitations ran out on his crimes years ago."

He smiled and licked his lips. "But what if he helped me hide the body of my first victim? That would make him an accomplice to an ongoing crime. You could arrest him for that?"

"I can't arrest anybody for anything," I said. "I'm a dog trainer, not a cop."

"But you could contact the authorities in Canada for me and tell them about it."

"Why? To give them this phony affidavit you've cooked

up as revenge? Remember, Clay, you have to tell the truth."

His face contorted. "But you don't realize! I thought you understood about the horrible things he did to me!"

"If he really did them then I have pity on you, or at least I have pity for the child you once were. But—"

"Please? You have to make him pay for all the lives he's ruined. I'm willing to pay for *my* crimes."

I snorted. "Sure, because you don't have any choice."

"I know," he said sadly. "But I've come to terms with it. In a way I'm almost glad I'm in prison so I can't hurt anyone else. I just need someone to make him pay."

"Sorry, Clay," I said, "even if I knew for certain that it was your father who did this to you, I'm not lifting one finger to help you get revenge on him."

"But why? You know what he did to me."

"Yes, but he did it out of a sick compulsion. It's awful, it's sordid, and it deserves retribution, with maybe a grain of forgiveness mixed in because it *was* a sickness. If I were willing to be forgiving and understanding, the same might be said of most of the crimes *you* committed. All except one."

"Which one? Which crime can't I be forgiven for?"

"Clarence."

"What? Who's Clarence?"

"Julie Zimmerman's dog. Remember? She wrote you a letter? And to thank her for it, you killed her dog. You didn't need to but you did it anyway, just for spite."

"No, no, I couldn't help *that* either."

I shook my head. "You have to tell the truth, Clay. Those are the rules."

"Yes, all right. I did it to spite you, but I'm sorry about it now, I really—"

"It doesn't matter how sorry you are, that dog is still dead and being sorry won't bring him back. It won't do a damn thing to bring back the spring in his step or the happy look in his eye when he's chasing a tennis ball. You took all that away from that little guy, and that's unforgivable.

"Look," I went on, "I don't know what kind of gods or angels there are, or even if there *are* any—sometimes I wonder—but if they're up there, maybe some of them will forgive you for most of your crimes and twisted compulsions. After all, you got them from your father, or whomever it was that abused you, so maybe you're only partially responsible. Who knows? But I do know one thing: No one in heaven or on earth—and I mean no one—will ever, ever forgive you for killing that little dog."

"But—"

"That's it, Clay. This conversation is over."

I got up. He screamed at me and pounded on the glass but I didn't look back.

I'd once told Farrell Woods, semi-jokingly, that anyone who mistreats dogs in this life would be reincarnated as a fire hydrant, but even that would be too good for Clay Henry.

I pondered this for a while as I drove home, and the best scenario I could come up with was some cross between Greek tragedy and the Bill Murray film *Groundhog Day*: The dog abuser would have to spend eternity re-living the same day of his life, over and over, always knowing that sometime during that endless, awful day he would find himself being relentlessly chased down, attacked, and then slowly and painfully ripped to pieces by a pack of wild dogs. Then he would wake up again the next morning knowing that the same thing would happen to him again that day, and the next, and every day after that for the rest of eternity.

No, I thought, that's still too good for someone like Clay Henry. But by then I'd gotten bored with designing the perfect revenge scenario, and all I wanted to do was go home and play with my doggies.

Author's Note (aka Kelley's Soapbox)

As always, the training techniques Jack uses in this novel are based on *Natural Dog Training* by Kevin Behan. Rousseau once said, "Nature is never wrong," and I agree. I also think that what is most natural about the dog is what is best and is what should be nurtured and cherished. Therefore, spaying and neutering dogs—which is totally unnatural—should be avoided.

However, intact male dogs (like Clarence in this novel) will tend to roam, and will, therefore, frequently put their lives in danger and will also add to the over*pup*ulation problem in this country. So if you own a male dog and you're not in a position to guarantee his safety or to prevent him from propagating at will, you should have him castrated—no excuses.

If, however, you are a conscientious dog owner, committed to a training program that keeps your dog under strict control at all times, you should consider these facts: a) scientific studies show that natural levels of testosterone actually promote calm, non-aggressive behavior, b) there is no connection between healthy sex organs and the growth of cancer cells, c) in my fifteen years as a dog trainer, I've had many dog owners come to me with male dogs who only developed behavioral problems *after* they were castrated, and d) all dogs—male *and* female—are easier to train and control when they're left intact.

These ideas may seem controversial to many, perhaps even heretical to some, but there are many vets and working dog trainers who agree with everything I've stated above.

I'd also like to point out that Dr. Ian Dunbar was once quoted (in the *New York Times*) as saying that our shelters are full of unwanted dogs due in large part to the training practices of those who believe in dominating dogs in order to control them. If you've read any of my other novels, you know that Jack thinks the alpha theory is a fallacy, and that any training program based on any part of it is also fallacious.

The fact is, everything that we've been told about how dogs and wolves form social hierarchies was based on the unnatural behaviors observed in wolves who were thrown together in captivity and were not given the opportunity to hunt together as a pack. Kevin Behan stated in *Natural Dog Training* (1992) that the pack instinct only exists to enable canines to hunt large prey by working together as a cooperative social unit. Dr. Ray Coppinger, in a 2004 online discussion hosted by *The Washington Post,* agreed with Behan, and also said that wolves who settle near garbage dumps don't form packs. The fact is in canines Predation=Sociability. (This is also true of lions, by the way, who also hunt in groups, in a manner very similar to the way wolves do, and are the only social cat in nature.)

Dr. David Mech, perhaps our greatest expert on the behavior of wolves in the wild, has stated that "the concept of the alpha wolf as top dog is misleading," and that in wild wolf packs "dominance displays are uncommon." (*Canadian Journal of Zoology,* 1999.) In fact, Mech and others don't even like to use the word alpha anymore because "it falsely implies a hierarchical system in which each wolf assumes a place in a linear pecking order." (*Canadian Journal of Zoology*, 2002.)

If you live in a multiple-dog household, you may disagree with me (and Mech) on this. You may see a clear hierarchy in your dogs. What you should know is that such hierarchies are totally unnatural and only form when the animals are under stress. The best way to reduce that stress is through playing hunting games like fetch, find, hide-and-seek, and tug-of-war.

Nobel Prize–winning biologist Konrad Lorenz said, "All animals learn best through play." This is certainly true of dogs. Besides, it's a lot more fun than trying to force your dog to fit his energy into a nonexistent social hierarchy.

I'm stepping off my soapbox now.

Thanks for listening.

Contact Information

My website: www.leecharleskelley.com

Kevin Behan's website: www.naturaldogtraining.com

My e-mail address: kelleymethod@aol.com

Adopt a rescue pooch: www.StrayFromTheHeart.com